Party Girl

a modern fairy tale

By

Erin Shaw

After Midnight Press   *New Orleans, Louisiana*

For Maria, Malynda, Kara and Ashley:

Without whom this story might never have been inspired.

AUTHOR'S NOTE

A very sweet Manhattan mother once asked me, "Would you like some pizza and cake?"

"Sure!" I said, not realizing how much I would grow to hate this combination as the months rolled on.

What's wrong with pizza and cake? You might ask. *After all, it's the classic birthday party duo.* The answer: there's nothing wrong with it. Unless you're being offered pizza and cake every single weekend.

Imagine trying to fit into your tightly-laced up ball gown each weekend after you've been eating this meal eight times a month.

Once I figured this out, I found myself politely declining with, "Oh thank you, but if Cinderella wants to fit into her gown tomorrow..." which was always met with uproarious laughter from all the parents in the room.

I moved to New York City in 2008 to become a Broadway actress, but I quickly discovered that I didn't have all the right intel on how to go about doing this. I worked as a nanny and started a small business performing as a birthday party princess.

I spent many weekends doing this. I'd ride the subway in my street clothes, wearing a ton of makeup, a wig and a tiara, always smiling politely as my fellow passengers looked at me in the jaded, yet slightly intrigued way New Yorkers look at odd things. I would carry my ball gown in a garment bag that looked like it was about to explode. My shoulder bag was filled with face paints, stickers, cardboard crowns, storybooks and glitter.

The subway ride home was always better. I'd wipe off the exotic-dancer-eye shadow and let my crumpled hair down. The twenty-dollar tip in my pocket would whisper to me that I could go out to dinner that night with my friends instead of making Top Ramen.

For me, those afternoons became 'just another day in the life' of an aspiring actress living in the Big Apple, but they also supplied me with the inspiration for this book.

While some of this story is based on real experiences, *Party Girl* is a work of fiction. The circumstances and characters in the book are purely fictional. Any similarities between them and real individuals, living or dead, are coincidental. Some New York and Los Angeles establishments are mentioned, but again, these are written about in a fictitious manner.

PROLOGUE

I'm walking down West 4th Street in New York City. The streets are aglow as the sun makes its descent over the Hudson River and the street lamps switch on in the changing light. A chilly breeze taunts me with the promise of winter as it sneaks its way in between my collar and scarf. New Yorkers hurry past me with the excitement of heading out for the evening. In short, the city is perfection in all of its autumnal glory. Meanwhile, I have never been more miserable.

My bank account has thirty-seven dollars in it. I've just lost my job, I'm about to lose my apartment, and I don't even want to think about my love life.

To make matters worse, I came to this city with no real understanding of what it would take to make it here. The word *failure* is a broken record in my head, repeating itself with each step I take. I have bills to pay and I have groceries to buy. I will likely have to start selling my favorite clothes to make ends meet; or worse, call my parents.

Men in suits bump into me as I walk to the corner to hail a cab, and I've never felt like more of a loser. This was definitely not part of my plan. I'm still not entirely sure how this happened to me, or how I got here. Looking back, I have only a vague recollection of how it all started.

Part I: Summer

"Snow White longed for the fine apple, and when she saw that the old woman ate part of it she could resist no longer, and stretched out her hand and took the other half."

- Little Snow White
  by the Brothers Grimm

ONE

Once upon a time, in the far away land of unseasonably warm temperatures known as Los Angeles, there lived a young girl who had always dreamed of performing on the Broadway stage.

That girl is me. At twenty-four years old, I've just graduated with a performing arts degree, and I'm moving to New York City, where I have every intention of making my dream come true.

"Mom, it's going to be fine!" I say, standing near the ticket counter at LAX. "I'll call you when I land. I'm going to see you in a couple months when you bring the dog out. Plus, you've got Dad, here! Think of all the fun things you two can do now that he's retired."

"That's right, Linda," says my dad in his comforting way. "Audrey will be fine and we have a lot of things to look forward to."

"I know, honey. I know." She sniffs as she squeezes me

tightly to her, nearly breaking my spine. She's surprisingly strong, given her small frame.

"You okay?" I ask

"I'm sorry," she says, wiping the mascara-tears from under her brown eyes. "I must look like a mess."

"You're fine." I plaster on a smile while fixing her disheveled brown hair.

"It's just the first time you're going to be so far away from home."

"Well, you can come and visit any time." I cheerfully give her arms a squeeze. "It's not even a six-hour plane ride. We'll go eat bagels and real New York pizza and you can sit front row as soon as I book a show."

"You're right." She sniffs again. "Okay, my little Broadway star, have a safe flight and knock 'em dead."

"I will. I promise." I give both my parents hugs, grab my carry-on bag and make my way toward the security line.

Just before I head up the escalator, I turn once more to give them a final wave, and I see my mom start to lose it again, burying her face against my dad's chest.

I feel my eyes start to pinch slightly, but I take a deep breath and force the tears back. I hate seeing my mother sad, but my excitement is palpable as I hand the TSA supervisor my boarding pass and driver's license. He scrutinizes my documents and then waves me through. I head toward the stack of plastic bins, preparing to remove my shoes from my feet and my laptop from my bag. It's finally happening!

I arrive at JFK in the middle of a torrential downpour, and my stomach is in knots from the bumpy landing. *Who likes to fly again?* My slightly sour stomach takes a turn for the better only when I see the first sign in the terminal reading, 'Welcome to New York!'

I look outside the windows at my first East Coast summer thunderstorm. Most people might consider this sight annoying, but I find it endearing. Rain is a rarity in sunny Southern

California. As I walk down the terminal following the signs for baggage claim, I hear New Yorkers talking loudly on their cell phones, many of them with thick New York accents. I'm fully charmed. *These are my people!*

I walk toward baggage carousel number four just as the buzzer goes off to announce the arrival of our bags. I'm grinning ear-to-ear at the people standing next to me, checking their watches and tapping their feet impatiently, waiting for their bags to arrive as well.

I have the impulse to tap someone on the shoulder and say, *me too! I'm a New Yorker too!* But I'm pretty sure that wouldn't go over very well, so I refrain.

I'm already imagining the dingy smell of the cab I'll soon be jumping into, the one that will race down the Brooklyn-Queens Expressway and take me into my favorite place in the whole world - Manhattan.

For all the times I've visited, it feels so different being here and knowing I won't be leaving in a week. I feel so grown up and mature, taking the first big step in a new chapter of my life.

As the minutes pass, I realize that most of the people that had been standing next to me are gone. I've been lost in my new-New-Yorker-reverie and haven't really been paying attention to the baggage carousel. I stand there for another ten minutes before I head toward the customer service desk, resigned to the fact that my bags are not coming down.

"Unfortunately, it appears your bags have been delayed in Dallas. We're not sure when they'll arrive," says Keisha, the disgruntled-looking airline employee whose top priority seems to be chipping away at one of her neon pink acrylic nails.

"Is there anything you can do?" I ask. "I just moved here. I don't have anything. Everything that isn't being shipped to me in a few weeks was in those bags."

"Honey, all I can tell you is that we'll call you as soon as your bags turn up," she says distractedly, in a thick Brooklyn accent. "What's your name again?"

"Audrey Princeton." I watch helplessly as she scribbles it on a form.

"We'll call you when we know."

"Okay thanks, I guess." I try to hide the dejection in my voice.

"Welcome to New York... Next!"

I leave the airline desk and head towards the curb. *At least I'll be in the city soon.* The doors open and I walk out into the monsoon-like weather conditions to see that the taxi line is about a mile long. *Great.*

I get in line feeling a little dazed when I am jolted back to reality by the sound of my phone ringing in my purse. Of course, I already know who's calling.

"Hi Mom," I answer.

"Audrey? Did you land okay?" She sounds panicked.

"Yeah it was a little bumpy," I say. "The airline lost my bags, but I'm sure they'll turn up. Thank goodness I have a spare pair of contacts in my purse."

"Oh no. Do they know when you'll get them back?" she asks.

"I'm not sure. Hopefully tomorrow," I say. "I'll have to wait and see. Hey Mom, I need to call Logan to let him know I'm on my way. Can I call you later?"

"Of course, honey! Just let me know when you get your bags. Your dad says hello!"

"Hi Dad," I say into the phone.

"We love you, bye!"

"Bye."

I open my messages to text my best friend, Logan.

Hey u. Landed. Bags are lost.
Anything that will fit me?

A minute passes before his text beeps through.

Think I have a few things
from my tiny dancer days.
Dinner's on the stove!

I finally make it to the front of the taxi line, and give the driver my destination, but the exhilarating ride into the city that I had imagined is replaced by a slow and painful crawl through heavy traffic. It takes over an hour to get into the city and my cab driver appears to have left his lunch in the cab all day. The smell of egg-salad mixed with body odor is thick in the air and enough to make me roll down my window in the pouring rain.

"Miss, could you please close that? Trying to keep my cab dry, okay?" says the cabbie, whose name is Mo.

"I'm sorry," I say.

"Whad'ya trying to do? Huh, Miss?"

"Can I just get some air please?" I ask, trying to stay composed. He turns the fan on, which only wafts the putrid smell back from the front of the cab towards me. "Actually, I'm good! I'm good. Thanks."

When I finally arrive at Logan's swanky TriBeCa apartment, I am feeling a bit dazed. But as I approach his floor, the amazing smell drifting into the hall from inside his door is enough to make me forget that I just had the cab ride from hell and currently have no possessions to my name.

"Holly!" he exclaims as he opens the door.

"Paulie!" I cry, and we hug.

"Thank God you're here already! How long have we been planning this?"

We were teenagers when Logan and I first met, he on the cusp of realizing, or at least acknowledging, that he was gay. I remember telling him that my mother named me for Audrey Hepburn when I found out that he was obsessed with *Breakfast at Tiffany's*. He started calling me Holly, as in Holly Golightly. I took to the nickname and started calling him Paulie, as in Paul Varjak. We hatched a plan to one-day move to New York City together. Now, here we are, like two bleu cheese-stuffed olives in a dirty martini.

As the moment of realization washes over me, I can't help but be proud of us. We've come a long way. Looking at Logan, I also realize that I had forgotten how handsome my friend is.

His tall, muscular frame is clad in the most stylish summer attire. His brown hair is perfectly coiffed and his skin is nicely tanned. He looks like something out of a Hampton's episode of *Sex and the City*. I suddenly feel a bit underdressed in my shorts, t-shirt and flats. My brown hair is disheveled from the plane ride and frizzed slightly from the humidity. I could definitely use a shower.

"Okay, let me give you the tour," he says.

I take a look around and see that something is bubbling away on the stove in a Le Creuset French oven. There's a huge spread of cheese and crackers on the table as well.

He catches me checking out the feast awaiting us.

"I know it's not really the right weather for Boeuf Bourguignon, but I figured screw it, we can eat it in front of the A/C unit."

"I'm game!" I say.

Logan gives me the tour of his apartment, which is admittedly much nicer than what most people our age can afford. Logan's father passed away a few years back, leaving him with a sizeable trust fund and giving him a fair amount of disposable income. Logan shows me the guest room where I'll be staying. On the bed, he has already laid out a pair of shorts and a t-shirt for me to change into.

"I figured you'd want to take a shower," he says. "Don't worry, I have all the hair products you'll need."

"You're the best," I say.

"I'm going to fix our drinks while you get cleaned up." He hands me a towel from the linen closet. "And how many olives do you want? Three or four?"

He knows me so well.

I stand under the amazing showerhead and let the water wash away the discouraging start to my new life. It's funny how a good shower can really improve a bad day. As I choose from Logan's vast array of salon-grade shampoos, I hear the sounds of taxis beeping outside and the occasional rumble of thunder.

There is a small window in the shower and I open it slightly to see the alley behind his building. The sky is tinged gray and the rain is still falling. The sounds of the city outside make me smile and by the time I'm wrapped in the buttery soft towel and drying my hair, I'm already feeling refreshed and ready to embrace this new experience once more.

After I change into the outfit Logan has laid out for me, I comb my long wet hair out and walk back into the living room.

"Drink's on the table, Holly!" he shouts from the kitchen. Logan has French music playing on his stereo and he's lit candles in his living room. The A/C unit is blasting cool air into the room and his couch is wonderfully comfortable. The furnishings in his apartment are modern and tasteful. He's become a very successful interior designer, all self-taught. I take a sip of my martini and the warmth from the vodka washes over my throat and makes me feel instantly at ease.

"So, tell me about your life," Logan says as he joins me on the couch. "How are you? How was your flight?"

"Long," I reply. "I hate flying in the summer... too many thunderstorms."

"Turbulence is *so* not cute."

"Not cute at all!" I say.

"And how's Brent?" he asks, but noticing the hesitant look on my face, continues, "Or maybe we should discuss that later?"

"Hard to explain... maybe after another drink," I say. "I'm just ready to have some fun and cut loose."

"Honey, you don't even know how much fun we are going to have," he says enthusiastically. "I have us slated to have drinks Friday night at the Laconda Verde, then dinner at Jewel Bako, and on Sunday, brunch at Le Bernardin!"

I'm not sure if he's even speaking English, but it sounds like exactly what I want to do. "Thank you so much for letting me crash with you," I say. "I just can't believe I'm really here! And I can't believe how swanky your apartment is! To have a second bedroom in New York City? Is that even legal?"

"You don't want to know who I had to kill to pull that off." The smirk spreads wide across his face.

I raise my glass. "To you, sweet friend!"

"To you, baby girl! I'm so ecstatic you made the move." We clink glasses.

"So, what's my first step in becoming a real New Yorker?" I ask.

"Well, as long as you don't have anything to wear, we should probably go shopping in the morning. Make you look like a proper East Coast girl."

We sit on the couch, eating the amazing Boeuf Bourguignon that Logan has prepared over a bed of Parmesan polenta. We sip our martinis and I fill him in on my life over the last six months. We talk about my senior voice recital, how my parents are and my brother's wedding. He tells me about the three most recent boys he's dated and how they are all dead to him now. It's wonderful just to sit and gab with him in person. It's been so long.

"Paulie, that was so incredibly delicious... do I even have to ask?" I say

"Of course it's Ina's recipe," he says, rolling his eyes. He sets his plate down on the coffee table and gestures to a shelf that contains several of Ina Garten's Barefoot Contessa cookbooks.

"Who else!" I laugh.

"So, now that you've had a couple drinks and you're well-fed, spill it," he says, prodding. "Let's talk about your love life."

I sigh. "There's not much to tell really."

"Brent seemed like a good guy," he says. "Wasn't he extremely tall? I just remember him being extremely tall."

I laugh. "Yeah, that's him. I guess we're still together? I'm not really sure. We decided we'd take it a day at a time and just see where we are come the holidays."

I'm still not entirely sure what's going on with Brent, and I hate explaining it to people. I always feel like I'm defending something that no one else understands, and why? It's my love life after all, isn't it?

Logan smiles a mischievous smile at me. "Well I always

think the best way to get over someone is to go get under..." He trails off at my look of disapproval. "But that's just me, honey."

"It sounds good in theory." I laugh. "But he still calls me all the time. We probably should've just had a clean break, but... Relationships are so freaking hard."

Logan jumps up and begins clearing our plates.

"Why doesn't he move to New York?" he asks. "Do you think he's the one?"

"I'm honestly not sure," I say. "He wants to stay in L.A. to pursue film. We're at a bit of an impasse with the locational logistics I'm afraid."

Logan begins to run the sink. "Well, you'll figure it out. Just make sure you're taking care of your own happiness."

I stand up from the couch and begin bringing our empty glasses into the kitchen. "I still love him. It sucks."

"Holly, I know you and I know that you love what's familiar," he says, rinsing plates and loading the dishwasher. "And you love the idea of being in love. You have a whole new life to explore now though! I think you should be open minded. You might meet someone special here."

"Who knows," I say dismissively, hoping he will move on to a new subject.

I'm not just in love with the idea of being in love. I know I'm not. It's more than that.

He closes the dishwasher, turns off the faucet and dries his hands. "How about we open some wine and move to dessert?"

"Sounds like bliss," I say.

After dinner, I get settled into bed and decide to call Brent. I know he'll be glad to hear from me. I know he still cares. Maybe he *will* even think about moving to New York, if I make it sound enticing enough.

"Hello?" he answers.

"Hi," I say, adjusting the pillows on Logan's guest bed.

"Hey you!" he says. "Sorry, I meant to call you earlier. I've been on a shoot all day with no phone service. How's the big city?"

"Oh, that's alright," I say. "I've just been hanging out at Logan's. He made me dinner. The airline lost my bags."

"Oh baby, I'm so sorry to hear that." He sounds distracted.

"It's okay, I'm sure they'll turn up," I yawn, realizing how tired I am after a long day of traveling.

"Hey Audrey, listen, I'm just heading out to meet some of the guys. Can I call you later?" he asks.

"It's midnight here." My eyes are starting to feel heavy. "And I'm pretty tired."

"We'll touch base soon then, glad you made it safely."

"Thanks," I say, still on the line as he hangs up the phone.

Too tired to ponder our relationship, I drift off to sleep, thinking about all the adventures and success awaiting me, the sounds of beeping taxis lulling me into a deep slumber.

The next morning, much to my relief, the airline hand delivers my bags back into my possession. I'm so thrilled to have all my clothes, but Logan quickly goes through my suitcases and concludes that nothing I've packed is suitable for my new life here.

He takes me shopping in SoHo for my proper East Coast wardrobe. Back in California, he explains, it's common to see people run to the store in yoga pants, but he won't allow me to be *that* New Yorker. In his opinion, successful people in this town dress the part and even my exercise clothes should have style.

I had never really considered myself all that into fashion. I dressed cute enough, and wore things that were in style, but I had never really learned much about buying 'wardrobe pieces' as Logan called them.

"Why would you buy five sub-par sundresses from *Forever pre-pubescent*, when you could buy one amazing one from Banana Republic that will make you look like a grown up woman and last for the next ten years?" he demands, as we walk along Broadway. "Or until you get pregnant by a hot stockbroker, whichever comes first."

"I guess I never really thought about it," I admit.

"Well it's time to start, my dear."

"What about H&M?" I ask.

"Don't even get me started," he says dismissively. "You need to start thinking about your wardrobe in a long-term sense. Don't waste your money buying crap. Buy well-made pieces that will last for a long time and are tailored to your body type and style. If you can find those pieces at less expensive stores, more power to you, but that requires a good eye and some serious digging."

In spite of my better judgment, we buy me audition outfits, outfits for going out, outfits for picnics in the park, New England summer ensembles and an adorable pair of boat shoes for me to wear in Fire Island in August. I know it's probably not the best idea to deplete my carefully budgeted savings buying clothes. The five thousand dollars I've been saving the last few years is enough to float me for a couple months, but I have every intention of finding a job soon, and most of these outfits will help to determine my success.

By the time we're done, my feet are killing me and I have so many shopping bags in my hands that there are tiny, permanent, red rope burns lining my palms.

Logan assures me that I'll get my 'New York feet' in no time, but as I limp down the street, I catch him looking at me sympathetically, and he suggests we stop for a drink.

Logan selects a Russian vodka bar called Pravda. It's dimly lit and cool inside, which feels glorious after a day of walking in the hot sun.

He orders us gimlets.

"So, when does your mom get into town?" he asks, as we sit at a small table in the dark bar surrounded by a sea of shopping bags resting at my very sore and blistered feet.

"Three weeks," I say. "She's bringing Baxter out as soon as I get a place."

"He's such a cutie. I love that you have a dog. It's so city-chic!" he says. "Now, what about your career? What's your plan for getting that cute little hiney on a Broadway stage?"

"I'm meeting my friend Sarah for coffee next week to go over my strategy," I say. "She's booked a ton of acting jobs since she moved here and she suggested that I look into some workshops at Actors Access."

"Well, I'm sure she'll help you book something right away," he says. "Especially with that dress from Theory. That peach color against your beautiful fair skin. You'll look dressed and ready for The Tony's."

As we drink our gimlets and laugh, I can't help but bask in the glow of our day. New York is my city, and I'm ready to take it by storm.

From: Registration <reg@actorsaccess.com>
Subject: Re: Welcome!
Date: June 10, 11:17:25 am
To: Audrey Princeton <princeton.audrey@gmail.com>

Dear Ms. Princeton,

Welcome to *Actors Access!* We are confident that your recent purchase of our 'Welcome To New York' seminar package will help you achieve your goals and theatrical pursuits.

This email serves as your receipt. Your MasterCard has been charged in the amount of $497.50

Please visit our website for a complete list of classes, workshops and seminars available to you!

Also personal one on one coaching is available through our affiliate's page.

If you have any questions, please let us know!

Regards,
The Actors Access Team

TWO

When I checked my bank account balance this morning, it was drastically lower than I thought it would be. Apparently my shopping spree for the ages with Logan made a bigger dent in my savings than I had accounted for. And after a very pleasant conversation with an associate at Actors Access, I purchased the 'Welcome to New York Package' of Broadway audition seminars. The package was five hundred dollars, but worth it when I consider the edge it will give me when I start pounding the pavement.

Two weeks have passed since I arrived, and it's a swelteringly hot and humid June day. I'm meeting my friend Sarah for coffee at The Grey Dog Café in Chelsea to discuss prepping for auditions.

The financial cushion I had is probably more of a throw pillow now, but as I walk into Grey Dog, I'm confident that Sarah will help me to find the perfect gig. She's a family friend who studied Theatre at a nearby university. She was a senior in college when I was a freshman, and she's been booking shows consistently for three years now. She's an outstanding dancer, beautiful singer and fine actor. It seems like every time I see her updates on Facebook, she's been cast in another smash hit show.

I scan the café for her bright red hair and head toward the counter once it becomes clear she hasn't arrived yet.

I glance up at the big chalkboard menu, contemplating what I want to order, when a guy appears from the back room and greets me.

"What can I get you?" he asks.

"Iced decaf Americano, please," I say.

"Anything to eat?" he asks, smiling.

"I'll wait for my friend to order." I smile back.

He's kind of cute, mussed-up brown hair, wearing funky glasses, and a button-down striped shirt. As I hand him a five-dollar bill and wait for change, I'm convinced that somewhere buried underneath all the bills on his desk is a half-written screenplay.

"There she is!" I hear Sarah before I see her. "You're a real New Yorker now!"

She walks over to me excitedly, her curly red hair bouncing with each step.

"Sarah, I'm so glad you're here!" I say as we hug. "I really need to book a job soon. Logan has insisted on renovating my entire wardrobe."

"Well then straight to business it is! We'll catch up after!" she says. "I brought my laptop so we can look at casting calls."

"What can I get you?" asks the guy behind the counter.

"Iced tea with lemon," she says.

"That'll be three fifty and I'll bring those right over," he says.

Sarah pays for her tea and drops her change in the tip jar. We sit down at a small table.

"Everything good so far?" she asks as she opens her laptop, heading straight to Playbill.com.

"So far so good," I say.

"Good!" she says. "Okay, here are some casting notices. How long have you had your Equity card?"

"Oh, I don't have it yet." I falter, feeling unsure for the first time.

The struggling writer guy walks over with our drinks.

"Oh," Sarah stammers. "Okay, well you know how Actors' Equity works right? It's like the stage actor's version of SAG. You earn points towards becoming a union actor with each professional show that you do. Have you earned any points yet?"

"I don't think so," I say.

"But you did summer stock theatre in college, right?" she says hopefully.

"I wanted to," I say. "But my degree was in classical voice, and my teachers thought doing musical theatre would confuse my technique."

"Audrey, you don't have a theatre degree? Why did I think you did?"

"I did theatre in high school," I say. "By college, I thought it would be smarter to major in vocal performance, so I'd learn proper technique."

"And your teachers never talked to you about how it would work in New York?"

"No," I say realizing how little I actually know. "I can tell you a whole lot about how to audition for a young artist opera program though."

"Okay, well, that's not going to help us much here. Let's just adjust our search parameters a bit." She selects the option for 'Non-Union.'

"Wait, I can't audition for Broadway?" Now I'm really getting nervous.

"Well, you're not Equity yet, so you can't request appointments for Equity auditions. You can try and crash them, but you'll need to line up to get your name on the list around five o'clock in the morning."

"What?!"

"I have to be honest with you, Audrey. If you're not in the

union yet, it's going to be very hard to get into a Broadway show."

"So, what are my options?" I can feel the panic rising. Surely, this can't be correct.

"You'll really need to consider performance options on tour and outside of the city."

"Leave New York? I just got here."

"Well, here's a listing for a non-union tour of *The Wizard of Oz*," she says. "It pays four-hundred-fifty a week. That's not half bad for a non-union tour."

"Any other options?" I ask, sipping my coffee nervously and squinting at Sarah's computer screen.

"These are all calls for males and highly experienced dancers, and it's a production in Philly," she says, scrolling down the list. "Do you want to intern at the Nederlander Theatre?"

"No!" I say, starting to feel my chest tighten.

"Don't worry, Audrey. It's the summer time and most of the summer shows and tours have been cast. There will be a lot more gigs when fall comes around." Sarah assures me.

Of course she's not concerned; she's leaving in a month to begin rehearsals at the Merry-Go-Round Playhouse, Upstate.

"Fall?" I squeak. "Sarah, what am I going to do? I can't wait until the fall to get a job, it's still June!"

"Well maybe you'll land the *Wizard of Oz* gig! I know it's tough, but you've got to have some money saved, right? It always takes about six months to get a job in New York. I figured you had a cushion." She looks at me as if this is as obvious as the sky being blue and the Earth being round.

How had I been so stupid? How had I not realized that I wasn't going to land at JFK, jump in a cab and all of a sudden magically be winning a Tony award? Why didn't my acting teachers in college tell me this? I'm devastated. I'm also soon-to-be-broke.

All I can do is think about dollar signs flying at me like daggers. Student loan payments! Astronomical Manhattan rent! Cabs! Brunches! New boots and coats for the fall I hadn't even bought yet! How am I going to afford all of this making four-hundred-fifty a week in the *Wizard of Oz*? Not to mention that to land this role, I'll be duking it out with about two-hundred other girls who look just like me, sound just like me, and also believe it is their birthright to grace Broadway stages with their impeccable talent and skillfully honed 'craft.' *Shit!*

"I think I need to go to the restroom," I tell Sarah, as I shakily make my way to the ladies room. I feel like I'm about ready to pass out, vomit, or scream. Maybe all three at once.

When you're in college and you're being praised by your voice teachers every semester, you almost just expect the transition to Broadway will be seamless. You have one great performance and think to yourself, *how on Earth could they not want me?* Now though, in that bathroom, I start to feel a very cold reality setting in. Even though it's eighty-eight degrees and ninety percent humidity outside.

Since my horrifyingly sobering meeting with Sarah, I've definitely gone into determined New Yorker mode. I may have spent that first week feeling sorry for myself and eating a fair amount of Ben & Jerry's ice cream on Logan's couch, but since then I've decided to suck it up and just go hardcore, nose to the grindstone. I've been checking Playbill.com every morning for casting notices and have been practically stalking the Equity office's casting call notice board. In spite of all my efforts, it's not looking too promising.

"So, what's your plan if you can't book a show?" asks my mom over the phone.

"Not sure," I say. "Apparently because we're in a recession, funds are tight in the Broadway community, and producers are hiring actors they already know because the work is so limited. At least, that's what I've been reading on the message boards."

"How did your last audition go?"

"It actually went very well," I say. "But there were tons of other Dorothy hopefuls there."

I guess it was naïve to think the recession wouldn't affect the Broadway community. I really thought there would be tons of auditions available to me - plenty to go around, but now I'm realizing that I'm new to a city that takes care of its own first and foremost.

"Starting out in any new city is hard," she says. "You'll get there. Do you want your Christmas money early?"

"No, Mom. You already gave me a thousand dollars for graduation. It's my fault that I didn't budget it well enough."

"Well some of that was Logan's fault," she says. "He should have known better."

"I just feel so bad," I say. "I'm twenty-four years old, and now you guys are offering to loan me money and taking care of my dog for a few more months. And all because I wasn't smart enough to learn how to get a job here?"

"Frankly, I'd like to contact the dean at your college. Someone should have talked with you candidly about what this experience would be like."

"I dunno," I lament. "Thinking back there was some kind of lecture in the spring about auditions, but I think I might have missed it to go to Disneyland with Brent."

"Oh, Audrey…"

"I know. I just thought I knew everything about auditioning! I've been doing juries and vocal adjudications for years!"

"Well you're certainly paying the price now, aren't you?"

"I know."

"Have you found an apartment yet?" she asks.

"Yeah, there's a cute studio in the West Village I'm looking into. The tenant is being shipped overseas for work in September, and he needs a nine-month sublettor. I feel bad I'd have to stay here at Logan's a bit longer than I initially thought, but the West Village place is miraculously rent-controlled."

"Why don't you and Logan just get a place together?" she asks.

"He's never leaving this apartment," I say. "And they don't allow pets here."

"I see."

"The place in the Village is fully furnished and he's fine with the dog, but I'm just not sure how I can afford it. Even with the utilities included, it's twelve hundred a month," I say hesitantly.

"Well, are you sure you need to live in Manhattan?" she asks. "Maybe you should look into a roommate? And isn't it less expensive if you live in Queens or Brooklyn, or maybe New Jersey?"

"New Jersey? Mom, are you kidding? I wouldn't be caught dead in Jersey!" I'm starting to feel irritated. Clearly my mother has no idea what she's saying. "I'll work it out, Mom. I gotta run anyway. I'm meeting Logan for drinks. Say hi to Dad, and tell John to call me back one of these days."

"You know your brother, always too busy to breathe." She hangs up.

On my way to meet Logan, I realize I've started walking faster and that I'm beginning to feel irritated with 'tourists' who are blocking my way to the subway. I take a small amount of pleasure in this shift, if only because it means I am becoming more of a New Yorker each day.

When I get off the N train at Prince Street, I yell at a taxi driver who nearly hits me, although I'm the one walking against the light.

I walk down Broadway past boutiques and shoe stores. It's evening time and the streets are filled with people in business clothes chatting away on their cell phones as they walk. The weather is warm, but there's a sweet breeze coming off the Hudson River. The sun is starting to set and the golden light is glowing through the cracks between buildings, illuminating the cobblestone streets of SoHo. I turn the corner at Spring Street and push open the heavy wooden doors of Balthazar.

"I think I'm going to have to move to Brooklyn," I tell Logan as we sip our cosmos and nibble on their famous French fries.

"Don't even speak the words or they might come true."

He looks horrified. "We don't ever use the 'B word' except when absolutely necessary."

"I mean it. I don't think I have the money to get that studio in the Village. Brooklyn can't be *that* bad! Maybe I can go somewhere that's decent like Boerum Hill," I suggest.

"Boerum Hill?" he gasps. "You didn't move to the greatest city in the world to shack up with all the roaches in Boerum Hill! Holly…if you can't get the studio in the Village, then we'll look somewhere else. But I insist you stay in Manhattan, at least for your first six months here. It's part of the experience to come to New York and actually live in the city. The absolute worst-case scenario, we'll find you somewhere on the Upper, Upper West Side. At least there's culture in Harlem!"

"Paulie, plenty of young artists live in Brooklyn. Hello, Williamsburg!"

"Hello, Holly! Being a hipster does not make you an artist."

"I think you're being unfair, but regardless, I have to just suck it up and get a day job," I say, while downing the second drink I can't afford. "Do you know a good temp agency?"

"Well, what happened with that *Wizard of Oz* audition? Your outfit was flawless." He pats my hand.

"Never heard anything. Maybe my song choice wasn't what they were looking for." I shrug.

"It's their damn loss. You're the Judy Garland to this queen's rainbow, so clearly they don't know talent when they see it."

"Thank you. But unless you want to start paying me to be your fag-hag, I think I need a real job."

"Why don't you just be a nanny?" He suddenly looks bright. "That woman on Park Ave whose bathroom I'm re-designing has a nanny who's an aspiring actress. She makes serious money, and the other day I heard her being offered some of the mom's old designer clothes. I'm pretty sure that bitch is going to make off with that Prada cardigan I had my eye on."

"Okay, first of all, I haven't even babysat since high school, so who would I list as a reference? And secondly, that sounds like a plot point right out of *The Nanny Diaries*. I'm not sure I want to get mixed up in something like that. Some of those Upper East Siders are a bit more than I can handle."

But even as I'm pouting, I feel that nagging tug of the truth pulling me in Logan's direction. The appeal of making cash under the table to make macaroni and watch *SpongeBob* is palpable. It might be a half-decent idea.

"I'll be your reference!" squeals Logan. "I mean, I detest children, but it would be fun to create a fake child with a whole backstory!"

"I don't know if that's such a good…" I begin to protest, but it's already too late.

"He'll have some fabulous name that will work perfectly whether he turns out to be straight or gay. He'll *love* Betty White and Beyoncé!"

"Earth to Mr. Vanderwood, come in, Mr. Vanderwood…"

"OH! He can have designer clothes and a collection of little bambino Prada shoes! And maybe we can have matching outfits! And…"

"PAULIE!" I shout.

"What?"

"Be realistic for a second! Who would ever believe that a real kid would love Betty White?" I say skeptically.

"Okay, well, I'll tone it down." He pats my hand. "Just list me as a reference. I'll sing your praises and I'll make sure it sounds completely believable."

Logan gives me a triumphant look as if he's already solved all my problems, and I cave. "Okay, okay. I'll look into it."

THREE

I can't believe I'm actually doing this. I'm actually about to be interviewed for a nanny job.

Logan actually found the agency for me. An operation run by women who seem as passionate about childcare as Kristy, Mary Anne and the rest of The Babysitters Club.

Judging from the short conversation I had over the phone, they seem convinced that being part of someone's staff is a dream job. Apparently I should feel honored that they would even agree to meet with me.

It's not a bad option really. They set up all your interviews for you, negotiate salary, process feedback and ultimately, draw up all the necessary contracts on your behalf. I'm slightly nervous because my nanny experience is obviously limited. As in, I have none. But I've always done really well with kids, especially my cousin's children. And when I did children's theatre in high school, the kids loved me there.

Something still tells me that all of this is going to fall a little short of the experience they are used to, but my fingers are crossed that Logan's glowing reference will somehow give them enough confidence to give me a shot.

Buzz

"Yes?" asks a voice on the intercom.

"Hi, I have an appointment at ten o'clock?" I say into the little speaker of a building on West 33rd Street.

"Name?"

"Audrey Princeton."

"Oh yes, we have you down. I'll buzz you in. Eighth floor!"

The door clicks open and I enter the lobby of a building that looks like a warehouse. I walk toward the ancient looking elevator, wondering how safe it is. When the doors creak open, I press the number eight and hold on as the lift jolts upward toward the offices of Spiffy Staff.

When I walk through the door of their office, I see the walls are plastered with giant identical pieces of funky art. They are framed maps with the outlines of Manhattan and Brooklyn filled in with the names of the different neighborhoods in giant type. CHELSEA. SOHO. BOWERY. GREENWICH VILLAGE. HARLEM. MORNINGSIDE HEIGHTS is facing sideways at the very tip-top of Manhattan. BROOKLYN HEIGHTS. DUMBO. COBBLE HILL. WILLIAMSBURG. FORT GREENE. BED-STUY. PARK SLOPE.

The waiting area is an eclectic mixture of sleek furnishings with colorful boho-chic accents. The couch is black leather with stainless steel legs covered in throw pillows that look like they have been made out of a variety of vintage pattern fabrics. They seem to want to make it clear that they are a hip and fun staff placement agency.

I'm the only one in the waiting area, so I sit down on the couch and look at all of the glossy magazines they have on the solid concrete coffee table. I try to ignore the fact that the table is covered in mason jars filled with those yellow flowers that look like small tennis balls.

"Good lord..." I mumble to myself. "It's like Etsy threw-up

in here…"

"Hi! You must be our ten o'clock," says a cheerful voice that jolts me to attention. "I'm Trisha. Lucy will be with you in just a few minutes. Can I get you a coffee? Tea? Water?"

"Water would be nice, thank you."

"Would you like a glass of our special Spiffy Water? It's made with mint, citrus, rosemary and cucumbers."

"Wow…"

"I got the recipe off Martha Stewart's blog. Don't tell anyone," she whispers emphatically.

"Ha." I force a laugh. "Your secret is safe with me."

"I'll get you some. It's great. Back in a jiff!"

"Trisha, do I just wait here?" I ask.

"Oh yes, our interviews are very informal. Lucy will just chat with you briefly here and then we'll have you fill out some paperwork. Standard stuff." She smiles.

"Great. Thanks." I can't help but wonder if Trisha was the bubble gum chewing, head cheerleader at her high school.

A few minutes pass and Trisha brings me my Spiffy Water. Then after about fifteen more minutes, Lucy greets me.

"So sorry to keep you waiting," she says in a smooth, composed voice as she sits down across from me. She is tall with dark hair and cat-eye glasses. She wears a mauve cardigan over a grey dress. She is 1950's housewife meets Madison Avenue executive.

"Oh, not a problem. I'm not in a hurry," I say.

"Lucy Sanders," she says extending her hand.

"Audrey Princeton," I say. We shake hands.

"So nice to meet you, Audrey. We're very excited to have you in today." She opens my file. "Your qualifications are a bit less than some of our other applicants, but you came very highly recommended. A Mr. Logan Vanderwood said you took care of his son, Thor, was it?"

Lucy looks up as I nearly spit out my Spiffy Water. *Dammit, Logan…*

"Um, yes… little Thor," I say, panicking. "Such a delightful child."

"I'll bet." Lucy smiles tentatively and I feel the need to continue.

"We read a book together about Norse mythology so I could teach him the story behind his name. After that, we took a trip to the Met to visit the sculpture garden. He's now versed in Greek and Roman Mythology as well." I study Lucy to detect if she's seen through Logan's fake reference.

"Oh, well that's quite impressive. Are you versed in different kinds of cultural mythology?" she asks. I panic for a moment thinking she must be waiting for me to elaborate on my extensive knowledge of golden apples, temples and sacrificial altars.

"Well, mostly in Norse and Greek. But I'm very interested in Asian Mythology." I lie smoothly "I've been reading a lot about Kwan Yin currently."

God bless my mother and her obsession with Goddesses!

"Very good. Most of our families really like their staff to instill a sense of culture," Lucy says with a proud smile.

She begins telling me the history of the company and how she started it with another friend who just felt it was so important to work with families. As she talks, I smile and nod but my palms are sweating slightly as I glance down at her folder, wondering what else Logan has said about me. Thank goodness I joined that improv troupe in high school.

"Mr. Vanderwood also mentioned that you and Thor spoke in French," she says reading on. "And that you regularly prepared him meals of Coq au Vin and cassoulet. My, my, what a developed palate for a little guy!"

"Oui, oui!" I reply. *Seriously Logan, I will kill you.* "I believe what Mr. Vanderwood meant is that Thor and I worked on French assignments that were prepared for him by his father. J'parle un peu d'française."

Lucy looks pleased and I'm grateful that I perfected the phrase 'I only speak a little French' when I traveled to France during college. "So, are you skilled at cooking cultural food?" she asks. "Any tricks for how to get a child to try cassoulet?"

"Oh yes!" I answer a bit too enthusiastically. *What the hell is cassoulet?* "However, Mr. Vanderwood really was firm about my cooking from his private stock of family recipes. You see, Thor's late mother… Madeline, God rest her soul, was French. So I must admit I'd never cooked some of those things before and he was very kind as to give me instruction."

"Well great! It sounds like you were an integral part in little Thor's success in life." *Wow. She's totally buying this.*

"Well, gosh I hope so!" I lay it on thick. "I mean, I really love children! You just learn so much from them. I don't think adults really give kids enough credit for how intelligent they are."

"So true," says Lucy, looking touched. "We feel very blessed to work with families."

I've got this now. "Just being a part of the family meant so much to me. I'll never forget the time that Thor showed me the little photo album he kept under his pillow that contained pictures of Mrs. Vanderwood. He once pointed to one where she was backed in sunlight and said, 'Mama is an angel now,' bless his little heart."

I take another deep breath and reach for a Kleenex to dab my perfectly conjured tears. Lucy looks about ready to cry herself.

"Wow. That is just so touching. That poor child. What a challenge to be that young and without a mother figure."

"Mmm hmm." I sniffle.

"But for you to step in and guide him through his pain, that is why we do what we do. I'm impressed," she says.

"Thank you," I say.

"Audrey, honestly I never do this without consulting my partners, but I would like to welcome you aboard," she says with a wink. "You have a bit less experience then we generally like but I think in your heart, you are absolutely Spiffy Staff material."

I walk out of the building feeling like I've just escaped a very sticky situation. I immediately pick up my phone and dial

Logan's number. He answers on the third ring.

"Thor? THOR?!" I shout into my phone as I'm walking back toward Broadway. "You almost killed me in there! I nearly spit my water on the woman when she said his name!"

"I'm sorry, but Thor is a good and strong name."

"Oh for the love of–"

"Well, did you get the job or not?" he asks, interrupting me.

"They're taking me on, yes. But I probably won't hear about any actual positions for a while," I say.

"I'm sure you'll get something great. And if you want, I can teach you how to make Coq au Vin later this week. Ina's recipe is everything."

"Of course it is," I say. "Okay, I'm going to go get a coffee and run to my acting class. I'll talk to you later."

"Okay, Mary Poppins! Congratulations! You're on your way!"

FOUR

It's a hot and sticky day in August as I'm boarding the Hampton Jitney on the corner of 84th and Lexington. With the help of Spiffy Staff, a family named the Branders has hired me for a trial month. They are bussing me out to the Hamptons to meet them and care for their three kids.

Humidity is one of those elements of New York summer life that I'm still getting used to. If I had to explain what it's like to someone who has never experienced it, I'd describe what happened to me this morning. I got out of the shower feeling refreshed, then got ready in front of Logan's A/C unit to stay cool and dry, then walked out the door and was instantaneously in a full body sweat. And that is exactly what has happened every day for the last month.

"I cannot believe you're gonna miss Fire Island! But then again, you get to go to the Hamptons. I'm so effing jealous!" Logan's voice on the other end of the line is flush with envy. "Who are these people again? Are they famous? Is the husband hot?"

"I don't know who they are. I Googled them and all that came up was a Times wedding announcement. I think the husband works for some stock brokerage? They have a house in East Hampton," I say.

I've already had a phone interview with Mrs. Brander and she seems nice enough. However, I was so desperate to have any work at all, I can't remember exactly what I've agreed to.

"I swear to God, Holly. If you meet Ina Garten before I do, I will one hundred percent un-friend you on Facebook."

"Understood. I'm getting on the bus and there's a sign that says no cell phones."

"Yeah, the Jitney is weird like that. Call me later and fill me in."

"I'll be back in the city next week sometime to get the keys to the studio in the Village. Dinner then?"

"Done and done." He hangs up.

I sit on the bus, listening to my iPod, wondering what this family will be like and what they will be having me do. I've heard so many things about the Hamptons from Logan; I wonder how much of my experience will be like what he's described to me. I wonder what their house looks like, and what my bedroom will look like. What the beaches will be like. I've never been to the beach on the East Coast before.

The ride out to the Hamptons is actually quite boring for the first ninety minutes or so. Getting out of Manhattan on a bus is cumbersome and nauseating. So many switch backs on the one-way streets.

Once out of the city, we drive through Queens and then through the inner parts of Long Island. I zone out to my music as we pass strip malls and grocery stores, banks, gyms, concrete parking lots… it actually looks like parts of the Valley in Los Angeles. But after about an hour and a half, I look out the window and notice that the scene has transformed into something out of a Nicholas Sparks novel. Huge cornfields stretch out along the sides of the highway, and we pass signs for foreign-sounding towns like Speonk, Quogue and

Tuckahoe. I silently attempt to pronounce these words. They sound so strange to me after growing up California, where every major city name starts with San, Santa, Las or Los. As we drive farther out, I notice the ancient looking cemeteries and tiny churches that dot the Montauk Highway. I've never seen anything like it.

When I arrive at the East Hampton stop, I'm met by Charlotte Brander. She has dark brown hair that is stick straight and piercing blue eyes. She's probably thirty-eight, but it's hard to tell with all the Botox she's surely had injected into her face. The fact that she weighs about one hundred pounds makes it even harder to approximate her age. Though in spite of her small stature, she gives off the air of someone not to be messed with.

With Logan's advice, I begin by scoping out her labels. According to Logan, you can always tell what kind of New York woman you are dealing with by the labels she wears. Chanel, Prada and Manolo Blahnik are in the clear. Louis Vuitton, Jimmy Choo, Versace, or Gucci, she's a bitch.

The first thing I spot is Charlotte's Louis Vuitton bag and Gucci ballet flats. *Shit.*

"Audrey! Hi! I'm Charlotte Brander," she says as she extends her tiny, emaciated hand my way. "It's so lovely to finally meet you in the flesh."

"Hi, Mrs. Brander. Very nice to meet you too." We shake hands.

I look down at her side and see an adorable, angelic child partially hidden by Charlotte's tiny thigh.

"This is Lily, our youngest."

"Hi Lily," I say.

"We are so glad you're here! Our last girl was a complete nightmare," says Charlotte as we pile into her car. "Today will be super easy because I just need you to take Lily over to a birthday party in Sagaponack. Her little friend Bridget is turning four and they're having a princess party."

"Oh wow! That sounds fun." I'm somewhat alarmed that this woman is going to hand her child off to me the first day she's met me, but I guess she has faith in the agency's background checks…or she simply doesn't care.

"Are you excited, Lily?" Charlotte asks loudly, as if her child is hard of hearing.

Lily smiles and nods her head in the back seat.

"She better be excited," Charlotte intimates to me. "This party is costing Bridget's parents a fortune. Spare no expense when it comes to birthday parties and weddings, right?"

She laughs, assuming what she's just said was very clever.

"Oh totally!" I try forcing my own enthusiastic-sounding laugh.

We turn down beautiful tree-lined streets dotted with elegant homes.

"Okay, here's the schedule for while you're here. We'll need you from eight o'clock in the morning until six o'clock in the evening most days. Some nights we'll be out late for events, in which case Mr. Brander will pay you extra for your time."

"That works just fine," I say.

"We need you here from Wednesday to Sunday, but if you'd like to stay on Monday and Tuesday to have your days off at the beach, we're fine with that," she says. "We just don't allow overnight guests, okay? Otherwise, we're pretty relaxed. You're welcome to a glass of wine with dinner."

"That's awfully nice." I smile. "And my boyfriend lives in California, so no problem there."

"So, you've met Lily, and you'll meet our sons Jet and Jax when we get home." She continues. "They're seven years old and I'm not going to lie, they're already starting to act like little pricks. But they're sweet boys deep down. At least, that's what their therapist says."

"Oh!" is all I can manage to choke out.

"You'll have access to our van and there's a GPS in there so you won't get lost. This is our street, Terbell Lane."

Charlotte pulls into the driveway of a huge home that is three stories tall and covered in dark wood siding. The garden is huge and lined with giant hydrangea bushes. Beyond the grass is a large body of water that looks like a private lake.

"What's that water over there?" I ask, pointing.

"Oh, that's Hook Pond. The kids can kayak in it, but make sure they wear life vests."

"That's a pond?" I ask in disbelief.

"Uh-huh," she says nonchalantly.

"Wow. It's really lovely here," I say, downplaying the fact that my mind is actually being blown as I speak to her.

"Yeah, it's pretty nice."

"How often do you come out here?" I ask.

"July and August every year, and then some weekends in the fall and spring. Our apartment in the city is on the Upper East Side; you'll see it in September."

Of course, they own a mansion that they use for only eight weeks out of the year. I forgot where I was for a second.

"Do you watch Food Network?" Charlotte asks with a smirk on her face.

"Sure," I say.

"Ina Garten's house is about a mile away. We see her in town a lot."

Logan is going to die.

Charlotte hops out of her SUV and right away gestures to me to un-belt Lily from her car seat, which I do graciously.

"My name is Audrey," I say to Lily. "I'm excited to be your new nanny!"

"Hi Audee." She takes my hand and leads me toward the house, following her mother.

When we walk into the entry hall of the house, I'm immediately overwhelmed by a wealth of tacky nautical-themed décor. Anchors, ropes, miniature sailboats, and even a dated wooden sign for the Montauk Yacht Club, which hangs on the wall.

"Are you a sailing family?" I ask.

"No," says Charlotte. "Let me show you the playroom."

"Oh, okay…" I follow her through the large living room and into the kitchen.

"We recently re-modeled to give the kids some more space."

The kitchen is huge and attached to it is a family room where there is a large TV, baskets of toys, several gaming systems, a pinball machine and an air hockey table.

The entire space is lined with windows that give a panoramic view of the backyard, pool and Hook Pond off in the distance. It's like a scene out of a movie. Basked in the golden glow of the afternoon sun, the view is absolutely breathtaking.

"Where are the boys?" I ask.

"They should be coming home from camp any minute," Charlotte says as she turns on the coffee machine. "Espresso?"

"No thanks. What kind of camp do they go to?"

"Lacrosse," she says. "Lily, why don't you show Audrey your room and you can get dressed for your party."

"Otay," replies Lily as she takes my hand. "C'mon, Audee."

Lily leads me over to a small staircase that's situated at the back of the playroom. We ascend the stairs together slowly, one foot at a time. I'm not sure about her mother yet, but I already know I like Lily. She's barely two feet tall with tiny brown curls all over her head. She has bright blue eyes that are the size of tea saucers and a shy, quiet demeanor.

Once upstairs, we walk down the hall toward the door at the very end. Bright pink glittered letters on it read, 'Princess Lily.'

"That's my room," says Lily pointing to the door, her voice timid and shy. Her R's sound like W's and I have to adjust my ear to note that she's pointing at her 'room,' not her 'womb.'

"It looks beautiful even from the outside," I say as we near the door. "How old are you by the way?"

"Fwee," she says, holding up three fingers. I can't help but grin.

I open the door to her room and my eyes are immediately assaulted by the color pink. The entire room is pink. Painted on the wall behind her bed is a huge mural of a castle, complete with pony-drawn carriages crossing over the moat, surrounding enchanted forests, unicorns running wild, rainbows, fairies, butterflies, and you guessed it – more glitter.

"Lily, I'm going to take a wild guess here and say that your favorite color is... pink?"

"Yep!" she replies enthusiastically. "I like purple too."

Her bed is a full-sized, four-poster bed, covered in the most beautiful pink gossamer quilts and pillows. My four-year-old self would have never left this room. Her princess dolls line the shelves and she even has a castle playhouse in the corner. But the pièce de résistance - the thing that would make any small female child the happiest child on the planet – is the giant dress-up box that is bursting at the seams with princess dresses, feather boas, costume jewelry and shoes.

"Whoa..." I say as I walk toward it. "Lily, is this your special dress-up box?"

"Yeah." She shrugs, like it's no big deal. Of course, to her it probably isn't. That box has likely been there since before she could walk. It's a part of a life she has become accustomed to that I never could have imagined at her age.

"Which princess do you think you want to be for the party today?" I ask.

"Not sure," she says very matter-of-factly. "Maybe Sleeping Beauty?"

"I think that's a solid choice. Shall we get you dressed, your highness?"

"Okay. Thanks Audee."

"Don't mention it." I open her dress-up box and we pull out her pink gown and tiara. Once Lily is dressed, I help her walk downstairs in her plastic heels. I'm also holding her wand, her handbag and her pink pony, whose name is Nicholas and who apparently goes to any special social engagement with her.

"You got Nicholas okay, Audee?"

"Yes, ma'am," I say. "He's right here."

"Oh good, you're all ready!" says Charlotte as we descend back into the kitchen playroom. On the ground I see what looks like a wrestling match, and I'm instantly ill at ease. "Audrey, I want you to meet the boys."

There they are. Seven-year-old twins Jet and Jax, wrestling and spinning around so fast I can barely make them out.

"Hi guys," I say with a small wave.

"Boys! Audrey is your new babysitter. I want you to say hello to her," says Charlotte with forced calm. "Boys, may I interrupt your little testosterone-fueled moment to introduce your new nanny?"

"Oh, it's okay, Mrs. Brander..." I attempt.

"BOYS!!!" she screams fortissimo.

"What?!" They both scream simultaneously in a way that makes me jump. Twins really are creepy.

"Say hello to Audrey, for God's sake!" shouts Charlotte.

"Hell-OH to Audrey, for God's sake!" They yell in unison, stopping only for a brief moment, before continuing their wrestling competition.

"You'll have a chance to get to know them at dinner tonight," says Charlotte. "Once they're tired out, they're actually very sweet to be around."

Right. "Great," I say half-heartedly. "So, which car do we take to the party?"

"Of course," says Charlotte reaching into a drawer. "Here are the keys to the van, and there's a GPS inside. The address for the party is on this invitation and the present for Lily's friend is in the entry hall."

"Sounds great. We'll see you for dinner then at what time?"

"Just be home by six-thirty and Nina will have dinner prepared. Do you eat lobster?"

"Yep, love it."

"Lovely. See you later then."

"Say bye to mom, Sleeping Beauty," I say as we walk out of the kitchen.

"Bye mama!" shouts Lily.

Charlotte doesn't answer her.

When Lily and I arrive at the birthday party, I pull into the driveway of a house that actually looks like a French chateau.

It's enormous and designed in the Tudor style. The front yard is covered in pink and purple balloon archways, and royal banners hang from all the upstairs windows. As I put the car in park, a valet dressed as Prince Charming greets us. Somehow the sight of a prince driving a Lexus minivan is just not that strange when you're in the Hamptons.

I snap a quick photo of the house and text it to Brent.

Thought Bel Air was nuts...

He responds after a minute.

LOL. What have you
gotten yourself into?

Lily and I walk under a huge pink balloon archway tunnel and down the front path toward the entryway of the house. Before we can get to the front door, we are greeted by two more princes who hand us cups full of punch that contain floating blueberries.

"Welcome to Bridget's castle!" says the first Prince. "May we take your coats?"

I look at them awkwardly, then to Lily and myself and back to them, as if it's obvious that none of us are wearing coats but them.

"Um, no thank you," I say.

"The party is out back in the tent," says the second one, smiling and giving us a bow.

"There's a tent?" I ask, more to myself than to him. He just smiles some more and gestures toward a gate leading to the backyard.

I'm fully expecting a camping tent set up for the kids to play in, but apparently that's not how they roll in Sagaponack.

As we walk through the gate, my breath catches in my chest. It's impressive. The interior of the huge event tent is draped in a sheer pink fabric that billows down in certain areas on the sides creating an elegant, whimsical feeling.

Half the tent is filled with tables boasting extraordinary floral arrangements, while the other half of the tent is covered in cushions. The cushioned areas are separated into different stations. There's a face painting station, a wand making station, and a balloon station, each area manned by a princess. Sleeping Beauty is face painting, Cinderella is wand making, and Snow White is making balloon tiaras for the girls and swords for the boys.

"Audee, look! She's here," says Lily. "Sleeping Beauty!"

"Should we go say hi?" I ask.

Lily grips my hand and hides behind my leg, immediately shy at the sight of her favorite princess.

"I dunno…"

If I didn't already love this child, this would be the clincher. I reach down and pick her up, balancing her on my hip. "Well I want to meet her, but I'm a little nervous to meet her alone. Do you think you could come with me?"

"Okay," she says. "I'll go with you, Audee."

"Thanks, Lil."

We walk over to the face painting station where Sleeping Beauty is painting an elegant butterfly face on a small girl that Lily recognizes.

"That's my friend Avery," she says to me. "Hi Avery!"

The little girl looks up, carefully. "Hi Lily!" she says.

"Now hold still," says Sleeping Beauty. "We're almost done."

"Wow, that's really good," I say to Sleeping Beauty.

"Why, thank you!" she replies.

She finishes up with Avery and adds some glitter to her cheeks for a final touch. Then she looks over at us. "Sleeping Beauty, this is Lily," I say.

"Hi Lily, so very nice to meet you." Her voice is melodic, as only a princess's would be.

"Hi…" Lily says quietly. "You my favorite princess."

"Well, thank you very much! Would you like me to paint your face today?" She smiles.

"Okay!"

"Would you like a butterfly face? Or a flower princess face?" Sleeping Beauty asks.

"Butterfly please."

I watch Lily have her face painted, marveling at how careful she is to hold still. Occasionally her eyes dart over to me and I smile, giving her a thumbs up. She returns a shy smile and nods whenever Sleeping Beauty asks her a question.

When Sleeping Beauty finishes, she brushes glitter on for the finishing touch. Lily stands up and gives Sleeping Beauty a big hug.

"Can I snap a photo?" I ask.

"Of course!" says Sleeping Beauty.

"One, two, three, cheese!" I say as I take the picture with my iPhone. "Mommy is going to love that, Lily! Thank you very much, Sleeping Beauty."

"You're very welcome! Enjoy the party, and don't forget the princess show starts in an hour," she says.

As she sits back down, she straightens her skirt and I catch a glimpse of her shoe. I recognize it from my shopping trip with Logan. It's a pink, sparkly Chanel ballet flat. *Holy crap! Those are like seven hundred dollar shoes!*

Lily and I enjoy the rest of the party, making wands, building ice cream sundaes and finally singing a long with the princess show, but even as we drive back home, the image of those Chanel flats keeps popping back into my mind. I begin racking my brain trying to figure out how a party entertainer, no older than myself, could afford such expensive, designer shoes.

FIVE

I'd be lying if I said I don't relish the two days a week I'm off and back in the city. Not knowing anyone else in the Hamptons is a bit challenging. I've tried making friends with some of the other nannies, but a lot of them are from the Caribbean and their English is hard to understand. My second week, I made friends with another girl who worked for some friends of the Branders. We started getting coffee in the mornings while the kids were at camp, but a week later, she left to take an African safari with her parents. Since then, I've been spending a lot of my Hamptons nights in reading, watching Netflix and having Skype dates with Brent.

On one of my free Monday nights back in the city, Logan and I sit chatting over seaweed salads at Jewel Bako. The minute I got off the bus this afternoon, I felt like I could breathe again. Even now as we sit in this lovely restaurant, the sounds of taxis beeping outside is such a comfort.

"I hate being out of the city," I say.

"The Hamptons can be very isolating," he agrees.

"I just feel like there's no one my age that I want to hang out with there," I say. "And the minute the kids are in bed and I'm off, I just want to get away from their mother as quickly as possible. There' something about her that creeps me out. She's totally sweet on the surface, but something is off."

"How do you like the kids?" he asks

"I love the little girl, Lily," I say. "She's adorable… but the twins are a friggin' nightmare."

"Twins are a nightmare no matter the age," says Logan, sipping his saketini.

"These two are particularly bad," I say. "They're studying martial arts or something, and the other day one of them said he wanted to elbow me in the neck so I'd pass out."

"He's compensating for something…" Logan stifles a laugh.

"I was sort of worried that the two of them might corner and attack me. They're pretty strong for seven. Oh! And one of them always runs out of the shower and plays his wiener like a guitar."

"Oh, every little boy does that," says Logan dismissively.

"Alright does every little boy try to pull off their nanny's bathing-suit top in the pool?"

"Well, I certainly did not!"

"They're identical and I can't tell them apart and they're always saying that one is the other and confusing me. It's awful!"

"Can't you just mark one of them with a Sharpie or something?" asks Logan.

I laugh but ignore the question. "I'm telling you, there is something about the mother. I took Lily to this princess party and when I brought her home the mom went nuts because her daughter had face paint on. I mean it's a freaking birthday party!"

"Expensive towels probably…" he says.

"Even so! I showed her a picture I took of Lily with Sleeping Beauty, who by the way is Lily's favorite princess, and

Charlotte didn't even care! She acted like she couldn't be bothered by this precious moment her daughter had."

"Holly, I'm telling you, some of these New York mothers are a breed of their own."

"It's so sad," I say.

"What's the dad like?" Logan asks.

"I haven't met him yet. He hasn't come out to the house once."

"Mistress in the city probably," he says matter-of-factly. "Or if he's really dirty… in Jersey."

"Oh stop it! That's crazy," I say. "People don't actually do that."

"Keep babysitting for them, you might change your tune," he says. "Families who seem perfect on the outside are seldom perfect on the inside."

"Their entry hall is just covered in sailing memorabilia," I say. "Anchors everywhere…"

"Stop it!" says Logan with a slight cough. "I might not be able to keep my dinner down."

"It's bad," I say with a laugh.

"Do they sail?"

"No!"

"I hate them already."

"But Lily is so perfect. I don't want that crazy upbringing for her." I protest. "She's perfect. I'm telling you. If they don't want her, I'll take her. I'd go single mom status for that kid."

"She won't want for anything I'm sure," he says. "And she'll go to the best private schools."

"I don't think that's enough," I say. "My family is crazy, but in the normal way. And I love them. I can't imagine how life will turn out for Lily…"

"You know why these New Yorkers have so many kids, right?" says Logan under his breath.

"Because children are a 'blessing from God?' I have no idea…why?"

"Because it ensures a better divorce settlement when they catch their husbands cheating."

"What?" I shout. "No way!"

"New York pretty recently followed California's lead and is now a no-fault state for divorces," says Logan. "Which means that a wife can no longer sue her cheating husband for breaking his marriage vows. They split everything fifty-fifty unless there's a prenup in place. So the best way for her to get compensated for being cheated on is to get extra child support money."

"That's terrible."

"You'll know she's discovered her husband is cheating on her when she gets pregnant in the fall."

"Paulie! Stop it… That's horrible."

"Okay, okay." He concedes. "But hey, just another week until you're back in the city and move into your new apartment! Are you excited?"

"Oh my God, I cannot wait! It will be so great to switch from live-in nanny to after school nanny. I feel like this Hamptons gig has put everything on hold!"

"It'll be great to have you back," he says.

"I can't wait to be back to auditioning and start sleeping in my own bed, in my new place." I say. "I'm sorry I've had to store my shit in your guest room for so long. I feel bad about that."

"Yes, it will be nice to have that back so I can make it into a gift wrapping room just in time for the holidays," he quips, just as our waiter shows up asking if we need another drink.

Two days later I arrive back in East Hampton to do my final five-day stint at the beach. Charlotte has already dropped the boys off at camp, and Lily to a play date with a friend, and has given me instructions to pick up groceries from Citarella.

"So this week the boys have fencing lessons on Saturday afternoon and a Lacrosse match on Sunday afternoon. Also, Hugh will be coming out this weekend so he and I are going to Sag Harbor for a couple nights."

"Oh," I say, taken aback.

"I know we haven't asked for you to be on duty for forty-eight hours, but we'll certainly pay you extra for your time."

Dear lord... forty-eight hours with three kids? "Right, okay," I say, not daring to argue with the source of my desperately needed income.

"We decided to cut Jet's hair in a buzz-cut and leave Jax's long so you'll be able to tell them apart. And Mr. Brander and I fully support you if you need to reprimand or discipline the boys, obviously within reason, but you're the expert here," she says with a laugh.

"Well, I just want to enforce the family rules," I say.

"Audrey, I'm going to be frank with you. I'm at my wits' end with the boys," she says with desperation. "When Hugh isn't around, they are a nightmare. I don't know why they hate me so much! I mean, I carried them in my womb. I lost my six-pack abs for them! Why are they so angry? I'm hardly even home, so what could I have possibly done to them?"

I don't bother answering that question, because I already know the answer. Instead, I give her a sympathetic nod and will this conversation to be over.

When we get back to the house, Nina is already in the kitchen making it spotless. Amidst all the Brander-crazy, Nina is a lighthouse in the storm. She is Pacific Islander, very small and stout, very calm, but strong as an ox. She has a thick accent and wicked sense of humor.

"Hey, Nina," I say as I set my overnight bag down in the guest room off the kitchen.

"Hello, pretty lady!" she calls to me. "How you doing?"

"Good! Thanks," I say.

"City good?" she asks.

"Yep." I walk back into the kitchen.

"Alright, I've got a massage at ten-thirty, so I'm heading out," says Charlotte. "Nina, if you can just make sure we use that chicken tonight, Audrey will get some more food for the week."

"Yes, okay," says Nina nodding.

"Audrey, thanks so much." She hands me the keys to the

van. "I'll be back later. You'll need to pick the kids up this afternoon. I've left a schedule on the table in the entry hall with the addresses and pickup times, and grocery list. Please buy the exact brands I've listed."

"Sounds good," I say. "Thanks."

"Okay, ta-ta ladies!" And with that, Charlotte disappears out the door.

Nina waits until she hears the engine of Charlotte's car roar to life before she starts laughing. "Ta-ta?" She giggles. "She crazy."

"I didn't realize that 'ta-ta' was back in vogue," I say laughing.

"I need to ask you question." Nina gestures me toward the laundry room, still giggling.

"Sure," I say.

"I not sure if I should throw these away? Or try to sew." She begins reaching into the laundry hamper. "What you think?"

Nina holds up something white and lacy and I burst out laughing.

"Nina," I say. "Those are crotch-less panties. They are meant to be cut like that."

"These not broken?" she asks, looking confused. "They make like this?"

"Yes!" I say through fits of laughter. "They are supposed to be sexy or something. Easy access."

"Oh…" says Nina, now laughing herself. "I thought Mister Hugh...he rip–"

"Stop it!" I squeak out, laughing so hard I'm actually crying. "Oh my God, Nina!"

Nina and I continue laughing as we walk back into the kitchen. I pick up the keys from the counter and grab my purse. "I'm glad you here, Miss Audrey," she says. "I like you. No one seem to stay very long here."

"Really?" I ask.

"I think Mrs. Brander like you though. Poor Lily always ask why her babysitter leave all the time."

"Poor thing," I say.

"These kids just need love," says Nina. "Their mom just don't want to be a part of their lives. She be sorry someday."

"You know, I honestly think they act out because they are starved for attention."

"Yep."

"Well, I'd better head out." I say.

"Okay. I make fried chicken tonight because the kids love it and Misses Crazy hate it," she says, winking at me.

"Sounds perfect," I giggle. "I'll be back later."

I walk into the entry hall and find Charlotte's list of groceries, alongside the pickup locations and times for the kids. I head out to the van with my plan already decided for me.

Driving through the Hamptons is actually very soothing. Endless cornfields, expansive lawns, and beautiful crisp white homes topped with dark wooden roofs. Some of the streets are covered in a thick tree canopy and each entrance to an estate is lined with hydrangea and oleander bushes.

I drive out of the neighborhood and turn onto the Montauk Highway, heading toward Citarella, listening to the radio with the windows down, enjoying the warm summer air. I make a firm vow to myself that I'm going to do whatever I can to help these children be nicer and more well-rounded individuals. Lily already has my heart, and I've seen Jet and Jax when they've fallen asleep on the couch watching TV. They're harmless when they're unconscious. If only there was some way I could convince them to stop acting out.

As I walk through the aisles of Citarella, I pass a small stationary aisle and my brain starts ticking. I turn my cart down the aisle and grab a white poster board, a black marker, and as luck would have it, I see blue circle stickers on the next row of office supplies. My plan is already forming as I pass the cookie aisle. *What's the biggest motivator for a spoiled child?* Sugar.

As children, my parents were always bribing us with dessert. Ice cream after getting vaccinations at the doctor, cookies after dinner if you finished all your vegetables. My brother and I were never grounded or spanked when we misbehaved, instead we were restricted from sweets. It was the biggest blow imaginable for a kid. *Maybe, just maybe.*

By the time, I pick the boys up from camp and Lily from her friend's house, my strategy is fully formed. And as we drive back to the house, I decide to implement it. The kids are particularly mellow after a full day of running around, so I feel like this is as good a time as any to give them the news that there's a new sheriff in town.

"Alright, guys. I want to have a little meeting just the four of us," I say. "I want you to listen very carefully because there are prizes involved."

I look in the rearview mirror and see their faces suddenly perk up.

"What kind of prizes?" asks Jet skeptically.

"Yeah, Audrey, what kind of prizes?" asks Jax.

"Seriously boys, can we just nix the surround sound?" I say sarcastically. To my surprise, they actually laugh. "Okay, listen up!"

"You boys better listen to Audee, or I'm gonna be the best and win your prizes," says Lily. My biggest fan.

"Okay, we're listening," says Jax.

"I am going to make a chart." I start out. "And the chart will contain your goals for each day. You guys don't have to do much because Nina is a huge help, but there are a few things you have to do to win your prize."

"Like what?" asks Jet defiantly.

"Like being nice to each other, and keeping your voices to a reasonable decibel. Cleaning up your games and toys when you are done playing. Finishing your vegetables, getting yourself in the shower and ready for bed when it's time and going to sleep when it's lights out," I say. "Does that sound doable?"

"What do we get if we do all that?" asks Jet.

"Well," I say. "If you don't do all those things, you are restricted from dessert and all sweets for the entire week."

"WHAT?!" the twins yell in unison.

"Hold on," I say. "If you mark off all your goals for the day, you'll get your regular after dinner popsicle... but if you mark off all your goals for the week, then you get to choose either a king size candy bar at the store, or you can get two scoops at the ice cream stand…with sprinkles."

"YEAH!" yells Jax.

"NICE!" yells Jet.

"Audee, I don't like sprinkles." Lily chimes in.

"That's okay, Lil. We'll work something out," I say.

"Audrey! You're awesome!" says Jax.

"But, I'm serious you guys," I say. "Your mom and dad have already agreed to this, so I'm not yanking your chain here. If you put one, I mean one toe out of line, I will throw every ounce of sugar in your house in the trash and you won't see another cookie or drop of chocolate milk until you're a teenager. And you'll have to drink soy milk and have carrots for dessert."

The car falls silent and as I glance in the rearview mirror again, I feel satisfied. I've adequately terrified them. They're taking me seriously.

After we arrive home, the kids and I take a little time to swim. At first the boys start roughhousing and splashing me and Lily, but I remind them of our deal and they slowly start to turn it around. After an hour, they're starting to play nicely.

"Audrey, Nina isn't feeling well and left early, can you heat up dinner for the kids? I'm heading out for book club!" shouts Charlotte. The kids and I exit the pool, and I wrap them all in beach towels. "I'll probably be late tonight."

"Okay," I say. "Do you mind if I rinse off in the outdoor shower before prepping dinner? Little chlorine allergy, need to get it off my skin."

"Oh, okay, no problem. Will you rinse Lily off too?"

"Sure!" I shout back. "C'mon, Lil."

Lily and I stand in our bathing suits under the warm outdoor shower and I help her soap up. As I'm lathering her hair, I hear one of the twins call my name.

"Hey Audrey, can I talk to you for a sec? You guys still in

your bathing suits?"

"Sure, what's up Jax?" I say as he rounds the wooden partition, his long hair giving him away.

"Well, I was just thinking about our goals because I really have a craving for a cookie tonight," he says. "So Jet and I were thinking maybe we should take quick showers in the outdoor stall after you guys? So that way we've already got that out of the way before dinner."

"I think that's a very smart idea," I say with a smile. "Lil and I will be right out and then you boys can jump in."

"Thanks, Audrey," he says with a smile, reaching his hand up to give me a high-five. *Holy shit. It's already working.*

After dinner, I marvel at the fact that the boys have not only showered and Jax has combed his hair, but their dinner plates are clean. We had a brief moment, mid-meal, where Jax threatened to catapult peas at me with his spoon, but all I had to do was get out the carton of soy milk, and he stopped. Now they sit at the table all looking up at me expectantly.

"Wow, you guys," I say. "I'm actually very impressed. Not only do you get dessert tonight, but I think we can make it a special night and pop some popcorn and watch a movie before bed."

I'm pretty thrilled to see three jaws hit the table and then curl up into smiles.

As we sit on the couch, the kids munch on their cookies and popcorn and I scroll through the channel guide.

"Oh!" I shout. "This is one of my favorites from when I was a kid!"

"What's it called?" asks Jet.

"Homeward Bound," I say. "Oh, it's so good. It's about two dogs and a cat that get lost in the wilderness and have to find their way back home. It's the first movie that ever made me cry when I was a kid."

"I dunno, Audee," says Lily.

"Well it's one of my favorites and I think you guys will really like it. How about we watch fifteen minutes and if you don't like it you can pick something else?"

"Okay," says Jax. "I'm game."

"Me too," says Jet.

"Me fwee!" says Lily.

The boys snuggle closer to Lily and me on the couch. They are already in their pajamas and I'm feeling pretty tenderly toward them. *These poor kids are just starved for some structure and TLC.*

"Okay, that's Chance," I say pointing at the screen. "And that's Sassy and Shadow. He's my favorite."

"Why don't their mouths move when they talk?" asks Jet.

"Because this was before CGI," I say.

"What's that mean?" asks Jet.

"Computer Generated Images," I say. "It's how they make animals look like they're talking in movies now that aren't animated."

"Wow, so this movie is like... a classic," says Jet.

"Old school," says Jax.

I laugh. "Yes, very old school."

"Cool," says Jet.

As we watch the movie, Lily falls asleep against my side and soon Jet and Jax are slumbering peacefully next to her. I decide to sit and watch the rest of the movie myself, and as always, I bawl my eyes out as a mud-clad Shadow limps his way back into little Peter's arms at the end.

"Dammit, Shadow..." I whisper to myself.

When the movie ends, I gently wake the boys, and they wander sleepily toward their bedroom. Then I pick up Lily and carry her upstairs to her room. I tuck her in with Nicholas the pony and turn on her nightlight before carefully closing her door.

As I make my way back down the hallway, I hear a voice up in the boys' loft on the third floor.

"Audrey, can you tuck us in?"

I walk into the boys' huge room, and there they are, lying in their beds and looking toward the door in the dim light of their nightlight.

"Of course, guys," I say as I tuck their blankets in and give them both hugs. "You guys did really well today. I'm very proud of you. Let's keep up the good work, okay?"

"Okay."

"Okay."

"Goodnight," I say, and I walk out of their room and close the door.

I've so got this, I think with a smile.

SIX

Fired? *Fired??* They fired me?

"Why would they fire me?" I say to Lucy on the other end of the phone. I'm pacing around my apartment, frantic. "We just got back to the city! Everything was going great!"

"She said she just didn't feel like it was the right fit and something about a chlorine allergy. I'm so sorry. This does happen, but we'll find you the right family," says Lucy. Her candy-coated optimism sets my teeth on edge.

"I only told her that I had a slight allergy and that I wanted to shower off after swimming with the kids. I was there a month! She never said anything," I say, stunned.

"Sometimes it's just about chemistry."

She's ready to get me off the phone as soon as possible.

"This can't be real!" I shout. "I gave those kids structure! Their manners were improved overnight because I set up a system of rewards for good behavior. I'm sorry, Lucy. I know this is going to sound totally unprofessional, but this is bullshit."

"Audrey, I understand this is a shock…"

"A shock? No, this is an outrage!" I yell. "That woman is out of control! Don't even get me started about the adult devices she and her husband left laying around for the housekeeper to clean up my last week there!"

I only hear silence on the other end. Clearly I've said too much.

"…Well, I think that's information that should not be shared. That's a violation of your confidentiality agreement with the Branders."

"Oh, screw the Branders!" I say exasperated. "And if I'm fired than that confidentiality agreement can go to hell. They're not even a high profile family!"

I'm so furious I can't see straight. I suddenly remember a snippet of the conversation I had with Nina, *No one seem to stay very long here… Poor Lily always ask why her babysitter leave all the time.*

"Audrey, I know this is upsetting…" Lucy interrupts my thoughts.

"Lucy, level with me," I say. "This isn't just about a chlorine allergy is it? This is about them not wanting to pay your hiring fee, right?"

Lucy sighs on the other end of the phone. "It would be unprofessional of me to—"

"The housekeeper mentioned something to me about the house being kind of a revolving door with nannies," I say. "Is this just what they do? They circulate girls through on trial periods and then shuffle them out the door when you guys are ready to collect?"

Lucy is quiet for another moment before I hear her taking a deep breath. "We have had a few placements with the Branders not work out, so it's possible," she says. "We were really hoping they'd love you, but we may not work with them again. I know you were excited, doll, but sometimes it just doesn't work out. They did pay you in cash for the month, yes?"

"Yes, but I'm hemorrhaging money on rent. Can you get

me another interview this week? Or something temporary?" The panic in my voice can't be masked.

"I'll give you a call tomorrow, I'm sure we can line something up for you with a great family."

"Okay…"

"Don't worry, Audrey. We'll work this out."

She hangs up.

I sit on my bed absolutely stunned. I had done so well with those kids. I had given them direction. I had driven them around to camp and pool parties. Jet and Jax's behavior was improving, and Lily… I had grown to care for her so much already. I can't believe I'm never going to see her again. And seriously, I was a great fit for them! How could they fire me? How can I be fired from my first job in New York for no reason?

I look around my beautiful apartment. I've only lived here for twenty-four hours, and now I'm not sure I can stay. In fact, I know I can't stay. There's no way I can afford this place now. I'll have to move at the end of the month.

I pick up my phone and dial.

"Logan?" I'm about to cry. "I'm coming over. I need a drink. And I'm moving to Brooklyn."

"I have vodka in the freezer and *Breakfast at Tiffany's* on demand. See you in ten."

Within five minutes, I'm outside hailing a cab to take me down to TriBeCa. I should probably save the ten dollars and just take the subway, but I'm so stunned by what's just transpired that I don't care. *Fired?*

"I've never been fired before!" I lament to my cab driver, Rajesh, as we drive down Varick Street.

"I'm sorry to hear that, miss. Perhaps there is a silver lining that you simply cannot see yet," he says in his thick accent.

"I hope you're right. Right now I just want a drink."

"Sometimes that helps as well," he says.

"Can you just pull over on the far corner there?"

"Sure thing," he says.

I hand him a ten-dollar bill. "Keep the change and thanks for the advice," I say.

"Good luck to you, miss," he says as I close the door to the cab.

I buzz Logan's apartment and the door clicks open. When I arrive at his floor, he's already standing at the door with two martinis in hand.

"I cannot believe those poor excuses for Manhattanites fired you! Rude!"

"Right? They just wanted to get out of paying my hiring fee," I say, accepting a glass and a kiss from him on the cheek.

"You can never trust rich people. Sometimes they're the cheapest ones. Come on in. The movie's already queued up and I have some snacks."

Logan and I sit on his couch and nosh on pita chips and crudité. By the time the film is nearly over, we're on our second rather large and strong martini.

"I wish I could write an exposé about them and send it to the New York Times. 'Goldman Sachs financier has weird fetish!' " I take a sip of my drink. "Then they could determine that Lily needs to be taken into protective custody by 'Audee,' her wonderful ex-nanny."

"I'm more concerned about that poor housekeeper. She'll never be the same again after some of the stuff you've told me," he says.

"Seriously…When I was there the last week, she asked me what to do with some of Charlotte's delicates. Apparently she thought the crotch-less panties had been torn and needed sewing."

Logan bursts out laughing. "Oh, bless her!"

"Aw, Nina. I loved her," I say. "She had to clean up their sex toys…"

"You just really can never tell with people, can you?"

"You sure can't…"

"How's Brent?" he asks.

"Haven't talked to him in a few days." I immediately want to change the subject. "God, they just don't make movies like this anymore!"

"Preach, girl."

"Oh! This is my favorite part!" I squeal.

Holly and Paul are sitting in the yellow cab. She's just been released from jail and is ready to leave for Brazil to find a rich husband. Paul looks at her with great intensity.

Logan jumps right in, reciting the dialogue. "Holly, I'm in love with you."

"So what?" I recite in my best Hepburn voice.

"So what? ...So plenty!" He waits a beat. "I love you. You belong to me."

"No... People don't belong to people," I say.

"Of course they do!" Logan shouts emphatically. We are perfectly in sync with the movie after years of practice.

"I'm not going to let anyone put me in a cage." I gesture theatrically, my martini spilling over the rim of my glass.

"I don't want to put you in a cage. I want to love you!" He grips my hand.

"It's the same thing!" I cry.

"No it's not! Holly!" He protests.

"I'm not Holly!" I shout. "I'm not Lula Mae either! I don't know who I am! ...I'm like Cat here. We're a couple of no-name slobs. We belong to nobody and nobody belongs to us; we don't even belong to each other!"

I swing my legs over Logan's lap as we watch Paul tell Holly off and toss the ring box to her in the cab. We hold our breaths as we always do, while she chases after him and then begins searching for Cat, finally finding him amongst the stack of crates in the movie set alley. We both wipe our tears as she finds Cat and puts him in her trench coat and then notices that Paul is standing there, watching her in the rain. I squeeze Logan's hand as Holly and Paul kiss and "Moon River" plays us out.

"What does it say about me that this is like my dream marriage proposal?" I say.

"That you were born in the wrong era, since the idea of having a man shame you turns you on?" he says.

"Maybe. I dunno. There's something about the fact that he doesn't give up on her that I love. And he just calls her out on her shit and then walks away. That's a real man, a man with some balls. That's what I want."

I'm feeling better as I walk back to my apartment from the subway. It's September and the air is cooling down fast. The drinks and movie date have made me feel a little better, but I don't think reality has fully hit yet.

The sidewalks in the West Village are damp from the bit of rain we had today and the pavement is dotted with fallen leaves. I breathe in the crisp, clean air and feel the hollow disappointment as I walk up to my building. It's so beautiful! But now, knowing that I won't be living here very long, the sight is bittersweet. October first, I'll have to relocate to the outer boroughs.

I reach into my purse for my keys and fiddle with the lock.

"Hey, can you hold the door?" I hear a voice behind me.

I turn to see a man carrying a box that looks heavy. He appears to be slightly older than me, tall with dark hair, a beanie, and hip-looking glasses. He's the guy that works at Grey Dog!

"Hey, I know you!" I say as I hold the door open for him. "You work at Grey Dog in Chelsea, right?"

He studies me a moment. "Yeah, have we met?"

"No, not officially. Sorry, I came in a few times a couple of months ago with a friend."

I see his eyes light up with recognition. "Okay... Yeah! You're the girl who drinks iced decaf Americanos with that very loud redhead."

"Yes! Yes! That's my friend, Sarah!" I realize I'm being a bit loud myself after my two martinis. "Sorry, I'm coming home from drowning my sorrows."

"Ah, gotcha."

"Are you moving in?" I ask.

"No. I just like to carry heavy boxes around the Village."

"Naturally," I say. "As do I."

He laughs. "Yeah, just moved in from Williamsburg. Thanks for holding that by the way, and sorry if that joke came out douchey," he says, walking through the door.

"Nah, you're fine. Heavy boxes are indeed funny."

"I don't know why I insist on moving my entire library with me every time I get a new place." He offers up as explanation.

"Oh, I totally understand. I'd never part with my books either." I smile.

"A kindred spirit." He smiles back.

"Seems so."

"I'm Jake by the way, 4C." He extends a finger, as it seems to be all he can spare.

I shake his finger with a laugh. "I'm 4B, but I won't be here long."

"That's quite a name." He teases me.

"Sorry, I'm Audrey." We start walking in unison towards the stairs. "Do you need some help with that?"

"Nah, I got it. Thanks though," he says as we ascend the first flight. "So, why are you leaving, 4B? Is this building more rat and roach-infested than normal New York apartments?"

"No, it's great! I just got fired from my job today. So... can't really afford to stay."

"I'm sorry to hear that."

"Whatcha gonna do, right?"

"What did you do?" We have just started walking up the second flight.

"I didn't do anything. They fired me because I have a slight chlorine allergy and need a shower after swimming with the kids for hours. Go figure."

He laughs. "No, I meant, what did you do for a living? I'm torn now between swimming instructor who is in the wrong profession, or something to do with childcare?"

"Oh! Sorry... Yes, I was a nanny," I say laughing. "Well actually, I'm an actress. The nanny thing is a side gig, while I audition."

"An actress, huh?"

"Aspiring," I say. "Anyway my nanny agency is looking for another position for me, but I guess pickings are slim. Most nannies get placed before the school year starts. So I'm pretty much S.O.L." And with that, we have reached the fourth floor.

"Well thanks for holding the door for me, Miss 4B. Don't be a stranger." I watch for a moment as he sets his box down and unlocks his door.

"Yeah, nice to meet you Jake. Welcome to Manhattan," I say as I open my own door and walk inside.

I shut the door behind me and set my bag down. He seems like a nice guy, I think to myself. Not really my type, but nice. I walk into my bedroom and kick off my shoes when I hear a knock at the front door. I walk back to answer it and see Jake smiling down at me.

"Hi," he says. "Listen, I know we just met, but would you like to come in for a beer? I'm just unpacking books and would love some company, and you seem like a nice, normal person. Plus, you didn't take offense to my dumb jokes."

"Don't you have any more boxes to bring in?" I ask.

"No, that was my last one." He smiles.

"Hmm," I say. "I am already a little buzzed from earlier, so I'm not sure I should..."

"Well then how about I have a beer and you have some water," he suggests. "I promise I'm not a serial killer, but if you feel more comfortable, we can keep our front doors open and just talk through the hall."

"That won't be necessary," I say with a laugh. I slip on some sandals I keep by my door and walk across the hall with him.

His apartment is really nice, slightly bigger than mine and with a bay window facing the street. The living room wall is exposed brick, which I love. The floors are lined with boxes and there's a bookshelf and desk in the corner of the room.

"So, what do you do, Jake? Other than slinging coffee at Grey Dog?" I'm surveying the boxes and wondering what's inside.

"I'm a photographer," he replies. "I mostly shoot travel photography, but I've just been contracted with New York Magazine."

"Oh wow! That's cool," I say.

"Thanks," he says, looking humble.

"So Grey Dog is *your* side gig then," I say.

"Yeah, sort of. I needed to make some extra cash so I could afford to move back into the city, and my friend Greg is the manager there. He let me sneak in a few shifts earlier this summer."

"That's handy," I say. "What kind of travel photography projects do you generally do?"

I walk around the room observing his digs.

"Is this an interview?" he laughs.

"Sorry." I blush. "You mean you didn't ask me over to interrogate you?"

He smiles. "Well, my dream would be to cover the Far East. I'd love for my photography to give me an excuse to leave New York. I want to travel more anyway."

Jake walks into the kitchen and I hear the snap of a beer bottle opening as well as the sound of the faucet.

"That sounds pretty cool," I say. "Have you been many places?"

"I mean, a few. I've been to South America and Mexico. I've done the Caribbean and Europe too. But I'd love to do Alaska and photograph the Northern Lights, parts of Asia and a few other project ideas I've got up my sleeve."

"Ambitious." I take up a place on the floor and lean against a large box.

"Just know what I want," Jake says, as he returns to the living room with a beer for himself and glass of water for me. "As promised."

"Thanks," I say, taking the glass.

"Anytime."

"Traveling is one of my goals too," I say. "I haven't been to many places outside of the country. Just London and Paris in college. I want to do Spain, Italy and South of France, then I don't care where."

"Well don't be afraid to jump way off the map and hit those places up later on in life," he says.

"I'm afraid I'll die before I get there though," I say.

"That's pretty morbid."

I shrug. "Yeah."

"You do need to eat in the Basque country and wander around the cathedrals in Rome. They're definitely worth seeing, but everyone starts with Western Europe and then never really goes back."

"Huh. Do you think that the more you travel, like if you get to all the places you want to see, that the world somehow feels smaller to you? Because it's not this vast unknown anymore?"

"Ah, a philosophical actress," he teases.

"Sorry." I blush. "Too much too soon?"

Jake looks thoughtful before answering. "I think the more you travel, the more you realize what's out there. But truthfully, while I love to travel, I also hate the fact that you can never see everything. It always feels like you're chasing your shadow."

"Hmm... So where's next on your list? If you could go anywhere, spare no expense," I ask, sipping my water.

"I've really been wanting to go to this little island off the coast of Vietnam called Can Dao. The landscape is supposed to be amazing. I'd also like to spend a week in Hanoi."

"Wow, Jake. You're quite ambitious. I'm super jealous, not gonna lie."

Jake laughs. "Thanks. So, how did you like Paris?"

"I loved it, but I was only there for a couple days. I ran around like crazy trying to see everything. I did the Louvre, the Musee d'Orsay, Notre Dame, Sacre Coeur, Montmartre, the Eiffel tower, Arc de Triomphe and the Tuileries. Ended up with a broken pair of sandals and a few blisters, but I got it done."

"I'd say that's pretty ambitious," he laughs.

"It was weird not to be there with someone though. I went

alone, and walking along the Seine, seeing all the people picnicking, drinking wine, couples kissing and listening to musicians play at dusk, it made me feel lonely." I take another sip of my water. "Sorry, I'm totally over-sharing! Can we blame the two martinis I had earlier?"

Jake chuckles. "My trip to Paris was actually pretty short as well. I have this idea to go back and do a series of photographs exclusively about the café culture on the left bank."

"That sounds amazing," I say. "All I did when I was there was eat Nutella crêpes and ham sandwiches off carts. I was too chicken to go into any restaurants alone when my knowledge of French is so pathetic."

"Terrible."

"I know. My friend Logan is a huge foodie and he got me very into French food. He was equally horrified when I told him. Man, I would have killed to eat Boeuf Bourguignon in a real French brasserie. I shoulda just gone for it…"

"Well, there's always next time." He reaches his bottle over toward my glass. "To seeing the world… and to new neighbors."

I laugh. "To Manhattan. I will miss it so."

I take a sip of my water and hear the small chiming sound of a ringtone.

Jake looks up with recognition. "Sorry, that's my girlfriend's ring," he says. "Do you mind? She's traveling for work, and her movers are bringing her stuff tomorrow so I should probably talk to her."

"Oh… yeah, sure," I say. "Totally fine."

Jake walks into the kitchen and I hear him answer the phone.

"Hey babe. How's Sedona?… I'll bet…Just moving stuff into the new place, met one of our new neighbors… How long do you think you'll be there?"

I pull out my own phone. Nothing from Brent today. Nothing from Brent for a few days. He must be really busy with work. I decide to send him a text anyway.

Hey, miss u.
All going well?

I stare at the screen, watching to see if a reply will pop up, but nothing comes through.

Jake is still on the phone in the kitchen. "Okay, no of course that's fine. Just let me know when to expect the movers. No, I won't unpack your clothes until you're back. Okay, you too. G'night."

I take another sip of water then look back at my phone. Still nothing from Brent. I'm starting to feel a little bit irritated when Jake walks back into the room.

"Hey, sorry about that."

"Oh, no problem." I set my phone down and Jake crouches to open his box of books. "What does your girlfriend do?" I ask.

"She's a model actually," he says. I balk, and he notices. "I know, I know. I'm not one of those modelizer types; we just happened to meet on a shoot and got along really well."

"Makes sense. My boyfriend, or whatever he is, is trying to break into the film business in L.A. Lots of travel involved there too." I smile.

"Yeah." He stands up and starts placing books on his shelf. "So, why the 'whatever he is'?"

"Well, we sort of decided to leave things open-ended when I moved. I grew up in Los Angeles, and I just got here in June. He wanted to stay in L.A. to do film, but I guess neither of us wanted to break up? So we're still kind of together, but who knows. I haven't heard from him in a few days."

"Well, just because a guy doesn't call or text for a few days doesn't mean you should panic," he says.

"My friends always say that," I reply. "But the truth is that not communicating is always the first sign that something has gone wrong."

"Don't jump to any conclusions," he says.

"You know what the problem is? We're just too conditioned to want instant gratification," I say. "That's the problem with Facebook, Twitter and texting. It's ruined our generation's ability to be patient. Or maybe, my generation... How old are you anyway?"

"I'm twenty-nine, and I would have to agree with you entirely there," Jake says, continuing to shelve his books. "How old are you, 4B?"

"Twenty-four," I say. "But seriously, I mean think about it, during World War II when soldiers were fighting in France, it would sometimes take weeks to get a letter from their girlfriends back home. Weeks. Can you even imagine? And I get uncomfortable if I don't get a reply to an email within an hour. It's so lame."

"Again, nothing I can really argue with," he says. "Such a shame since I'm a big fan of playing devil's advocate."

"Do you want some help with the books?" I offer.

"I'd take you up on it, but I'm sort of OCD about the order they go in."

"Wow, well in that case, I'm just gonna enjoy the view from my box couch."

"Hah. Chloe's furniture is getting here tomorrow. My last place was mostly furnished."

As I sit on Jake's floor getting to know him, I feel my spirits lift slightly. I may have to move out of my apartment in a month, but I've made a new friend tonight. At least that's a silver lining to my shitty day.

Hi Audrey,

So sorry to hear you won't be able to stay, but I completely understand your situation. Thanks for giving me advanced notice.

I've got a couple other potential sublettors who I'd love to have stop by and see the place over the next week. Sorry that I can't show it myself. Hard to do that from across the pond, lol.

Would you be willing to let them in and give them the tour? I can get you your deposit back as soon as we secure a tenant.

Hope you're staying in New York!

Cheers,
Charles

SEVEN

September is arguably the most beautiful month in New York and while I'm trying to enjoy living in my dream apartment in the West Village, the glaring signs that I actually will have to move are hard to ignore. I keep attempting to convince myself that I'll be back as soon as I book a show, but I can't help but feel like I flew into JFK with more naivety than wisdom.

In my efforts to stay calm, I've been leaning on my parents a lot. I refuse to accept any financial help from them, but I think my mother has received calls from me every four or five hours whining. It's helpful when you have a retired therapist for a mother. She's particularly great at calming me down.

"Hi Mom," I say in a dull melancholy tone.

"Hi baby, how are things going?"

"I'm okay." I mope. "I'm officially moving to Brooklyn in October."

"I'm sorry, honey," she says. "But, I think maybe this will

end up being some kind of blessing in disguise."

"I dunno," I say. "I love this apartment. It's perfect. I was kind of hoping that Charles, the tenant, would end up staying in London and I could just take over the lease. I even have a really cool neighbor."

I can hear Jake playing records next door. He's listening to John Coltrane.

"That's good. How's Brent?"

"Not good. I guess," I say. "I don't know. We haven't talked much. I feel like everything is going wrong. I waited outside for five hours the other day for a casting call, finally got my name on the sign in sheet, and then they typed me out before I even had a chance to sing."

"Typed you out?"

"It means they took one look at me and decided I was wrong for the part."

"Honey, I know it feels crumby right now, but I'm sure this will all be for the best. If you need to, in the meantime, write your feelings down in your journal, or make a vision board collage with magazine scraps so you can see your goals in front of you. And if neither of those work, maybe try the old trick of screaming into a pillow," she suggests, trying to sound optimistic. "These are those trials and tribulations that people are always saying make them stronger in the end."

"How's Dad doing?" I need to change the subject.

"He's doing alright. The doctor has changed his heart medication and told him he has to lay off red meat for a while. He's thinking of going vegetarian, and just cutting it all out, so we're going to have one last dinner at Saladang tonight as a farewell to meat."

"God, I miss Saladang," I say. "How's John doing? We're still playing phone tag."

"Oh you know your brother, working hard as ever. He's taking a teaching fellowship at Stanford in hopes that he'll be offered a permanent position there, and he and Sophie are still trying. You should text him, he's good about responding to those."

My brother John and I were never very close growing up, but as we've gotten older we have become good friends. He's several years older than me, so I think he always thought of me as a naïve child. Until I had intelligent ideas to contribute to our conversations, he pretty much ignored me. I always sort of thought he was a pompous ass until he met and married Sophie. I could not ask for a cooler sister-in-law, and she's definitely mellowed him out.

"Is that Audrey?" I hear my father's voice.

"Can I say hi to Dad?" I ask.

"Of course! Howard, pick up the extension!"

"Hi, Princess," he says. His favorite nickname for me.

"Hi Daddy," I say. "You're going vegetarian?"

"Oh, Linda. You told her?" he says.

"I didn't know it was a secret!" my mom replies.

"It's not a big deal, Daddy, but that means no more chicken curry from Saladang. Where will we eat when I come home to visit?"

"We can still go out for Thai, but I'll just order the vegetarian curry." He sounds hopeful.

"That's pretty boring," I say.

"I know, Princess. I hope you can find it in your heart to forgive me." I can hear him chuckling.

"I mean... I guess..." I'm giggling too now. My father, a vegetarian? He was always Mr. BBQ.

"Audrey is moving to Brooklyn, Howard. She lost her job." My mom shares this news so offhandedly.

"Mom!"

"I didn't know *that* was a secret!" she says.

"I'm sorry to hear that, Princess. What happened?" At least my dad sounds sympathetic.

"Nothing," I say.

I explain the situation to my father. The Branders, the agency fee. I'm getting so tired of explaining it to people. It always feels like I'm making excuses for screwing up.

"Positive thinking," says Mom in her best therapist voice. "We have faith in you, honey. Don't you worry."

"Thank you, Dr. Princeton," I say.

"Audrey, if money gets tight, just let us know," says my dad.

"Thanks, Daddy, but I'll be alright." I hear a knock at my door. "Hang on one second, you guys."

Jake is in my doorway with a wooden spoon in his hand. "Okay, this is kind of embarrassing, but taste this." He holds the spoon out to my mouth. "I'm practicing making marinara sauce for when Chloe gets back."

I taste the spoon. "Tastes good. Add more pepper," I say.

"Cool, you wanna come over for spaghetti in an hour?"

"Sure," I say.

"Great, see ya then." He disappears back into his apartment and shuts the door.

"Who was that?" asks my mom, unable to help herself.

"That's Jake, my neighbor." I close the door to my apartment and head back over to my desk.

"Is this a love interest?" She *really* can't help herself.

"Mom, no! He has a girlfriend; he's practicing making her dinner for when she gets back from Milan."

"Milan, wow. Maybe he'd like to date someone who lives a little closer."

"She's a model. Trust me, I'm not his type and he's not my type. We're just friends."

"Hear that, Linda? They're just friends," says my father with reproach.

"Okay, okay," she concedes.

"Alright you guys, I need to jump in the shower. But let's have a Skype date soon, okay?"

"Oh good idea! I love the Skype!" I can hear my mom's enthusiasm.

"We love you, Princess. Chin up!" says my dad.

I hang up the phone and head toward the shower.

After our spaghetti dinner, Jake and I sit on his couch with our laptops. He's editing photos and I'm searching Craigslist for apartments.

"Not sure I like the saturation on this one," he mumbles.

"Not sure I wanna live in Queens," I mumble.

"What part of Queens?" he asks, turning to me, suddenly alert.

"Woodside?" I say, skipping through the ad.

"Not terrible, what's the apartment like? And how close to the train?"

"Pretty small and nine-hundred a month," I say.

"For Woodside?" He balks. "No, look in Brooklyn, that's crazy."

I'm starting to feel frustrated. A month ago I thought I had it all figured out. Life was starting to make sense and I felt like I finally had my head above water, like things were starting to go my way. Still, even in spite of the struggle, it's a comfort to have someone like Jake across the hall.

"Are we still gonna hang out after I move?" I ask.

"Sure," he says, looking up from his computer. "You're welcome here anytime."

"Thank you, sir."

"You're welcome, kid."

"So, I have a theory." I change the subject.

"Yes?"

"My theory is that I graduated from college thinking I knew everything, and now after a few months flat on my ass in New York City, I'm realizing I don't know anything and I might as well have about a zillion back up plans going forward."

"Yep, that tends to happen."

"Did it happen to you?" I ask.

"Sure did! I used to think I was going to be a screenwriter," he says. "Paid a lot of money for a film degree I'm not using."

"I didn't know that!" I say.

"Yeah, but we learn and we grow. You get to a point where you realize it's alright to give yourself permission to do something other than what you dreamed of at eighteen."

"Right now my dreams are sort of tabled," I say. "Priority numero uno is that I need to figure out a way to make money."

"I know it's stressful," he says. "But, you'll figure something out. You're smarter than you look."

"Hey!"

"Kidding!" he laughs. "It'll happen. Just stay positive."

I hear a ping on my computer and look down to see the number one in my inbox.

"I got an email from Brent!"

"What did he say?" asks Jake, looking up.

"Oh…" I mumble. "It's just a spam link. Apparently he's been mugged in London and needs me to wire funds."

"How touching."

"He just loves me so much, Jake!" I say with mock sincerity. "Our love is real and true!"

"Definitely real and true!" he says.

"I wonder if he's tried to call at all." I giggle, reaching into my bag for my phone. I look down and notice I have a voicemail from Spiffy Staff. "Hey, the agency called me."

"What did they say?" he asks.

"Not sure," I say. "Hang on."

"Hi, Audrey. It's Lucy. I have an interview for you! I think this is going to be the perfect fit. Great Upper West Side family who lives near Lincoln Center, two kids and mom just needs help after school until bedtime. This is a rare one, so call me as soon as possible so we can get this set up. Thanks!"

"Sounds like she's got an interview for me!" I say.

"That's great! Well done," Jake says. "Hey my friend just texted that there's a bar in Midtown doing an early Oktoberfest thing, you wanna go?"

"I should go start packing and maybe email about a couple of these apartments," I say hesitantly.

"Packing is for sissies! Let's go get a couple beers and then I'll help you pack in the morning."

"Fine, I'm in. But I gotta make a call as we walk to the subway," I say.

"Done and done. Go grab your jacket; it's chilly out there.

Jake and I walk down the street toward the West 4th Street. station. The evening is crisp and there's a slight chilly breeze blowing by. Around us, college students are running about hopping in and out of bars, talking loudly with friends or on their cell phones. The city is a bustle now with families having returned from the beaches and students back for the fall semester. I feel a longing twinge in my heart to be back in school. What I wouldn't give for the days when my success was solely dependent upon completing assignments and projects given to me, instead of being determined by finding a job in one of the most competitive cities in the country.

I dial the number for Lucy's cell, which is already programmed into my phone, fingers crossed in my pocket.

"Hi Lucy, it's Audrey," I say into the phone.

"Oh, Audrey! Thank God! I've got the perfect family for you and I want to set you up for an interview as soon as possible," she says. I feel my heart leap into my chest. An interview!

Lucy proceeds to tell me about this "wonderful family" that is looking for a part-time nanny for two great kids afterschool and maybe some weekend hours if I'd like them.

"Great! Sounds awesome. When can they meet?"

"Tuesday morning would be ideal," she says excitedly.

"Tuesday morning it is!"

I feel an instant spring in my step. Finally, something going my way!

"Audrey, I want to make it very clear that this is the holy grail of nanny job opportunities," she says, sounding grave. "Especially considering it's the middle of the September."

"I understand," I say. Although, I'm anxious to know what makes these people so special.

"They are a rare breed for us, and I say that with love for all of our other clients of course, but these are not your typical New Yorkers. They are extremely down to earth and the kids are a delight. Just go and be your normal wonderful self, and maybe do us both a favor and don't lead with the chlorine allergy thing, okay?"

I laugh. "Right, got it. Okay, no problem. Thanks, Lucy!"

"You're welcome, doll! I'll email you the specs. Let us know how it goes right after." She ends the call.

I turn to Jake smiling ear-to-ear, and he looks at me expectantly.

"Interview Tuesday!" I squeal as we walk down the stairs into the subway. "She says it's the holy grail of nanny jobs."

"Awesome!" Jake envelops me into a big bear hug. "Proud of you!"

"Thank goodness!" I say as Jake lets me go and we swipe our metro cards to walk down the tunnel.

We approach the uptown side of the platform and wait for the train.

"It would be nice to work for people who are normal," I say hopefully.

"That's the dream," he says. "How are auditions going, by the way?"

"Not great," I say with a shrug. "I've been so frustrated by the process, I haven't really gone to as many casting calls as I should."

"That sucks," he says.

"If I could just get in front of someone and have them hear me sing, I think I would have a shot, but I'm not Equity, so I can't seem to get past the waiting room."

"Sounds frustrating," says Jake, as the wind from the incoming train rushes through the tunnel and blows our coats around. "You wanna take the C or wait for the A?"

"Wait for the A," I respond.

We sit down on a bench.

"So if you land this new nanny gig, will you make enough for you to stay in our building?"

"Probably not. It's part-time, and I have student loan payments coming in soon. I think I've gotta be smart with my money and just suck it up and move to Brooklyn."

"Bummer. I was enjoying having a buddy in the building."

"Oh, don't worry, I'll be visiting frequently," I say.

"Good. Come by anytime," he says with a smile. "And

you'll meet Chloe soon. As soon as she gets back."

"How's that going anyway?" I ask.

"Alright. I'm getting pretty sick of having a relationship with my phone though, ya know?"

"I hear that. Although, as you already observed, my love life is all kinds of wonderful."

"Have you heard from him at all?" Jake asks.

"He tends to call late at night when I'm asleep and leaves messages saying how busy he is, but that he misses me."

"Sounds a little suspicious. Is this late night calling the only time he communicates?"

"Yeah. He used to text me during the days, but now he says his days are jam-packed." I shrug. "I have a feeling he knows that if he catches me, we'll actually have to talk about us."

"Do you want to end it?" Jake asks.

"I think it's taking that course, naturally. We just have to have the conversation," I say. "At this point, I know this is bad, but I'm kind of getting a sick pleasure out of just watching what happens. How many more excuses he'll come up with before he gets the balls to just end it."

"Horrible." Jake laughs. "I'm sorry to hear that, but maybe it's for the best, huh? Fresh start?"

"Yeah, I think so," I say. "Logan has been telling me to break up with him for months. I guess it's just been a comfort thing. Knowing I have someone to call or text at the end of the day or if something happens that I want to share."

"Except for the fact that he's not taking those calls?"

"True. That kinda blows a hole in that theory, doesn't it?" I say. "Jeez. What's wrong with me? Why am I so afraid to let go and be alone?"

"Being single in your twenties can be good for you," he says. "Helps you figure out who you are. Does that sound too much like an after-school-special?"

"Maybe. Anyway, for now I don't wanna think about it." I watch as the A train comes barreling into the station. "Let's go drink some beer and if things get wild, maybe eat some sauerkraut."

Jake and I are giggling as we return home several hours later and make our way up the stairs to the fourth floor. We've both enjoyed a few of the Hefeweizen and I'm feeling much better about life.

"Everything is gonna be a-okay, Jake!" I say enthusiastically.

"I think you're right," he laughs.

"I'm gonna get this nanny job, I'm gonna go back to auditions, and I'm gonna make my parents real proud of me." I reach for my keys in my purse.

"I think you definitely will," he says. "And I'm gonna get laid as soon as my girlfriend comes back from Italy!"

"Yeah, ya are!" I say as we reach my door and I fumble with the lock. "I on the other hand, am as celibate as a nun right now, but it's all fine, man. It's all good."

"Well you get some sleep, kiddo." He gives me a hug and unlocks his apartment. "I'll see you tomorrow and we'll pack."

"Yes, packing." I lament as I walk into my apartment. "Night!" I take off my coat, kick off my shoes, and head toward the bathroom to brush my teeth.

I'm walking through Central Park. The sky is indigo blue and the grass is brilliant green. My movements are slow and my vision is slightly blurred. I hear my father's voice, *"I'm sorry to hear you lost your job, Princess."*

"Thanks, daddy!" I call out, but I can't seem to see where he is.

Suddenly I see the Sleeping Beauty from the Hamptons birthday party, sitting beside a tree.

"Oh, hi!" she calls.

"Sleeping Beauty," I say as I approach her. *"You had Chanel flats on, how did you afford them?"*

"I make good money doing princess parties," she says. *"We get tipped very well!"*

"Spare no expense for birthday parties and weddings, am I right?" I hear Charlotte Brander's voice off in the distance.

The scene melts away and I'm sitting in a brightly lit living room on the floor. A dozen happy little girls surround me.

"Who can tell me their favorite color?" I ask.

"Blue!" shouts one.

"Green!" shouts another.

"PINK!!" shout several others.

"Very good! Who can tell me their favorite fairytale princess?" I ask.

"Sleeping Beauty!" shouts one.

"Snow White!" shouts another.

"Mermaid!"

"You! You're my favorite, Cinderella!"

I jerk awake and sit bolt upright in bed. *I've got it!*

Part II: Fall

"Then the little mermaid drank the magic draught, and it seemed as if a two-edged sword went through her delicate body: she fell into a swoon, and lay like one dead. When the sun arose and shone over the sea, she recovered, and felt a sharp pain; but just before her stood the handsome young prince. He fixed his coal-black eyes upon her so earnestly that she cast down her own, and then became aware that her fish's tail was gone, and that she had as pretty a pair of white legs and tiny feet as any little maiden could have."

- The Little Mermaid
by Hans Christian Andersen

EIGHT

It's a crisp October morning and Logan and I are in my new apartment in Parkside Brooklyn, unpacking boxes and getting me settled. I still cannot believe I've managed to get him out here. For as much as he was adamantly against my moving to Brooklyn, he's been incredibly helpful. The Park Avenue woman he's been working for allowed us to borrow her driver for a couple hours to transport my boxes. And being without a job, I was grateful not to spend the thirty-dollar cab fare.

"Okay, I need to ask you something," Logan says, sounding exasperated.

"Why did I have to move to Brooklyn?"

"No… well yes, but that's not what I want to ask," he says.

"Okay… shoot," I say as I begin shelving books.

"Ugh. I'm just gonna say it." He sounds hesitant. "Okay, who is this Jake character that you've been hanging out with all the time? Are you replacing me? Because, so help me Holly, if you've found another fag to your hag…"

"Seriously?" I laugh. "He's my neighbor. Or he was, before I had to move to freaking Brooklyn. Why doesn't your building allow dogs? We could have been roomies!"

"Holly, let it go."

"Fine."

"Is Jake hot?"

"He's attractive, in a nerdy kind of way."

"Is he gay?"

"Most definitely not. And he has a girlfriend, so don't start your conspiracy theories about how I should break up with Brent and start dating someone in New York," I say.

He gives me a look. "Well, just because he has a girlfriend doesn't mean I'm wrong about that."

"I'm waiting for Brent to have the balls to end it. But even once he does, I'm going to need some time before I can just meet someone. Jake seems to think maybe I should try being single for a while. That maybe it will help me figure myself out or something."

"Well, that's pretty insightful of him, but I'm still not sure I approve of your new friend," he says skeptically. "You've been spending all this time with him and not me! I'm your number one, remember?"

"I know baby," I say, patting his back, "But you've been working a lot, and he lives, or *lived*, across the hall."

"That's no excuse," Logan whines. "You're supposed to not do anything fun unless I'm free."

"I'll remember that next time, and now that I've moved, Jake won't be so nearby. So you can untwist your panties."

"I can't believe you live in Brooklyn," he says. "Now we'll never see each other."

"I know… there's no way you'll come and visit me after today…You don't ride the subway and you never drop more than thirty-five dollars on a cab unless you're going to the airport."

Logan pulls open a box of my shoes and begins arranging them in the closet.

"Honey, for you I will brave the Q train. I promise." He gives me a sincere look, but I know he's lying.

"Uh-huh."

"Any new job prospects?" He changes the subject before I can force him to buy a monthly metro card.

"Well, I had this kind of crazy idea," I say. "But I need you to tell me your honest opinion."

"Okay," he says. "Are we talking my actual honest opinion, or the one that you want to hear?"

"Actual, actual," I say. "I mean I hope you'll think it's a good idea… I think you'll like it."

"Oh my God, Holly, out with it!" I can see him arranging my shoes according to color.

"Okay, okay!" I say. "I'm thinking about doing princess parties."

"Like bachelor parties?" he asks.

"No! Like for children. I'm thinking of performing at parties for kids," I say laughing.

"Oh," he says. "Actually, that's not a bad idea. How'd you come up with that?"

"Remember when I was working for the Branders, and I took their daughter to a princess party?" I ask.

"Yes, and Mrs. Crotch-less Panties threw a fit about her daughter's face being painted."

"Right! Well, when we left the face painting station, I noticed Sleeping Beauty was wearing those pink seven-hundred-dollar Chanel flats."

"She might actually also be a stripper, but go on," he says.

"Think about it," I say. "It's creative. It's performing. I can sing and work on my improv skills and I can do it on weekends."

"Sounds like a good idea, honey," he says. "Have you found any companies here in the city?"

"I wrote to a couple companies, but no one is hiring," I say. "And to be honest, I think I can do it better myself."

"So how are you going to start it up?" he asks.

"I'm not exactly sure yet. I've got to figure out a business plan and create a website or something. Get some costumes. I'm hoping Jake can help me with photos."

"Of course. Jake to the rescue," he says slyly.

I give him a reproachful look. "Stop…"

"Sorry, so are you thinking you could make enough money doing this that you won't need to nanny anymore?"

"No," I say. "I think I'll still do that. I actually had a great interview the other day with this family on the Upper West Side. They are extremely cool and the kids are pretty funny. I'm still waiting to hear."

"Well, that's good," he says. "If this all pans out, you'll be back in Manhattan before you know it!"

"I'm not so sure of that," I say. "But fingers crossed."

"So, who's your new roommate?" Logan asks as he starts hanging up my clothes in the closet.

"Her name is Mallory. She's a ballet dancer or something. I don't think she's home very much. Her boyfriend lives in the city."

"And if she has a brain, she's in the city as much as possible and only returns here twice a week to pack clean clothes."

"I know," I say with a laugh. "I do sort of feel like a stranger in a foreign land here. But I think I'll get the hang of it. And I'll be in the city every day for work and auditions."

"And to see Jake and not me," Logan pouts.

"Oh hush."

The next day, I spend some quality time exploring my new neighborhood. While it's not as blissfully quaint as my former West Village digs, it has some perks. I'm right near the Q train and the park is just down the street. If I feel like strolling across the park, I end up in Park Slope, which is a very charming family community that is full of cute restaurants and shops.

As I pass a sweet little coffee shop on 7th Avenue in Park Slope, I note that it would make a great place to work on audition materials. I silently make a promise to myself that this will become a daily routine for me.

I decide to have a late lunch in a small deli near the coffee shop and do some research on what I'm affectionately calling Project Princess. I do some browsing online to see how much it would actually cost to start up my own business. The truth is it *would* be simpler to join another troupe of performers, but if no one is hiring, there's not much I can do but take matters into my own hands.

I make a list of all the birthday party activities I enjoyed as a kid, excluding the crappy ones like pin the tail on the donkey and the bean bag toss. I search online for costume options and wigs. I browse Oriental Trading Company's website for party supplies.

I'm typing furiously and feeling pretty excited when my phone rings, interrupting my focus.

"Hello?"

"Audrey! It's Lucy. You got the job!"

"Oh my gosh, that's great news! Thank you!" I squeal with delight.

"Keep it down, eh?" says the man behind the counter, giving me a look.

"Sorry, I just got a job," I say.

"Eh, good for you sweetheart! These are tough times, these." He goes back to slicing cold cuts.

"Sorry Lucy, so when do I start?" I ask.

"Well, they'd like to have you come do a trial day with the kids this weekend so you can get a feel for the house and the neighborhood," she says. "Can you work on Saturday?"

"I don't like the word trial, but of course," I say. "That sounds great!"

"Don't worry, doll, this won't be a re-run of the Branders."

I sigh and smile. "Oh thank goodness, Lucy, this will be so helpful."

"Good! And they seem very understanding about you being an actor and pursuing that too; she said she's open to being flexible if you have an audition or something."

"Wow, that's pretty generous," I say.

"I know! I told you, this is the perfect nanny job! Alright, doll, you did it! I'll email you their address and the time for Saturday."

"Thanks, Lucy!"

I'm on cloud nine. Finally something going my way! If I can get this company going, I might actually be able to get some financial security! I'm just about to text Logan when my phone rings again. This time it's Brent.

"Well, this day keeps getting better and better," I say as I answer the phone. "Hi! I have great news!"

"Hey." His voice sounds a bit stiff.

"I just got a job!" I squeal.

Silence on the other end of the line.

"Hello? Brent?" I say.

"Yeah, sorry. Listen...I think we need to talk."

"Did you not hear me? I just said I got a job."

"Yeah, that's great, Audrey. Congratulations, it was definitely only a matter of time. But I need to talk to you..."

"Alright," I say tentatively. I knew this call was coming, but for some reason, I feel instantly irritated that he's about to break up with me and rain on my 'I got a job' parade.

He sighs. "Look, I know I've been distant lately and part of it is work, but the other part of it is me pulling away because I just don't want to do the whole long distance thing anymore."

"Uh-huh."

"I've just got a lot on my plate right now and it's hard," he says. "I mean, it was fine when you first moved, but it's just getting to be a bit much and...I just think it would be better if we just... Shit, I don't want to lie to you, Audrey. I met someone."

For a few seconds I can't even speak. Then I choke out, "You met someone... When?"

"A while ago. I've been trying to slow our conversations in hopes of helping you to get over any feelings you might still have for me."

"Excuse me?" I say.

"Audrey, I'm sure you've been dating."

"Actually, I haven't been," I say hotly. "I've been waiting to see what happened with you before I brought someone else into the mix."

"I just...I knew you'd get upset and I was trying to avoid a moment like this," he says. "I was hoping if we put some distance between us that it would make it easier for you to move on."

"Okay, I think it's time to hang up now," I say. "I don't really want to say something I'll regret later, so let's just leave it at this. Thanks for your honesty, Brent."

I end the call.

I don't even set the phone down; instead, I take a deep breath and open my messages and send two identical texts to Logan and Jake.

I'm officially single.
The Half-Pint, 6pm?

Logan is the first to respond.

Vodka makes everything better.

Jake's text comes back a couple minutes later.

Sorry kid, see you there.

It's the first time that Jake and Logan will meet, and as I walk into the bar I see them both waiting on opposite ends of the entry area, clearly not knowing that a third party will be joining us. It's kind of amusing to see my two friends in the same room, not knowing each other.

"Jake! Logan!" I call out as I see them both. They give each other a strange look before walking over to my side.

"Hi, kid," says Jake.

"Hi, honey," says Logan.

"Brent broke up with me, and I figured you two should just

meet already, so that's why we're here. Logan, Jake. Jake, Logan."

Jake extends a hand to Logan.

"Hello, replacement friend," Logan says sassily. He tentatively shakes Jake's hand.

"Logan, let's just clear one thing up," says Jake as he grips Logan's hand firmly. "There's no way I'll ever look as good as you, so there's no way I could ever replace you."

Logan's skeptical face breaks. "Okay, I like him!"

"Thank goodness," I say. "Now let's talk about my tragic love life."

We grab a booth in the back and a server approaches and asks for our order.

"Two dirty martinis with bleu cheese stuffed olives and a Brooklyn Lager." I order for the group.

"And some fries," says Jake.

"Sweet potato fries," says Logan.

"Nice call," says Jake.

"Coming right up," our server replies.

Jake looks at me with a more serious face. "Okay, tell us what happened? You've got the floor."

"Get. This." I say, allowing for a suspenseful drum-roll-please-silence to wash over them before I continue. "He's been dating someone else!"

I'm expecting a big reaction, but neither Jake nor Logan flinches

"Not surprised," says Logan.

"Sounds about right," says Jake.

"What the hell, you guys! *I* haven't been dating anyone else!" I protest.

"Honey, I've been telling you since you moved that you should be dating a stockbroker," says Logan.

"I have no opinion on who Audrey should be dating, but clearly Brent isn't the guy," says Jake.

Our server brings Jake's beer.

"Oh! This was my favorite part of the whole conversation," I say. "He said he's been ignoring me for the past few weeks in the hopes that it would help me stop having feelings for him."

"How charitable of him," says Jake.

"Because, clearly I wouldn't have been able to make it through without his assistance," I say.

"Oh, Holly... you're better off," Logan groans.

Jake looks perplexed. "I'm sorry to change the subject, but...Holly?"

"That's Logan's nickname for me," I answer. "Holly, as in Holly Golightly, from *Breakfast at Tiffany's.*"

"I'm not following," says Jake, looking confused.

"Audrey here, is named for Audrey Hepburn," says Logan. "And that's her character in our favorite movie."

"We've seen it probably a million times and we can recite most of the lines," I say proudly.

"Wow... See, Logan. No way I could ever replace you," Jake jokes. "I don't think I've even seen that film."

"You have a film degree!" I interject. "That's criminal!"

Logan looks suddenly serious. "Well, you have to see it! It's a classic. Audrey calls me 'Paulie' after Paul Varjak, who is Holly's love interest."

I jump in. "Well, technically Holly calls Paul 'Fred' in the film, but we were in high school when this started and we liked the fact that Holly and Paulie rhymed."

"Interesting." Jake starts to pick at the label on his beer bottle.

"Okay, can we get back to me now?" I pout.

The server brings our martinis and the fries.

"Audrey, you will be fine," says Jake firmly. "You are fine. Break-ups suck, but I refuse to throw you a pity party here. You're an amazing girl and will always have a group of guys to choose from. And you should never let a guy define who you are, even if it's only for a short while. It's a waste of your time."

"I completely agree with him," says Logan.

"Well... wow. Okay." I smile. "Thanks for that, Jake."

Logan lifts his martini glass. "To your new freedom! And your new business venture!"

"Business venture?" Jake looks perplexed.

"Our girl here has a great idea to start a princess party company," Logan boasts.

"And I got a new job! Forgot to mention, I got the Upper West Side gig!"

"Way to go, kid!" says Jake. "I can't wait to hear more about this business venture. I knew things would turn around."

"See Holly, there's always something to celebrate in New York," Logan raises his glass. "To you!"

"To you… Holly," Jake says with a wink.

"To New York." I raise my glass with my boys, suddenly feeling so much better. "Anything is possible."

Two weeks later, I'm picking Baxter and my mother up at JFK. When I told her my good news about the job and my idea for the company, she jumped on the computer and booked a flight.

I'm so glad she's here to help me get the business off the ground. My mother is truly great at throwing parties and she's already come up with some fantastic ideas for activities we can offer.

"When you and John were little," she says as our taxi pulls out of the airport. "Your father would always play that game, 'we're going on a bear hunt' with you two and you loved it!"

"Oh my gosh, I totally forgot about that," I say.

"So I was thinking, since you're going to have little princesses *and* knights at these parties, you could maybe do, 'we're going on a dragon hunt' and do it that way. I think they'd really like that."

"That's brilliant, Mom!" I say. "Really a good idea."

"Well, I just thought it would be good to accommodate the boys that are going to be there, so they don't feel left out."

As we drive along the BQE, I hold Baxter in my lap and stroke his soft brown fur. I'm so happy to have my dog with me again.

"I just don't know how you can live in a city that has no

greenery," my mother says looking out the windows of the cab. "Everywhere you look is concrete."

"Mom, most of L.A. is concrete too," I say. "And it's fall, nothing is green right now."

"Yes, but we have yards in Pasadena. Thank God," she says. "Where do children play here?"

"Well, you'll see tomorrow when you come with me to pick up pick up Amelia and Evan," I say. "They live right across the street from Central Park! It's the biggest backyard a kid could ask for."

"I guess that's something," she says thoughtfully. "How do you like the kids so far? How old are they?"

"Seven and eight, and I've only done a few days with them," I say. "But they appreciate my sarcasm."

"You? Sarcastic?" My mother teases.

"My first day on the job, when they asked if they could have candy for dinner, I told them yes and they actually fell over laughing."

"Kids like you, Audrey." She smiles. "You always did well with your cousin Emily's kids."

"Well, anyone who thinks I'm funny automatically gets a point in the winning column."

"And when will I be seeing Logan?"

"Soon as we get home," I say. "He's been in my kitchen all day cooking us dinner, naturally."

"Naturally."

"And your roommate?"

"She's never home, her boyfriend lives in the city," I say. "It's kind of like living alone."

"And what about that boy who lived across the hall at your last place?" she asks. "Anything happen there?"

"No." I laugh. "Jake is still with Chloe and we're just friends."

"I see," she says.

"I was hoping you two would meet," I say. "But he's actually in Philly this week for work."

"We'll meet at some point I'm sure," she says.

"He's really been a huge help to me," I say. "He's helped design the website, which I'll show you when we get home. He's come up with business cards, which are in the mail. And once you and I get the costumes sorted, he'll do some quick character photos before we launch."

"Sounds like a very good friend," she says.

"He's really a good guy!" I agree.

When we reach my apartment, Logan comes out and helps us bring my mom's luggage in. I take Baxter for a short walk up and down the block so he can get used to his new home, while Logan gets my mom settled inside.

Baxter sniffs every tree and wags his tail excitedly as he takes in all the new smells.

"I hope you're ready to become a New Yorker, buddy," I say to him.

He smiles up at me.

When we get back to the apartment, Logan and my mother are in the kitchen chatting busily, a bottle of chardonnay already opened on the counter.

"Linda, you're going to love this pasta I'm making," says Logan standing at the stove. "The chopped heirloom tomatoes have been sitting in olive oil, chopped garlic and a chiffonade of fresh basil all day. Then when it's time to serve, I'll add about half a cup of fresh chevre to the bowl and place the hot linguine on top."

"I'm already salivating," she says, peaking over his shoulder.

"The hot pasta will melt the goat cheese, which will create a delicate sauce with the garlic, basil and tomatoes. It's everything. And perfect with a nice Brunello, like the one I purchased from Dean and Deluca this morning."

"Do you think we should get that bottle out and let it breathe?" she asks him.

"It can *breathe* between the rim of the glass and my lips, but if you want to open it now, feel free."

The next day, my mom and I walk to the subway together. We're heading into the city to pick Amelia up from school and then Evan from a friend's house a bit later. My mother spent the entire morning meditating in Prospect Park, fulfilling her need to commune with nature.

"I just feel so much better having spent some time in nature," she says as we buy her a metro card from the machine.

"I'm glad you're zen, Mom," I say. "You'll need it. We're heading to the Upper East Side."

We swipe our metro cards and head down to the platform of the Q train.

"I had some ideas for your costumes," she says.

"Oh yeah?" I ask.

"It was smart to buy used prom dresses."

"eBay," I interject.

"The bodice's are great and we can embellish the skirts with a bit more tulle, lace and satin and then create collars and sleeves."

"Sounds good," I say.

"I know you didn't want your Christmas money early during the summer, but I think considering the start up costs for this new business venture, we'd like to go ahead and give it to you."

"Thanks, Mom," I say. "I think in this case, that would be really great."

"When you start making money, you might think about hiring a costume designer to make nicer costumes for you, but this will be a good start."

"Thank goodness Logan has a sewing machine we can borrow," I say with a grin.

"That's our boy!"

We take the Q to Union Square, transfer to the Uptown 6 train, and finally return to the surface at 96th Street. I walk my mother down Madison Avenue and we stop at Yura for a quick snack before heading down to Amelia's school. I grab a couple rice crispy treats for her and Evan.

When we pick Amelia up, she is her usual cheerful self. I introduce her to my mom and they instantly love each other.

"Amelia, tell us what you think about this," says my mom as we walk towards the park. "Audrey is thinking of starting a company where she does princess parties for little girl's birthday parties."

"Really?" says Amelia. "Cool."

"Pretty neat, huh?" says my mom.

"Yep!" says Amelia. "Hey Audrey, I thought of this really cool name today!"

"Oh yeah?" I ask. "What's that?"

"I think it's going to be my secret identity."

"Why do you need a secret identity?" I ask.

"Just 'cuz," she says. "So, I think it's going to be Gertrude Yolanda Gonzalez."

My mother looks at me and I laugh. "Welcome to my world," I say.

We stroll through the park over to the Westside, and grab Evan from his friend's house on 85th and Columbus, and then hail a cab to take us home.

"So, I was thinking, since my mom is in town, maybe we could play a board game with her after you guys finish your homework," I say.

"Okay," says Amelia.

"What game?" asks Evan.

"Whatever you feel like," I say.

For the rest of the cab ride home, my mom regales Evan and Amelia with embarrassing tales of my childhood. They nearly lose their minds laughing at me, but I'm glad that they're enjoying my mother and she's enjoying them.

When we reach the apartment, they ask if we can take my mom up to the roof, so she can see the view of Central Park. We show her the roof deck and the view and then we begin cracking away at their homework.

"Audrey, if you're going to do these birthday parties," says Evan, working on his vocab. "Make sure you have a guy character, because not all boys are gonna like the princess thing."

"That's good thinking, kiddo," I say. "I'll see if we can hunt down a prince or a pirate."

"Or the Hulk," he says.

"Sure," I say.

"And make sure you also include Princess Gertrude Yolanda Gonzales," says Amelia, working on her math sheet. "She's the prettiest!"

"Amelia, you're so weird!" says Evan.

"G-Y-G!" says Amelia dancing in her chair. "G-Y-G!"

"Okay, girly, let's focus on that math sheet and we can talk about Princess G-Y-G a bit later, alright?"

"G-Y-G!" she says again.

"When Audrey was little she had an imaginary best friend named, Collina," says my mother.

"What?!" says Amelia finding it hilarious.

"Mom!" I protest.

"And, she used to blame Collina if she didn't do her chores," says my mom.

"You're giving them ammunition." I warn her.

"You know," says Amelia in her tiny silly voice. "I've heard that Gertrude Yolanda Gonzales and Collina are BFF's!"

"Hey!" I say. "I have two rice crispy treats in my purse for two kids who finish their homework in the next twenty minutes."

"G-Y-G!" chants Amelia. "Sorry, that was Collina."

I give my mother a look and she chuckles.

When Evan and Amelia finish their homework, we make our way into their living room and begin digging through the closet of board games. We decide to play Monopoly, but Evan insists that he has to be the banker because he wants to handle all the money and doesn't want to owe rent to anyone. And judging by the meltdowns I've seen when Evan doesn't win at a board game, I opt to allow it.

After another hour, their mom, Alexandra comes home early to relieve my mother and me, and we head out to dinner to scheme the rest of our strategy to begin Project Princess.

From: Suzanne Richards <s.a.richards@timeout.com>
Subject: Article Is Live!
Date: November 1, 7:01:45 am
To: Audrey Princeton <princeton.audrey@gmail.com>

Audrey,

Just a quick note to say your article just went live, Party Girl!

Get ready for a huge slew of calls and emails today! I'm sending you a copy of the magazine and you can view the online version by clicking here.

We went ahead and listed your email address and your website, but I left the phone number we had on file for you out of the final article because I figured you might want to set up a Google voice account once you get really busy.

Let me know if you need anything else! Give Jake a hug!

Suz

From: Dana Bixby <d.bix@bmpartners.com>
Subject: Party Dec 1
Date: November 1, 08:26:15 am
To: Audrey Princeton <princeton.audrey@gmail.com>

Hi Audrey,

I just read the article about you in Time Out New York and I'm so excited to have found you! My daughter, Laura's birthday is December 2nd, but we are having the party on the 1st this year to accommodate the grandparents who will be visiting from out of town. We are in Gramercy Park.

Can you let me know your rates and do you have Snow White available?

Thanks!

Dana Bixby

From: Nick Peterson <nickatnight@ymail.com>
Subject: Long Shot
Date: November 1, 09:34:16 am
To: Audrey Princeton <princeton.audrey@gmail.com>

Hi,

In serious need of a sexy, Arabian Princess! Do you do bachelor
parties? What's your bra size?

Nick

From: Carl Denison <cdenison@goldmansachs.com>
Subject: Help Save My Marriage!
Date: November 1, 09:47:11 am
To: Audrey Princeton <princeton.audrey@gmail.com>

Good Morning,

Please help! My wife says she's going to divorce me if I can't find someone to dress up as Cinderella for our daughter's fourth birthday next week. Can you please help me save my marriage?

I love my kids and I don't want to go back to living in a walk up. That bitch'll take everything!

Name your price!!!

--
Carl Denison
Senior Account Executive
Goldman Sachs and Partners

Hello,

My daughter loves Sleeping Beauty and her birthday party is tomorrow. Is there any chance you could come to Park Slope? We'll pay you extra for the last minute notice.

Have heard great things in Time Out!

THANK YOU!!

Elisa Peretto

NINE

Ah, the sweet sound of success! A steady ping of emails coming into my inbox as hungry Manhattan parents vie for my magical services. Okay, maybe that came out wrong...

I've had a big number of reservations coming in after Jake's contact at *Time Out New York* printed an article about me in the kid's section. She was extremely kind in talking me up, and so far people are excited by what they've read. Some might be a bit *too* excited...but that comes with the territory.

"I can't believe it's your first party!" Sarah says over the phone, one of our first conversations since our last Grey Dog lunch in the summer.

"I know!"

"I still think it's hilarious that you're all chummy with that guy from Grey Dog now, and that he has connections at *Time Out New York*!"

"He's been a life saver, and Logan left a ton of business cards with each of his Upper East Side clients too," I say, brushing on a third application of mascara.

"Everything is falling into place," she says. "I'm sorry I haven't been more available to help... that Merry-Go-Round gig pretty much usurped my whole summer."

"It's alright, Sarah," I say.

"I don't know when I'll see you next! I'm heading to London next week to do Phantom, but I have a good contact for you at a restaurant uptown that I think will be perfect for parties. I'll email you details."

"Sounds good!" I say. "Listen, I should probably get going in a minute here, and I need to leave soon."

"Of course! Break a leg, sweetie!"

"Thanks so much!" I hang the phone up and check my reflection in the mirror. Baxter is sitting on the bathroom floor looking up at me.

"Okay, Bax. What do you think? Do I look whimsical enough? Or is it too much? ... Is it stripper-makeup?"

Baxter yawns and rests his head against his paws. He couldn't care less how I look; he always gives me those adoring eyes.

As I throw all of my makeup back into the drawer, my phone rings again. It's Jake.

"Hey buddy!" I say as I answer. "Only got two minutes, gotta go be magical."

"I know, kid, just wanted to call and wish you luck. Can I buy you dinner later to celebrate?" he asks.

"I thought you had plans with Chloe this weekend?"

"I saw her for about twelve hours last night, and then she left again this morning for Hawaii."

"Oh gosh, I'm sorry," I say.

"It's alright," he says. "We had a fun night."

"Good," I say. "Still can't believe I haven't met her!"

"I know," he says. "I keep telling her about you and she wants to meet you!"

"Well, maybe when she gets back," I say. "What do you feel like for dinner? Grimaldi's?"

He chuckles. "Exactly what I was going to suggest."

"Done. See you in line around six-thirty?" I say.

"Yup! Go be magical!" he says.

"Roger that! Over and out!" I hang up the phone smiling.

I grab the garment bag with my freshly dry-cleaned princess dress in it, blonde wig and tiara, plus the pink canvas bag that contains twenty-five paper crowns, about a zillion stickers, face paints, story books and glitter.

"Show time, Bax!" I grab my coat and keys and head towards the door.

As I walk out onto the street, a crisp breeze is blowing. The day is overcast and crisp – perfect fall weather. I'm feeling fortunate because the birthday party is in Park Slope, so I can easily walk there from my place. I've got plenty of time to stroll through Prospect Park at a leisurely pace, admiring the deepening fall colors.

"You just don't see this in Pasadena," I say to myself as I take in the lovely scene.

Trees on each side of the path are standing in various shades of red, orange and gold. The color is striking with the grey backdrop of the clouds behind it. One particularly beautiful tree sheds tiny golden leaves that rain down gently onto the grass that is filled with kids and dogs running around playing. I'm surprised to see so many people out and about, given the moisture in the air, but I guess it is a Saturday afternoon. And I've been told that most East Coasters don't hibernate until it's below freezing.

I smile as I walk. Brooklyn has grown on me in spite of myself. But, I'll never tell Logan that. I exit the park on the Park Slope side feeling confident. I know these kids will love me. The brownstones along the park stand proudly and parents walking with strollers are everywhere I look. I pull out my phone to check the address as I turn left down Prospect Park West.

I arrive at their brownstone twenty minutes before I'm scheduled to start entertaining. I'm feeling very pleased with myself as I dial the mother's phone number to let her know I've arrived and need to be let in to change.

The phone rings and I wait for the mom, Elisa, to answer. Four rings. Five rings. Six rings.

"*Hi, you've reached Elisa. Please leave a message.*"

I hang up and call a second time. Three rings. Four rings. Five rings. Six rings.

"*Hi, you've reached Elisa. Please leave a message.*"

"Okay," I say quietly to myself. "Let's try a text."

Hi Elisa, I'm here and need
to come inside to change.
Thanks! - Sleeping Beauty

As I wait for a reply from her, I walk toward the front of the building to see if I can flag anyone down through the window. The sky starts to darken and I feel a sense of foreboding. I need to get inside!

The living room is directly on the other side of the glass and every child guest of the party is running around. I quickly walk past the window so they won't see my bright pink bag. I now only have fifteen minutes before I need to start performing.

I check my phone, but no reply from Elisa. I'm starting to feel nervous. A light rain starts to trickle down through the trees and I grab an umbrella from out of my bag. If I go to the door, all of the kids will see me, and the parents will have to try and explain to them who I am even though they won't see *me* the rest of the party. What I need is for the parents to distract the children so I can sneak inside and change, but there's no way to get a corroborating parent to help me without getting Elisa on the phone.

"Dammit, Elisa" I curse under my breath. "What the hell am I going to do?"

I start looking around the street to see where I can change. The rain is coming down harder and I hear the distant rumble of thunder. If I take my gown out in this weather, I'll ruin it. There isn't a single restaurant on the block and no lobby or doorman in a tiny brownstone.

"Shit, shit, shit." I cannot believe I'm about to blow my very first party. Eleven minutes before I will officially be late. I check my phone again, but still nothing from Elisa. I send a second text to her.

> Hi Elisa, I'm outside and
> need to be let in to change.
> Princess rescue required! — SB

Another two minutes pass without a reply. I'm ready to resign and try my luck at the front door when an illuminated blue and red sign at the end of the block catches my eye.

Citibank.

I make a run for it as the clouds burst. It's a Sunday afternoon so they'll be closed. But maybe, just maybe, I can get into the ATM lobby. At least it will be dry. I reach for the door to the lobby and jam my debit card into the security card reader. The light on the reader turns green and I hear the door lock click open.

"Thank you, Citibank!" I run over to the table where the deposit slips lay and throw my bags down. I look at my watch. I've still got eight minutes. I've got to work fast. As I remove my coat and sweater quickly, I give myself props for having already put my leotard and leggings on. I won't have to strip down completely naked in a transparent glass room on the corner of a family street. Which is good, because there are families with strollers rolling past the window at this very moment. Why the hell are these people still out when it's raining anyway?

Zzzziiiip

I unzip the garment bag and yank the giant pink ball gown out of it, throwing it over my head. I'm tightening the corset strings when I hear the *click* of the door open and freeze. A man walks in, takes one look at me, and his expression turns to instant bewilderment. Probably the first time he's seen a half-dressed princess at his bank.

"Hey, how ya doin'?" I say. "Birthday party."

"Oh. Right," he says, still looking confused.

I give the corset a final tug, tie the strings into a bow and grab for my make-up bag. I pull out two bobby pins and pin my bangs back before snatching a rubber band and putting my hair up in a ponytail.

I hear Mr. ATM pressing buttons as he completes whatever kind of transaction he's making and I grab the blonde wig and swing it up on top of my head. A quick glance at my watch tells me I have five minutes. I take the tiara out of my bag, fix it to the wig and pin it in place.

"Well, good luck!" says Mr. ATM as he exits the lobby.

"Thnk-oo," is all I can get out with six bobby pins between my teeth. I check my reflection in the tiny mirror of my compact, making sure none of my brown hair is showing. I throw on some extra red lipstick, toss everything else back into my garment bag, hike up my skirt, grab my umbrella and make a dash for the party.

I feel like I'm in an episode of *Seinfeld* as I run down the street in a full princess gown through the rain. I hear gasps as I pass people on the street, and "Look! It's a princess!" I can't help but laugh to myself. I cannot believe I'm going to pull this off.

I hit the front doorstep of Elisa's house at one o'clock on the dot. I ring the doorbell and hear twenty-five pairs of tiny feet rush towards the entry hall.

As the door opens, I'm greeted by a resounding chorus of tiny voices: "SLEEPING BEAUTY!!!"

The party is a complete success. The kids are completely enchanted with my costume and they love all the activities. Some of the parents comment that they've never seen their little ones so well behaved and joke that maybe they should start parenting in costume.

By the time the hour is over, I've painted twenty-five designs on cheeks and hands, we've made crowns together, sung songs together, and taken an adorable group photo. As the kids sit down at the table to eat their pizza and cake, I give the birthday girl final hug, wave goodbye to all the guests, and slip into the parents' room to change as instructed.

On my way out, Elisa catches me in the hall.

"Just a little something extra as a thank you," she says. She reaches her hand out and gives me a clump of money. "You were wonderful!"

"Thank you," I say, pocketing the cash.

"We'll be telling all our friends about you," she says giving me a hug. "Thanks again."

I walk out the door into the rain, open my umbrella and reach into my pocket to see how much she's tipped me. Seventy-five dollars.

Nailed it.

Jake is in stiches as we wait in the line for Grimaldi's Pizza, under our umbrellas.

"You changed in a bank ATM lobby?!"

"I know!" I laugh. "I didn't know what else to do. I was going to be late or spoil the surprise."

"That's quick thinking, kid!" he says, still chuckling. "I'm honestly impressed. Did anyone come in?"

"Yeah. A very confused older man," I say.

"Did you say anything to him?" he asks.

"Sure! I said hi and 'birthday party.' I think he got the gist."

Jake lets out a full chuckle. "This seriously made my day. If I didn't know you better, I'd think you were full of shit."

"And yet, it really happened," I say giggling.

"So how did the rest of the party go?"

"Great! The parents were ecstatic and the kids loved me. Tipped me seventy-five big ones."

"Wow! So you're buying tonight, then."

"Actually I think I will," I say. "But I'm only buying one round of beers, if you want a second one, that's on you."

"Fair enough," he says. "Well, I'm proud of you, kiddo. You moved to New York and started a successful small business." He puts his arm around me in a sideways hug.

"With help! And let's not get ahead of ourselves." I protest. "One happy client does not a successful business make."

"Sure, but it's only a matter of time," he says. "What a day."

"A new classic fairy tale," I say. "The Adventures of Sleeping Beauty and the magical ATM lobby."

TEN

Sarah was right about having a great connection for me. Before she left for London, she introduced me to her friend, Pamela Thompson, who is the manager at Wonderland Teahouse. Wonderland has two uptown locations. Sarah thought it would be the perfect place for me to do Alice tea parties, and she turned out to be right!

I met with Pam several weeks before and we discussed ideas for how these parties could work. We've landed on a pretty solid concept, and I performed the first party a week ago, on the heels of my epic Sleeping Beauty ATM save. The party took place at their Westside location and was a smashing success.

The little girls were so delightful and starry-eyed. We sat around the table and I read them the story of Alice, while they sipped their tea and ate their tea sandwiches. I painted their faces, we made jewelry, and I got dozens of hugs plus a fifty-dollar tip. It was such a fantastic experience that I cannot wait to relive it today at their Eastside location!

"So, the host will arrive in about half an hour and then we'll go ahead and start your meet and greet time," says Pam.

"Great," I say. "I'll go ahead and get changed."

"How is this business venture of yours going anyway?" she asks. "We all think it's so cool!"

"It's actually going pretty well!" I say. "Consistent reservations for the next few weekends. I'm getting so busy I might need to hire on another performer."

"So exciting, Audrey! I know Sarah is majorly proud of you."

I walk into the back of the restaurant, which is known for their amazing baked goods, and prepare to change in the back room.

I don my blue dress with white pinafore, long blonde wig, black shoes and black headband. I look perfectly the part. I exit the changing room and head back to the hostess stand where Pam is waiting.

"Today's party is going to be slightly bigger than last week's," she says. "A few boys will be here too."

"Okay," I say. "No problem."

Pam and I head upstairs to the party room to set up my supplies. Today we'll be doing face painting, story time and crown decorating. I have cardboard crowns and a variety of adhesive jewels so the kids can create royal masterpieces and wear them during the party.

As the guests begin to arrive, I stand and welcome the children into the space with the proverbial, saccharine-sweet "Hello there! How are you today?" greeting. The first four guests to arrive have little daughters who are instantly shy and adorable.

The mothers are busily chatting about a variety of subjects that I can overhear - charity galas, school events, field trips, soccer clubs, typical New York City mother conversation topics. The little girls are seated at a small table at one end of the room while the mothers immediately congregate at the adult table on the other side, pitchers of mimosas and Bloody

Mary's awaiting them. This isn't their first time at the rodeo.

Finally, a woman who I assume is the host approaches me. She is tall and slender with freshly bleached-blonde hair. She's impeccably dressed from head to toe and wears delicate accents of gold jewelry on her fingers and wrists.

"Hi," she says. "I'm Monica, Claire's mom."

"Very nice to meet you." I extend my hand, which she takes in a weak, half-hearted handshake.

"So far, a few of the girls have arrived. Some of the brothers will be here shortly. I brought some wands for the girls and swords for the boys," she says. "I thought it would be a nice touch."

"That sounds great," I say. "I'll go ahead and lay out the crown activity and then when the boys arrive we can start the face painting."

"That's fine," she says distractedly, walking back to the table of moms.

I sit down at the table with the young girls who are all around the age of five. They are dressed in their best party dresses and they look up at me expectantly. I see Monica's clone. She must be Claire, the birthday girl.

"How old are you today, Claire?" I say, addressing her and hoping I've guessed correctly.

"Six," she says.

"Wow! Six years old today, what a big girl!"

"My mommy says that you're not the real Alice," Claire says matter-of-factly. "She says you're an actress."

"Well–" I start.

"She also says that an actress is not a real job and that she won't let me be one."

I'm too stunned to speak. Is a six-year-old really talking to me this way? Is a six-year-old really insulting my profession? I don't care if it's her birthday; I'm not taking any shit from this little brat.

"Well, Claire, that really hurts my feelings that you'd say I'm not the real Alice," I say. "Is there anyone else here who doesn't believe I'm real?"

"I believe you're real, Alice," says a tiny little girl with red curls and green eyes.

"Thank you," I say. "What's your name, sweetheart?" I ask.

"Shannon," she answers.

"Well, I guess it looks like Shannon is the only one here who wants to believe in magic," I say. "I guess if no one else wants to believe in magic except for me and Shannon, that's fine."

I watch as the rest of the girls' skeptical faces turn to concern. The 'believing in magic' tactic is one of the best tricks I've learned with older kids, especially in New York City, where most six-year-olds have SAT-level vocabularies.

"I believe in magic, Alice!" shouts another of the girls.

"Me too!" shouts another.

"Claire, I have to say, your mother seems like a really smart lady. I'd find it very strange if she asked someone who wasn't the real Alice to come to your party."

"Yeah, Claire!" says another of the girls. "Why wouldn't you have the real Alice at your birthday party?"

I watch Claire. She studies me for a second, her face screwed up in thought. "Well, I guess you must be the real Alice, or how else would you be here," she concludes. Her rationale makes absolutely zero sense, but I'll take it because now the girls are all on my side.

I look over at the table of mothers to see if they've just witnessed this completely stellar turn around I've maneuvered, but they are all gabbing with each other drinking mimosas and laughing loudly.

"How *did* you get here, Alice?" asks Shannon.

"The Q train," I answer honestly. "Now, who would like to decorate crowns?"

My question is met with a resounding chorus of, "Me! Me! Me! Oooh me!"

I begin to lay the crowns out when all of a sudden I hear a thunderous noise coming up the stairs. I watch in horror as a dozen boys explode into the party room. A man who I'd bet is Claire's dad and a frantic Pam bring up the rear. Pam runs up to me and explains in a panicked whisper that there were only supposed to be five more children, but apparently some of the older siblings were invited last minute.

"Just do what you can!" she says, with a very real look of terror in her eyes.

Monica jumps up from her seat and kisses the older man on the cheek, her husband I assume. She motions him towards a bag in which I see the hilts of a dozen foam swords sticking out. *Please, God. No.* I think as he reaches down and starts pulling the swords out and distributing them to the boys, who are all jumping up and down, screaming.

No sooner does Monica's husband distribute the swords, does he sit down with the ladies and pour himself a Bloody Mary, completely ignoring the army of mayhem that he has just unleashed upon me.

I freeze as the boys run at the table where the girls are making their crowns and start hitting my little princesses with foam swords. The girls squeal and grab their foam wands from the table and begin fighting back. All it takes is that brief moment for me to lose complete control of the party.

For a minute all I can see is children sword fighting on one end of the room and oblivious adults drinking heavily on the other end. I find myself wishing I could join them and ignore this mess I've just been heaved into.

C'mon, Audrey. Get your shit together! I scold myself under my breath. "Okay everyone, can we sit down quietly, please!" I clap my hands three times and some of the kids respond by clapping the pattern back to me, a subconscious response ingrained in most young children. At that moment, Pam re-emerges from downstairs and helps me choral the kids into an orderly line so that we can begin face painting, while a few of the other children sit down at the table and continue decorating their crowns with as many sticky jewels as they can fit. *Greedy little bastards.*

"Okay, can everyone please line up for Alice?" Pam shouts.

"I sit down in my chair and open my face painting kit, but I'm already starting to feel claustrophobic. I'm surrounded by at least fifteen children who are all shoving to get to the front of the line and who all push forward to see what I'm painting on each child in front of me. I give them all the option of a heart, star, spider or butterfly, so I can get through them as quickly as possible.

When the oldest boy comes forward, he gives me a look that is unsettling. There is something in his eyes that looks almost evil. My first impression of him is that he's the kind of child who makes life a living hell for his parents.

My suspicions are confirmed when I ask him what he'd like painted and he responds, "Blood."

"I'm sorry?" I say, thinking maybe I've not heard him correctly.

"I want you to paint blood on my face," he says.

"Well, why don't you choose between a spider or a star?" I suggest.

He looks at me for a half a second before he erupts, "I WANT YOU TO PAINT BLOOD ON MY FACE!"

I startle at the volume of his voice and look immediately over to the parents in hopes that they'll reprimand him. Instead, his mother looks at me exhaustedly and says, "Just paint the blood, Alice," as if she's been the victim of this kind of outburst for some time. I nod at her and watch as she goes back to sipping her Bloody Mary and talking to the other moms.

I grab my red face painting crayon and start painting droplets of blood on the boy's face.

"Make it good, Alice!" he says firmly as I work.

"What's your name?" I ask.

"Gunnar," he says.

"Gunnar, I'm not sure I like the tone of voice you're using when you speak to me," I say in my best character voice. "That's not a nice way to speak to someone."

"You're just a dumb clown in a dress." He spits back at me. "Finish the blood, clown."

At this point, all I can think of is marching over to the adult table, slapping each unconscious parent and then pouring the entire pitcher of Bloody Mary's over Gunnar's head and shouting, "That bloody enough, ya little bastard!?" But instead, I keep diligently working on Gunnar's bloody face as Pam tries to encourage the other kids to stop hitting each other with swords and sit down at the table to work on their crowns.

When I finally finish all the kids' face painting, I walk shakily back to the table where they are all huddled together around a plate of cookies that Pam has brought up to distract them.

"Is everyone ready for story time?" I ask. I'm so frustrated I can barely get the words out, but I know I have to keep it professional and try and close this party strong.

The servers finally get the kids to sit down by setting plates of grilled cheese sandwiches and more cookies on the table. Most of the kids sit obediently and eat, but the older boys are still running around the table playing duck, duck, goose and hitting each other with their plastic swords. Parents' table: completely oblivious.

"Let's all listen to Alice's story!" shouts Pam, to no avail. I give her a desperate look and she gives me a sympathetic one back.

I grab the *Alice in Wonderland* book and begin reading. For the first two pages, the room quiets down from a cacophony of screams to a dull roar.

"Alice sat reading on the hillside one afternoon!" I begin. But just as I am turning the page I hear Gunnar's voice rise above the crowd.

"GET ALICE!!!" he screams, raising his sword. All the boys rush at me and start hitting me with their swords while laughing maliciously.

"Okay, that's not very nice!" I yell, panicked. "Please stop that now!"

"Please!" shouts Pam.

"DIE, ALICE! DIE!" shouts Gunnar, as he attempts to poke my eyes with his sword.

"That's quite enough!" I shout. "If we can't be nice, Alice is going to have to leave the party."

I look desperately over to the parents' table, but they are just watching the scene laughing as if this is a typical Saturday brunch for them.

"We don't want Alice to leave!" yells a desperate Pam.

"SHE'S JUST A CLOWN!!!" Gunnar screams, rallying the other boys who begin chanting. "Die, Clown! DIE, CLOWN!"

As my ears begin to ring, I see red, and finally shout at the top of my lungs, "IF YOU DON'T STOP RIGHT NOW, ALICE IS GETTING BACK ON THE Q TRAIN AND GOING HOME TO BROOKLYN!!!"

At that moment, a few of the servers walk into the room holding Claire's cake and singing the birthday song. I attempt to regain my composure, as the boys are suddenly far more interested in consuming sugar than beating me with foam swords.

Finally, after the candles are blown out and the cake is cut, Pam tells the guests that it's time for Alice to leave. I walk downstairs feeling furious and on the brink of tears.

I sneak into the back room and change out of my costume and back into my street clothes. After a few moments, Pam comes down and knocks on the door.

"Audrey?" she says. "Are you alright?"

"Yeah, I'm fine." I open the door to let her in.

"I'm so, so sorry about those people," she says sincerely. "They were absolutely out of line."

"It's alright," I say, but deep down, I'm feeling a little bruised. Literally. Am I fooling myself attempting to be an actress in New York City? I'd never imagined it would be so hard. Even now that I'm making money doing parties, I still don't feel like I'm exactly living the dream. How could a couple of bratty kids make me question my purpose here?

Pam pays me out of the drawer for the party and I walk down Madison Avenue toward 57th Street, so Alice can get back on the Q train and go home.

It's the next day when I walk out of the building on Central

Park West and 75th Street and see Logan and Jake sitting on a bench directly across from me, along the park. Still reeling from the disaster at Wonderland, I got up this morning and performed an Indian Princess party. I tried to teach the kids the term, Native American, but they didn't seem to get it.

As I cross the street, the image of my two best friends sitting and chatting together is exactly what I need. I'm so happy that they have become chummy. Ever since my break-up with Brent and the formation of the company, they have bonded in their joint mission of helping me to succeed.

"Your majesty!" Logan yells at me as I cross the street.

"Ow!" Jake shouts, before blowing a cat-call whistle at me.

"Excuse me you two, I'm trying to keep a low profile so the paparazzi don't find me!" I tease as I walk over to their bench.

"Speaking of which," Jake says, picking his camera bag up from the bench. "Just got done with a shoot. I texted you to stay in costume so we could take your picture in the park."

"Well, you're in luck Mr. Demille, I didn't see that text, but I was in such a hurry to get out of there, I just threw my coat on over it. The Indian Princess costume hides well."

"Photo. Shoot. Now!" says Logan gleefully.

"Excellent," says Jake. "Let's take a walk."

As Logan, Jake and I walk into the park together, I regale them with the events of the party. I tell them how the birthday girl had been terrified of the birthday song, or anyone even saying, 'Happy Birthday' to her, so when the cake came out, we all stood there silently. After she blew out the candles, everyone clapped and then she just lost it anyway.

"Ugh, I can so relate." Logan chimes in. "That child gets it. There's absolutely no reason why we should celebrate aging. Never wish me a happy birthday or I might do something drastic."

"We'll try to remember that," says Jake. "Go on, kid."

"Well, that was basically it," I say. "The parents apologized for her but didn't tip me. Maybe this weekend is just cursed for parties, or maybe I didn't look Native American enough for their liking..."

"Honey, your complexion is flawless." Logan interrupts me. "You're like Rachel McAdams. You can pull of any hair color. Besides, not every Native American girl spent all day in the sun. You could have just been the one that stayed in her wigwam all day working on fabulous beaded garments."

Jake chuckles and I start giggling too. "How about over there?" says Jake. "There's a nice tree."

"Looks great," I say. "Let me put the wig back on." I grab the long black wig from inside my garment bag and put it on over my ponytail.

"Fierce," says Logan as I smooth out the long black tendrils. "You look like a young Madeleine Stowe."

"Okay, let's make this fast because it's chilly," I say as I take my coat off, revealing my Indian princess dress, and set it on a park bench with my bag.

"Alright kid, can you climb over the wall and stand back by the tree trunk?" Jake asks.

"On it," I say. I climb over the stone wall and walk back a dozen yards or so into the space next to the tree. "How's this?"

"Looks great!" Jake adjusts his camera and I stand there for a few moments before he gives me some direction. "Okay, go ahead and look like you're pissed at me for taking over your land and giving you syphilis!"

I laugh and Jake starts snapping photos.

"Show me those fierce, cork-husking hands!" shouts Logan, and I raise my arms above my head as if I'm embracing the trees. I switch the pose a few times looking demure, sweet, serious, and fun. Jake continues snapping photos. Finally, after he's convinced we've got enough business material, he decides to play around a little bit.

"Okay kid, give us day-after-a-late-night-rendezvous with John Smith," he shouts.

I laugh and tussle my hair, coyly lifting my skirt a tiny bit up my thigh. "You guys are terrible!" I shout. "Some people might consider you a little bit racist right now!"

"Let's see that Pocahont-ass!" shouts Logan. "Can you pose with your back to us like you're looking in the tree for that stupid raccoon?"

"I guess so!" I shout back as I turn and face the tree looking up. "Like this?"

"GO!" is all I hear as I turn around and see Logan and Jake grabbing my coat and bag and taking off running.

"Hey!" I scream, running back toward the stone wall. "You guys! You suck!"

Logan and Jake run around the path towards the lake laughing hysterically as I scramble to climb over the wall and then sprint after them.

"This isn't funny! IT'S COLD!" I run down the path surrounded by families starring, laughing and pointing at me.

"Look honey, it's Tiger Lily!" I hear as I round the bend towards the lake.

When I finally catch up to Logan and Jake, they are sitting calmly on the benches overlooking the lake, shoulders shaking hard from their laughter.

"You bitches are going to pay for that!" I yell, laughing now too. "Jerks!"

"Can't believe you fell for that, kid." Jake is chuckling. "Indian Princess isn't very smart, is she?"

"Well, her coloring looks a bit more appropriate now," says Logan. "I think we figured out what made the red man red."

Jake reaches over his fist and Logan bumps it.

ELEVEN

With Thanksgiving nearing, the temperatures have really begun to drop. It's a cold and gray day, and I find myself in a very elegant brownstone on the Upper West Side. In spite of the crummy weather outside, I'm glowing.

This party is a complete success so far, which is a welcome change after the Alice-bashing and crying birthday girl incidents. Today's birthday party came as a referral from Alexandra, who is here with Amelia.

The birthday girl, Vianne, is one of Amelia's friends from school and she has two fabulous gay dads, whom I'm already in love with. The afternoon gets even better when I meet a very influential friend of theirs.

I've just finished my mermaid song. Amelia made sure to mention to me how weird it was, before joining the rest of the kids at the table for pizza. I'm organizing my supplies when a tall and slender man wearing wire-rimmed glasses and a cashmere sweater approaches me; he's holding a glass of white wine.

"Wow, that was really quite good," he says.

"Thank you." I give him a smile.

"I assume you're an actress?" he questions.

"Yes," I answer. "Well, trying to be."

"Are you Equity?" He takes a sip of his wine. I love how New Yorkers drink at kid's parties. It must make it so much more bearable.

"Sadly, no," I say. "Still trying to figure that out."

"Well, that might work in my favor," he says. "I'm co-producing a reading for a new show and we're looking to fill a couple parts with non-union actors for budget reasons."

"Oh wow," I say.

"Would you like to come audition?" he asks.

"Yes! I'd love to!" I realize too late that I've been a bit too enthusiastic. "Sorry. Yes, that would be great."

"Great!" He laughs. "I'm Jeffrey Chamberlin, and we'd love to have you come in. Here's my card."

"What's the show about, if you don't mind me asking?"

"It's a period piece," he says. "A musical. You'd be great."

I take the card from him and my heart swells. "Thank you! I'm Audrey by the way. So nice to meet you, Jeffrey."

"You too, Princess! Enjoy the party." We shake hands, and he walks away.

The rest of the party, I'm floating on cloud nine. I have an audition with a Broadway producer! For a Broadway reading! I can hardly contain myself.

As I leave the party, buzzing with excitement, I decide to splurge on a cab instead of taking the subway. I already know where I'm headed. Downtown.

"Hey." Jake answers my call on the second ring.

"Jake! You won't believe what just happened!" I squeal into my cell phone as the taxi cruises down Central Park West.

"Chloe and I broke up," he says dryly.

"What?"

"I'm fine… I think," he says. "I could use a drink."

"Oh God, of course, I'm on my way down," I say. "Want

me to invite Logan? He's great at being snarky and wonderful in the face of a break-up. He'll probably use the C word a lot."

"Think I just want it to be the two of us. That alright?" He sounds low. I feel instantly concerned.

"Of course," I say. "I'm on my way now. Half-Pint?"

"Sounds good. Sorry, what was your news?"

"Oh, it's nothing important. I'll tell you when I see you."

Twenty minutes later I'm getting out of the cab on Sullivan Street and walking into our bar. Jake sits in the corner, looking downtrodden, sipping what appears to be a whiskey. In spite of our three months of friendship, I've still never met this elusive Chloe. She hasn't been back to New York for longer than a day since I met Jake, and now she's broken his heart. I'm not even sure what happened, but the sight of Jake looking so defeated has me feeling fiercely protective. I might even just hate her a little bit.

"Hi," I say as I take up a seat beside him and give him a hug. "You okay?"

"Yeah." He breathes into my neck. "Thanks, kid."

"What happened?" I ask, pulling away from him and arranging my bags on the bench. I've never seen Jake like this. He's always so upbeat and happy, and now he looks like Eeyore. His face is tired, he's got a five o'clock shadow and the light in his eyes has gone dull.

"Honestly, I think it just ran its course." He takes a sip of his drink, but I can tell he's holding back.

"That all?" I ask.

He hesitates. "She met someone."

"Oh, Jake…" I start.

"Another photographer," he says.

"Jesus," I mutter.

"She says that nothing has happened, but I know how she is, and I don't believe it," he says.

"I'm so sorry," I say. "How do you feel?"

"I'm alright." He shrugs. "I'm pissed off that I'm going to

have to move out of our apartment, but honestly I think I'm more upset that I didn't end it myself sooner. I knew it wasn't working and I didn't just get out. I'm pissed off that I stayed for so long, putting up with long distance bullshit, when I could have been living my life, uninhibited."

"I understand completely," I say.

"Instead." He continues. "I was making sure I was home at certain times to Skype with her, or that I had my phone in my pocket at all times in case she called or texted. And for what? Now she's screwing someone else! I mean, why even move in with me if she wasn't into it?"

"I'm so sorry."

"She's such a talent-whore," he says. "Apparently this guy's work is more impressive than mine, so she'd rather let him bed her."

"Did she actually say that?" I ask, aghast.

"Of course not, but I know her," he spits out angrily.

"I hate her for doing this to you." I take his hand and give it a squeeze.

I'm getting the clear impression that even though Jake is upset, as any guy would be, that another man has taken his woman, the bigger blow to his ego is the assumption that this new guy is more talented than him as a photographer. It's his professional ego that is taking the biggest hit.

"Long distance is so pointless." He continues. "Why put up with the bullshit that comes along with relationships if you're not getting any of the perks, ya know? I've gotten laid once in the last three months because she's been gone and I wanted to be faithful to her and build our home! If I'd known she was screwing some other photographer, I might have made some different choices."

"Well, the fact that you didn't speaks volumes about your character," I say. "You're a great guy and you have so many wonderful qualities. You deserve someone who sees all of those things and is stoked that you love her. Not to mention, your work is incredible!"

"Audrey, it's okay, you don't have to..." He starts.

"No, I'm serious. Let me finish my thought for a second." I'm starting to get heated. "You're incredibly talented, Jake, and your work *is* amazing. I wouldn't bullshit you. If I thought your photos were sub-par, I'd tell you. So don't let her bitchy, selfish choice make you feel insecure about your career. I'm sure this new guy's photos suck. It's probably just the novelty of something new, or maybe the initial appeal of the danger of getting caught. And it's quite clear that Chloe has a low IQ because only a moron would let an incredible guy like you go... Fuck her."

Jake is silent for a moment and then his mouth curls up into a slightly bashful smile. "Wow. You're really pissed off for me," he says.

"Hell yeah, I am!" I retort. "I hate this girl with a passion and I've never even met her. No one breaks my friend's heart and escapes being on my list."

"Thanks, kid. It'll be alright. I'm fine."

"Are you sure?" I ask, still waiting for my blood to stop boiling.

"Yes, you're actually quite adorable when you get heated and lose your temper," he says, still chuckling. "I'm feeling much better."

"Sorry," I laugh. "I can get a little overly passionate sometimes."

"It's a good quality, I assure you." He takes my hand and gives it a squeeze. "So, what was your news that I interrupted with my sad sob story?"

"Oh, gosh, it's not really a big deal," I say. I had almost forgotten my good news.

"Lay it on me." He smiles. "Don't let me rain on your parade."

"Really?" I ask.

"Of course," he says.

"Okay, I did a party this afternoon and one of the guests introduced himself to me. He's a Broadway producer," I say. "He asked me to audition for a reading of a new show."

"Holy shit! Audrey, that's huge!" he says. "You let me go

on about my stupid break-up when you've just had a huge break? I feel like such a douche."

"Are you kidding? A break-up is a big deal, Jake," I say.

"Whatever, this calls for a celebration," he says. "Let me close out my tab and let's go for dinner. My treat."

"Let's not get carried away." I laugh. "I haven't even got the part yet! I don't even know what the part is!"

"But you will!" He smiles. "You're talented and a great person; this is the start of something big and I don't want to spend the evening thinking about someone who isn't worth my time. I'd rather spend the evening with you."

"Jake, that's really sweet." I'm totally touched.

"Don't mention it, kid," he says. "Hey, have you had a night on the town with a guy since you got here?"

"Sure," I say.

"Logan doesn't count." He teases. "I mean like a night where a guy takes you out and treats you."

"Like a date?" I ask.

"Sort of, but in our case, a friend-date."

I laugh. "No, I haven't been on a friend-date with a guy other than Logan."

"Alright then," he says. "Let's do it. Two single people enjoying all that this city has to offer."

I'm stunned with how quickly Jake's demeanor has changed. The color has returned to his face and his eyes have their familiar twinkle once again.

"Well, twist my arm," I say.

Jake closes out his tab, I grab my bags and we walk outside and jump into a cab.

"Prince and Mercer, please," says Jake, and away we go.

Our first stop is the Mercer Hotel, where we decide to plunge into a dozen oysters and a couple cocktails.

"You have to try a Vieux Carré here," Jake says. "They make a good one."

"A voo-ca-what?" I ask, confused. Our stunningly beautiful server brings the plate of oysters to the table and waits for our drink order.

"It's a classic New Orleans cocktail," he says. "You'll like it. It's great for this time of year."

"Alright," I say somewhat skeptically. "I'll trust your judgment."

"Your man has great taste," says our server, smiling at me. "You guys are a such a cute couple."

"Oh, he's not—"

"It's okay," says Jake, cutting me off.

"We're just—" I start.

"Oh, I'm sorry," says our server. "I just assumed."

"Two of those," says Jake. "Thanks."

She walks away, looking embarrassed, and all of a sudden Jake and I find ourselves sitting in a completely awkward silence.

Our eyes meet and we smile. "So… that was awkward," I say.

"It's fine," he says with a laugh.

"Well, here we are… on a friend-date," I say.

"Yeah…" He clears this throat. "What should we talk about?"

I burst out laughing. "This is ridiculous! I see you all the time, why does this feel weird?"

"I dunno!" He laughs as well. "Maybe because it's the first time we've both been single?"

"This is stupid, Jake. You're one of my best friends," I say. "We just spent half an hour at the Half-Pint. We can do this! How is work going?"

"You wanna talk about work?"

"I dunno, I'm trying to ease the weirdness."

Just then, our server appears with our cocktails and we both reach for them gratefully. Jake is right that the drink is delicious. It's spicy and a bit sweet; it feels very appropriate for this chilly weather.

"Well, let's talk about this audition," he says. "When is it?"

"I don't know yet," I say. "I have to e-mail the producer guy I met today."

"What's the show?"

"He says it's a period piece, but a musical," I say. "I'm not really sure beyond that."

"Sounds interesting." Jake reaches over to our plate of oysters and begins dressing one with vinegar and horseradish.

"Hey, do you really think that oysters are an aphrodisiac?" I ask.

"What do you mean?" He raises an eyebrow and tips the shell to his lips, slurping the oyster down.

"Like do you think there's truth to the myth that oysters make you randy?"

"Randy?" he asks. "What are you, Austin Powers?"

"What?" I say laughing. "Do people not say 'randy' anymore? Is that not in the vernacular?"

"You're an odd one," he says, chuckling.

"You already knew that," I say with a smile.

"I know. I'm just realizing the full extent of it." He teases me.

"Fine," I retort. "Do you think that oysters make you sexually aroused?"

"I don't know. Can't say I've ever experienced that. Why? You feel something comin' on?"

"No!" I giggle. "Just wondering."

Jake and I finish our oysters and drinks. We fight for the bill, and he of course wins. I run to the bathroom to freshen up and then we gather my princess bags and head back out into the street.

"Where to next?" I ask.

"I'm thinking we go to dinner at Extra Virgin," he says. "Maybe sit at the bar."

"Sounds lovely," I say.

"Do you mind the walk?" he asks.

"Not at all," I say, adjusting my party supply bag on my shoulder.

"Here, give me that," he says.

"You want to walk around SoHo carrying a pink shoulder bag?" I ask.

"Just hand it over," he says. "I'll take one for the team."

As we walk down Bleecker Street, we fall easily into conversation and any tension that was there before is gone. The air is chilly, but not unbearable. A light breeze blows my hair a bit as we walk and I tuck it behind my ears. The rain has stopped and the rays of setting sunlight break through the remaining clouds, casting a golden hue onto the buildings.

When we get to Extra Virgin we are seated at the bar and we order two glasses of red wine. Jake then orders Brussels sprouts with pancetta, a truffle mac 'n cheese tart, a pistachio-encrusted goat cheese, watercress and endive salad, and a New York strip steak to share.

"Quite the spread," I say as the barkeep begins setting plates down in front of us.

"Not too shabby," says Jake. "The Brussels sprouts are amazing here."

"I've walked past this place a million times," I say. "Never come in before."

"Here's an extra plate," says the barkeep.

"Thanks, man," says Jake.

Jake takes the plate and serves me half of everything before setting it down gently in front of me.

"Thank you," I say looking at the feast before me.

The Brussels sprouts are wonderful, but then again so is everything we try. By the time our plates are clean, we're on our second glass of wine and I'm feeling rosy and content.

"So, what do you think the fascination is with princesses for little girls?" he asks me.

"What do you mean?" I ask. "Every girl wants to be a princess."

"But why?" he asks. "Aside from the pretty dress. Why do little girls love those movies so much?"

I think for a moment before answering. "I guess every girl wants to feel beautiful and special."

"Do you think every girl just wants to be rescued and taken care of?" he asks.

"Honestly, I think the being taken care of part, is more about being cared *for*. But don't all people want that? We can take care of ourselves, most of us, but it's nice to know that someone else has your back. And for a woman...well at least for me, it's nice when that someone is bigger and stronger than you. Makes you feel protected."

"You're pretty independent, kid."

"Well, sure," I say. "And I like that about me. But I remember being a little girl and not really dreaming about what my career was going to be, like other kids did. I'd just imagine falling in love. For as long as I can remember, I just wanted to meet my prince. And I loved playing make believe. Maybe that's why I became an actor."

"Do you think you've ever really been in love before?" he asks.

"I used to think I was in love with Brent, and maybe I was, in kind of a juvenile way, but in terms of like great love? Not sure I've had that yet."

"Just don't be dumb enough to ever settle," he says.

"Yeah, that sounds awful," I say. "Have you known great love?"

"I don't think so," he says. "I think its possible to have though."

"I think so too," I say. "I know it'll happen for me one day. I just haven't met the right guy yet."

"Sure," he says.

"It's weird too," I say. "This is the first time in my life I haven't like had someone in mind as a back-up, ya know?"

"What do you mean?"

"I mean like every time I've gotten out of a relationship, I've always had someone in mind to be a rebound, or be the next boyfriend. This is the first time I'm not doing that. I'm just happy hanging out with my friends and being by myself."

"Yeah," he says. "Listen, I'm gonna hit the men's room and then you wanna go to Milk & Cookies and call it a night?"

"Sure!" I say. "Thank you, Jake. This has been a really fun friend-date. I'm so glad to have you in my life."

"Don't mention it, kid," he says. "I'm glad you had a good time."

A few days later, I'm sitting in the waiting room at Ripley Grier Studios. When I emailed Jeffrey Chamberlin with the subject line, 'Mermaid Princess seeks audition,' he instantly remembered me and set an appointment.

It's the very first time I've had an appointment for an audition and it's so nice to be waiting inside and not outside in the cold. My voice is feeling nice and warm, my outfit isn't wrinkled and my dancing feet aren't blue. The room is filled with a dozen other girls, all looking very nervous. I try to make polite conversation with a couple of them, but they seem too nervous to talk, which doesn't suit me very well since I'm a nervous-talker.

I'm running lyrics over in my head and reading the sides Jeffrey emailed to me, which I've memorized. I remind myself of the top five things I'll need to remember when I'm in there. 1. breathe, 2. Don't lock my knees. 3. Shake the hands of each of the auditioners. 4. Set the tempo with the accompanist before we begin. 5. Say, "thank you" when leaving. And above all, to be myself.

"Audrey Princeton?" I jump at the sound of my own name and nearly have the inclination to shout, "Present!"

"Yes, that's me," I say, raising my hand.

"Right this way." She directs me.

"Let's do this," I whisper to myself as I grab my headshot, audition book and bag.

"Break a leg," says one of the other girls sitting and waiting. I give her a confident smile.

I walk into the room and look at the table. There are four people there, one of whom is Jeffrey. I flash him a smile and he returns it with ease.

"Audrey, very nice to see you again," he says. "I'd like to introduce you to the rest of our creative team."

"Hello," I say cheerfully as I hand Jeffrey my headshot.

"Thank you very much for having me."

"Whenever you're ready," he says.

I walk over to the pianist and shake his hand. I give him my sixteen bars and sing the first two measures in my desired tempo. He gives me an affirmative nod and I walk back to the middle of the room. Jeffrey makes eye contact with me and raises his eyebrows as a slight gesture of encouragement.

The piano starts playing my song and I immediately allow myself to get lost it in. I'm not sure what exactly this reading is for, so I've chosen a character piece, one of my favorite songs from a somewhat recent Broadway show. The selection is fun, melodic and showcases the hell out of my range.

When my moment to sing comes, I take a nice, calm breath and begin. I watch the faces at the table closely as I sing the bridge of the song. Each person's expression seems to convey the same message, *she's good*.

Charged with the positive reinforcement, I flow effortlessly into the final verse of the piece, hitting the high notes with the ease of a perfectly mixed-belt. This is literally what I've trained for. I'm shining and I'm feeling great about it.

When I finish, the creative team smiles at me.

"Thank you," I say.

"Audrey, we'd like for you to go ahead and read the sides that I sent you with Fiona here."

The girl who retrieved me from the waiting room walks over to me and we go through the scene that I've been practicing. I'm still unaware of the context of the scene, but it seems to be very exciting. My character has done something heroic and she is being praised by her mother for coming to the aid of the town.

When we finish, Jeffrey thanks me and I walk over to the table and shake everyone's hands.

"Thank you again," I say before walking out, and just like that, it's over. Six and a half minutes and I'm out of there.

I walk back into the waiting area, passing a dozen nervous-looking girls, and I breathe a sigh of relief. No matter what happens, I'm proud of that audition.

I walk out the door and into the hall and stop dead in my tracks. There leaning against the wall on his phone is the most beautiful face I have ever seen. He's tall with dark blond hair, ice blue eyes, a chiseled face and perfectly rosy cheeks. *Holy shit.*

He notices me starring at him, smiles and mouths, "Hi."

"Hi," I say shyly as I walk past him and out the door.

I walk up 8th Avenue with a spring in my step. I still have over an hour before I have to pick Amelia up from school, so I decide to stop at Argo Tea in Columbus Circle for a snack.

I walk into the shop and order myself a hot green tea and a muffin. I find a seat near the window next to a couple girls who are chatting busily.

"I'm telling you," says the first girl, a blonde. "The MTA is a friggin' conspiracy! Do you know how long it took me to get into the city on Sunday?"

"How long?" says the second girl, a redhead.

"Two god-forsaken hours," says the blonde. "From Prospect Park to Union Square. Are you freaking *kidding* me?!"

"What?" says the redhead. "That's nuts!"

"Yup! There were just no effing trains!" says the blonde. "I swear to God, I stood there for an hour, not a single one! It's like they think people who live in Brooklyn don't need to get into the city or something!"

"I hear that," I say before I can stop myself. They both look at me. "Sorry, I didn't mean to eavesdrop."

"You live in Brooklyn too?" asks the redhead.

"Yeah, I do," I say, still mildly embarrassed for interrupting their conversation. "Prospect Park Q train is my stop too."

"It's ridiculous, right?" says the blonde.

"It's awful," I say. "I do birthday parties every weekend, so I'm constantly on the subway coming into the city. I give myself two hours to get here just in case the trains aren't running, and I have a car service number in my phone as well."

"You do birthday parties?" asks the redhead. "Are you a magician?"

"No," I laugh. "I do princess parties for kids. I'm an

actress."

"Hey, us two!" says the blonde. "You just come from an audition? I like your dress."

"Yeah, I did," I say. "And thanks, I just went in for a reading of a new musical. My first appointment ever actually, and it went well."

"Good for you," says the redhead. "I'm Em by the way."

"Hi. I'm Audrey." I shake her hand.

"I'm Kay," says the blonde.

"Nice to meet you both," I say.

"So, how many people work with you in this princess thing?" asks Kay.

"For now it's just me," I reply. "But I'm getting so busy that I'll probably need more girls soon."

Em and Kay stare at me for a moment before they both break into smiles.

"I don't want this to seem forward or anything, but... you need to hire us!" says Kay. "We are both actors and singers and totally available."

"She's right," says Em. "We both went to Tisch, but that doesn't seem to mean much in this town anymore."

"It's so true," says Kay. "I mean, how much money did I give that damn school and not a single 'connection' has paid off for me beyond one summer stock gig."

"Well, would you guys be willing to email me your resumes?" I ask tentatively.

"Absolutely!" shouts Em. "I have a website with some samples of my voice on it."

"And of course I've got one of those too," says Kay.

They each scribble down their contact information on a napkin and hand it to me.

"What sort of activities do you do at these parties?" asks Em.

"Mostly performance-based ones," I say. "A little bit of face painting, but mostly singing, games, reading, arts and crafts, meet and great. Standard stuff, maybe a bit of improv required."

"Sounds simple enough," says Kay.

"Actually, I'm going to do a party at Wonderland Teahouse after Thanksgiving," I say. "God knows how it will go. But if you want to come observe, I'm sure that would be fine. The manager is a friend and they owe me after the last disastrous party."

"Oh jeez. What happened?" asks Kay.

"It's a long story," I say. "Suffice it to say a boy wanted blood painted on his face and then led the rest of the boys in a sword-wielding Alice mutiny that resulted in me completely losing my shit."

"Sounds intense," says Em.

"Oh, I want in on this so badly," says Kay laughing. "I would *love* to get paid to lose my shit in front of children."

I chat with the girls for another twenty minutes before I gather my things and get ready to head to Amelia's school. By the time I leave, we've become Facebook friends, and have made plans for them to come observe my party after the holiday. I like these girls instantly, and the idea of having backup performers appeals to me.

As I walk out of Argo to grab the train I'm bursting with good feelings. Sometimes the universe just conspires to bring all the right people into your life!

TWELVE

$\mathcal{S}$ometimes when things are starting to look up, life completely shits on you.

You feel hopeless and question every choice you have ever made leading up to that awful moment. You wonder why everyone else seems to have all the luck and why good fortune never seems to smile down upon you. Those are the days when it's an absolute struggle to get out of bed in the morning. And when the sun goes down, you just want to crawl back in bed with your shoes still on and disappear.

Today, however, is not one of those days.

"I'd like to propose a toast!" says Logan, raising his glass. "To Holly, our little star! Soon to be making her off-Broadway debut!"

"Thank you, Paulie," I say raising my glass. "I can't believe it's happening! We start rehearsals in two days!"

Logan, Jake and I are sitting at my favorite sushi restaurant in Midtown. I received the call from Jeffrey Chamberlain this afternoon telling me that I've officially been cast in the show, so we decided a celebration was in order.

"We're very proud of you, kiddo," says Jake. "I told you you'd get this one."

"Thanks, Jake." I smile. "You guys are the best!"

"Are you ready to order?" asks our server.

"Actually, we're waiting for a couple more people," I say.

"Excusè moi?" Logan raises an eyebrow as the server walks away.

"My new princess girls, Em and Kay, are coming to celebrate too," I say. "I told you about them."

"Ugh, honey, I'm so stressed with my client's damn bathroom tiles right now, I can't even remember my debit card PIN and it's only four numbers," says Logan. "In fact, I think it's my birthdate?"

"Are either of these girls single?" asks Jake.

"Yes," I say. "But hand's off Jake! This is business and I don't want you tempting my new Snow White with your poison apple, if you catch my drift."

"C'mon!" he protests. "I'm on the rebound. I need to see some boobs!"

"Gross," says Logan.

"You can find boobs at your local pub, my friend," I say. "These boobs are mine."

"Can we stop talking about boobs? I'm losing my appetite," says Logan.

"Sorry, Logan," says Jake. "By the way, I tried to watch *Breakfast at Tiffany's*, but I just couldn't get into it.

"Excuse me?" says Logan.

"What's up with Mickey Rooney playing that Asian guy? Isn't that kind of racist?"

"Oh, Mr. Yunioshi?" asks Logan. "That's classic!"

"I'm just not sure about the Holly character," says Jake. "I mean, don't get me wrong, Hepburn is a stunner, but the character is kind of… aggravating?"

"Oh, I can't hear this," says Logan.

"Jake, know your audience," I say.

"Jacob, I'm going to pretend you didn't just say all of that and we're going to move on," says Logan. "Can we please talk about Thanksgiving? I'm hosting dinner and I need to know how many to plan for. Jake, are you staying in town?"

"Yeah, and I'll be just one since Audrey won't share her princess boobs with me," says Jake slyly.

"I'll probably just be one as well, unless I meet some hot guy in my rehearsals," I say.

"Oh, I'm sure you will, but they are more likely to be interested in me than you, m'dear," says Logan.

"Ha-ha," I retort. "Thanks for rubbing in the fact that I'm going to die alone."

"Hey guys, can you excuse me for a second?" says Jake, suddenly serious, his phone vibrating in his hand. "I need to take this."

He stands up and walks outside the restaurant. Logan and I watch him out the window.

"What's going on?" asks Logan.

"No idea," I say.

Logan and I stare out the window. Jake looks pretty focused and serious, pacing around on the sidewalk, phone to his ear. Then finally, his furrowed brow relaxes and his expression turns to a look of elation. He's clearly just received some kind of good news.

"Looks promising," I mutter to Logan.

"Ugh, I hate suspense," he says.

After another minute, Jake hangs up the phone and walks back into the restaurant.

"Oh my God, what?" Logan blurts out as soon as Jake sits back down in the booth next to me.

"I think *I* have something to celebrate tonight too," Jake says, beaming.

"Yeah?" I say.

"Should we order first?" Jake says evasively.

"Spit it out, Jacob, or so help me!" says Logan.

"Okay, okay." Jake chuckles. "That was my boss."

"Uh-huh…" I say.

"I've been chosen out of my entire department to fly to D.C. to photograph the first family for a piece the magazine is doing."

"Jake! That is amazing!" I squeal, throwing my arms around him.

"Oh. My. God," says Logan. "You are going to be permitted to look directly at the First Lady?"

"Seems so," says Jake. "The best part is I won't have to move, at least for a while. This gig pays pretty handsomely."

"And the President!" I exclaim, still hugging Jake.

"FLOTUS. The most stunning one since Jackie?" asks Logan.

"Yep!" says Jake.

"And the girls and the dog!" I've practically crawled onto Jake's lap I'm hugging him so close.

"Her hair is flawless," says Logan, still on the First Lady train.

I remove my arms from around Jake's neck and give him a kiss on the cheek. "Jake, I'm so thrilled for you. I told you your work was amazing. Obviously your boss sees that too!"

"Thanks, kid," he says, laughing.

"Did we interrupt some kind of love fest?" I hear Kay's voice. She and Em have just approached the table. "Congratulations on your role, lady!"

"Thank you!" I say getting up to hug each of the girls. "Introductions!"

I introduce the Kay and Em to Jake and Logan and we all sit down to order dinner. Four yellow tail rolls, three salmon rolls, two orders of red snapper sashimi and several Sapporo's later, everyone is well acquainted and having a good time.

"So, what's the craziest thing that's ever happened during a party, Audrey?" asks Kay.

"God, where do I start?" I say laughing. "I'm not sure you wanna hear the half of it. You might not want to work with me anymore."

"Are you kidding? I love crazy stories," she says.

"Well, the other day I was doing a mermaid party," I start

out. "I don't know if I'm losing weight or something, but I'm sitting around in a circle with the kids and we're doing get to know you songs. Then all of a sudden, a mother catches my attention and points to my chest. I looked down and my shells had fallen off my boobs!"

"Seriously, enough with the boob talk!" says Logan.

"Luckily I had a leotard on!" I laugh.

"Bet there were a few dads who enjoyed that!" says Jake.

"Anything else good?" asks Em giggling.

"Had a drunk dad walk in on me changing accidentally-on-purpose once." I giggle. "He was so embarrassed after I called him out that he tipped me fifty bucks; I assume not to say anything to his wife."

"I didn't know that," says Jake. "Do I need to give this guy a call?"

"No, Jake, that won't be necessary," I say. "But thank you for being protective of me."

Two days later, it's the Friday before Thanksgiving, and our first night of rehearsals and I could not be more excited. I'm sitting around a giant table with the entire creative team of the show, as well as the rest of the cast. Today we're doing a table reading of the script to get familiar with the material, and we'll all be meeting for the first time.

I glance around the table and see Jeffrey Chamberlin and the other producers who I remember from the audition. But other than them, every face is new.

"Hello, everyone, and welcome to our very first reading of the piece," says a tall blonde woman. "My name is Annie Crawford and I'll be your director for this reading."

I look around the table and see that there is one empty chair in the circle. Just as I'm starting to wonder whose chair it is, I hear the door to the studio crash open and my heart stops. It's the beautiful guy that I saw after my audition.

"So sorry I'm late!" he says as he rushes to the open chair. "Sorry, Annie. Subway."

"No problem, Chace," she says. "Everyone, this is Chace Campbell, our leading man."

"Sorry everyone," he says, face flushed. "Didn't mean to be such a diva on the first day of rehearsals."

Everyone in the group kind of chuckles, smiling and nodding at the same time. I imagine that people don't stay mad at Chace very long with a face like that.

We begin reading the script and I quickly surmise that the play takes place during the American Revolution. It's loosely based on the signing of the Declaration of Independence. Chace will be playing a young John Adams. I play a bar wench who comes to John's aid, when a drunkard tries to hurt him, by dowsing the drunkard in beer and then hitting him over the head with the beer stein.

I watch Chace as he reads. I've never seen such a beautiful creature in the flesh. It's like being in the presence of a movie star. As we read through the script, I catch myself stealing glances in his direction. *He's so talented.* His voice is resonant, his comedic timing is perfect, his serious delivery is decisively sincere. He should be nominated for some kind of award just for this reading.

When it comes time to read the scene we have together, I feel my face flush as our eyes meet.

"Young lady, do you understand how much your simple act has aided our efforts here at home?" he reads.

"Mr. Adams," I say, glancing up and then quickly averting my gaze away from his piercing eyes and back to the script in my hands. "If there is anything I can do to help, it will be my greatest pleasure."

"Truly, the pleasure is…all mine," he says in my direction.

I peek up and give a shy smile, hoping that he'll think the color in my face is either nerves or some kind of acting method he's never heard of before.

"Alright, let's stop there and take five," says Annie.

I walk over to the drinking fountain in the hall to fill up my water bottle and regain my composure. I lean against the wall and take a deep breath, willing myself to pull it together and be professional. I begin to screw the cap back on my water bottle when a young girl approaches me. "Hi," she says. "I saw you at the audition. I'm Gillian."

"Hey," I say. "Audrey. Nice to meet you."

"Likewise," she says. "Nice to have some eye candy with such a crappy script, huh?"

"Huh?" I stammer.

"Chace Campbell," she whispers.

"Oh!" I say. "Yeah, totally."

"Not a terrible view, ya know?"

"Is he gay?" I ask.

"Nope," she says. "My roommate's friend used to date him."

"Wow, usually boys that pretty bat for the other team…" I say.

"Yeah," she says, lowering her voice. "He's totally straight and apparently he has somewhat of a *sizable* reputation, if you know what I mean."

"Really," I say before I can stop myself.

"That's what I hear," she says. "You two seemed to have some nice chemistry in your scene."

"Oh gosh, no…" I stutter. "I'm just a little nervous is all. It's my first show in New York, so I just don't want the producers to be sorry they hired me."

"You'll be fine," she says. "It's just a reading anyway. They're more worried about how the show looks and sounds than the individual performances."

"I see…"

"Chace is somewhat of a Broadway darling," she says. "Producers here love him, but he's never booked any major shows. I think he's kinda hoping he might take this one past the workshop phase."

"Makes sense," I say.

"But between you and me," she says. "I don't see this show getting picked up. It's pretty terrible."

"Well, I guess it can't hurt to show these producers our stuff and hope they remember us next time we're in the audition room," I say.

"You've got the right idea, girl," she says. "That's the only reason I'm here. Half the battle in this town is who you know…and Annie, the director, is well connected here. I'd cozy up to her if you can."

"Alright! Let's get back to it, folks!" says a voice in the other room.

"Guess we'd better start that cozying up process," I say, as we walk back into the rehearsal space.

As the long weekend of rehearsals continues, I'm completely and totally distracted from how stupid this show is by Chace. I catch myself watching him when we go on break, wondering who he's texting, becoming instantly shy and blushing when he smiles at me or says hello.

We've had brief interactions in the last forty-eight hours. He's come up to me a few times and told me I'm doing a great job, and he laughs if I make a sarcastic comment. But I feel like a schoolgirl with a crush. The few times we've had half a conversation, I seem to black out and can't remember what I've said afterwards. When he sings on stage, my stomach flips. There is a consistent chant in my head of phrases like, *You are such an idiot, Audrey!* And *Oh, now that was smooth!*

I don't tell anyone about my crush, not even Logan or Jake, because I feel like it would be unprofessional. But it's hard to keep things from your best friends.

"You guys, you don't understand, this actor in the reading with me is like worthy of a Tony Award," I say over our diner brunch that Sunday morning. "He's fierce."

"So basically, he's good looking," says Jake.

"Remind me again why we are eating in this establishment?" says Logan, distracted. "These hash browns were frozen, I'm sure of it."

"Logan, we can't always eat brunch at Sarabeth's!" says Jake, clearly agitated. "It's too expensive. I can't do lemon ricotta pancakes one more Sunday in a row, and part of the

New York experience is diner food! How can you not know that after you've lived here for so long?"

"Honey, my 'New York experience' is a bit more refined than yours," says Logan.

"Well, it was my choice this week and I like this place," says Jake with a bit of egg yolk in the corner of his mouth.

"He's going to win a freaking Tony! I'm telling you guys." I carry on while sipping my coffee. "He's *so* talented."

"We get it, kid. He's talented." Jake still sounds a bit terse.

"Ouch!" I protest. "What's wrong with you today?"

"Sorry." He backs down. "Sorry, I'm just tense about this D.C. assignment, and my dry-spell is not helping matters."

"I'm seriously convinced that the people who do the worst things in life aren't getting laid," says Logan. "That's why I make sure I always am, so I don't accidentally go postal on a crowded street, ya know?"

"Jake, you must meet women at work," I say. "You work at a magazine for goodness sake!"

"The women in my office are ball-busting, high power executives with very limited creative prowess."

"So, they're boring." says Logan.

"Exactly," says Jake. "Some of them are nice, a few of them are hot, but I want someone who I can have a conversation with."

"If you're just trying to quench a dry spell, what does conversation matter?" I say.

"She has a point," says Logan. "Sex is sex."

"I dunno," says Jake. "Maybe I don't want *just sex*, maybe I want to meet someone that gets me excited in other ways than just physically. Mental stimulation is half the battle for me anyway."

"I actually agree with that," I say. "I have a way better time in the sack with someone who I have a great intellectual connection with."

"See, Audrey knows what I'm talking about," says Jake.

"Well, I think you're both crazy," says Logan. "In a dark room after a bottle of wine, the last thing on my mind is whether or not we both vote Democrat. And honestly, Republican-hate-sex can be pretty hot."

A few days later Amelia and I are walking up Fifth Avenue after I've picked her up from school and I can't stop thinking about Chace. It could be the fact that I'm in the midst of a dry spell myself, but I find I'm day-dreaming about him multiple times a day. Fantasizing about us kissing on a blanket in Central Park, or sitting in a candle lit bathtub…

It's the day before Thanksgiving and a brisk wind is blowing through the trees along the park as we stroll down the block.

"Audrey, I have to play the best song for you when we get home," Amelia says. "It's so cool."

"Sounds good," I say absentmindedly.

Amelia is seven, so she's just learning about music, and when I say music, I mean terrible pop songs that are on the radio. I honestly can't judge her though, because I may have been the world's biggest Ace of Base fan at her age. Although in all fairness, "I Saw the Sign" is one of the quintessential songs of the early nineteen nineties.

"Why doesn't my mom ever let me wear skinny jeans?" she asks as we walk into the park at 96th Street. "You always wear them."

"Well, I'm an adult, so I guess I get to choose what clothes I buy and wear. When you're eighteen you can wear whatever you want."

"That's so unfair, that's like so many years away!" she protests.

"I think that boot-cut jeans are super cute," I say. "When you roll up the cuff, that's very hip and cool."

"Whatever, my mom probably told you to say that," she says.

In truth, her mom and I *have* talked about the skinny jeans issue, and I did tell her I'd say that when the moment presented itself. Amelia is such a sweet girl and kids grow up so fast in New York City. If there's any way to keep her from dressing like a teenager too soon, I'm all for it.

"What's Evan doing today?" I ask, changing the subject. "Squash or hockey?"

"He plays squash today," she says. "He has a really cool coach."

"That's right," I say. "He's pretty good looking, that coach."

"Audrey, that's *so weird*!" she says, laughing. "Why don't you have a boyfriend?"

"Well, I used to have one back in California," I say. "But we're not together anymore."

"Did you guys kiss a lot?" she asks, making a sour face. "I don't like watching movies where people kiss. It's *so weird*!"

"You'll probably feel differently about that in a few years," I give her a playful grin.

"What about that guy who's always texting you?"

"Oh, Jake?" I say. "He's just my friend; we're not dating."

"How do you know which guys you want to be your boyfriend and which ones are just friends?" she asks.

"A lot of questions today, are you interested in boys?" I tease.

"No!" she says, embarrassed. "I'm just wondering."

"Hmm… I guess you just know when you feel something more than friendship for someone," I say. "Like you feel something in your heart."

"Does that happen right away?" she asks.

"I think so," I say. "There's a guy in my show who I think is pretty cool."

"Do you like him?" she asks.

"I do, but I'm not sure if he likes me; that part is always hard," I say. "He doesn't know I like him yet and I don't want him to find out so I haven't told anyone really."

"What's his name?" she asks.

"Chace," I say.

"Like the bank?" she says laughing. "That's a *weird* name!"

"You're a *weird* girl!" I tease as I wrap my arm around her and tousle her hair. "What do you say we grab a cab on the Westside? It's pretty cold today."

"Good idea!" she says. "I can't wait to tell Evan you like someone named Chace, he's gonna laugh so hard."

"Well, I'm glad you and your brother can have a laugh at my expense."

We walk across the park to the Westside and over to Central Park West to hail a cab. As we get into the taxi, Amelia opens her window and starts chanting, "Audrey loves Chace! Audrey loves Chace!" and continues to do so the entire cab ride home. I find myself silently praying that Chace lives below 59th Street.

The next morning, Jake, Logan and I take the subway to 66th Street and then walk over to my work apartment on Central Park West. Evan and Amelia's parents have invited us over to watch the parade from their 5th floor apartment. The excitement in the air is palpable as we walk amongst the huge crowd of New Yorkers all wanting to get a peek at the famous balloons.

It's pretty satisfying knowing that we've been invited to an exclusive party and that we won't have to be huddled on the sidewalk, trying to squeeze in to catch a glimpse of the parade as it goes by.

"Holly, I officially love your job," says Logan as we walk through the doors of their 66th Street apartment.

The place is filled with families, many of whom I recognize from their schools, and there is a huge spread of food on the dining room table. We say hello to the parents. I introduce Logan and Jake, who graciously thank them for the invite, and then Evan drags us toward to the balcony's French doors, just in time to see Spider-Man go by.

"Hey Audrey, Amelia told me you like someone named Chace? Like the bank?" says Evan, giggling.

"Great," I say under my breath. *Why did I ever say anything?*

"Don't worry, I'll respect your privacy," he says. "But

Amelia made a sign."

"What?"

"Hey New York!" I hear Amelia yelling on the balcony. "Audrey Loves Chace! My babysitter loves Chace!"

I walk over to the balcony with Jake and Logan hot on my trail, to find Amelia holding a huge white sign that she's decorated with red hearts that reads, "Audrey Loves Chace!"

"This is not happening…" I mutter under my breath, mortified. "Please, God let him not be at the parade today."

"This is fantastic!" says Logan, walking out onto the balcony to join Amelia. "The first child I've ever admired."

"Who's Chace?" asks Jake.

"That guy in my show," I mutter

"Audrey loves Chace! Audrey loves Chace!" Logan and Amelia have the entire balcony chanting now.

"Gotta hand it to her," says Jake. "She's got spirit."

"Audrey loves Chace! Audrey loves Chace!"

"Holly!" shouts Logan, laughing. "The people on the street are chanting too!"

I walk out onto the balcony to see a huge crowd of people on the sidewalk, five stories below us chanting, "Audrey loves Chace!" with Amelia, Logan and the rest of our balcony. I'm ready to crawl into a hole and die.

About a week later, I'm standing at the bar of a small lounge in Midtown. We've opened the show and I'm pleasantly surprised by how much the audience enjoyed it. In spite of the marginal script, Chace seems to be winning over audiences with his charming portrayal of John Adams, and I have to admit that the musical arrangements have grown on me. Since it's a staged reading, not a full scale production, audience reaction is important and will dictate whether or not the show goes anywhere down the line. So, it's nice to see that we're being well-received.

The embarrassment of Logan and Amelia's raucous Thanksgiving parade chant is still freshly seared into my memory, but so far no one in the cast has heard about it, so I'm thankful for that. The party is dying down and I'm ready to call it a night when I hear a voice in my ear.

"You enjoying the party?"

"Oh my God, Chace, hi!" I choke out. "You scared me!"

"Sorry," he laughs. "Are you drinking anything specific?"

"Oh, just a good ole Sam Adams," I reply nervously.

"Sam Adams? You should be drinking John Adams," he says, and then blushes. "Sorry, that came out kinda dirty."

I laugh. "Oh, it's okay... good one!"

"Want another?" He smiles and it's unfortunate how dazzling his pearly whites are.

"Sure, I guess. Thanks," I reply. How do you deny the hot guy in your show buying you a drink at your opening night party? You don't.

"Here you go." He hands me a cold glass of beer, but then someone across the bar calls his name and waves him over. "I need to go say hello to some friends over there. Catch up with you later?"

"Totally!" I wish I could bite back the enthusiasm in my voice.

"Happy opening, Miss Audrey." He winks at me while walking away and I feel my knees turn to jelly.

"Yup! Way to go, you!" I hear myself blurting out. *Jesus-tap-dancing-Christ, Audrey...*

"Okay, I get it... he's beautiful." Logan appears by my side.

"That's what I've been saying!"

"Holly, take him home, poke holes in his condoms, and lock that shit down."

"Oh my God, whatever!" I balk. "He talked to me for two minutes."

"So..."

"Honestly, I don't think I'm his type. He probably dates movie stars, or something."

"Sometimes I think you underestimate your looks," says Logan.

"Well, thank you, love, but I still think I'm a bit out of his league," I say. "Anyway, I've got to do a party in the morning, so I better go. Are you staying?"

"Yes, one of your chorus boy's friends is totally in that closeted-but-open-to-exploring stage, and I'm hoping to be the America to his Columbus."

"Wow, lots of American History going on tonight!" I laugh. "You want the rest of my beer?"

"Is there vodka in it?" he asks, rolling his eyes.

"No…" I say.

"Then no."

I kiss Logan on the cheek before heading to grab my coat.

"Love you. Call me tomorrow for dinner. I'll come in."

"Okay, boo. Get home safe," he says as he makes his way back to the Columbus guy.

I get my coat and walk out of the bar and into the chilly night air. I reach inside my purse to grab my gloves and metro card when I feel my phone buzz. It's Jake.

"Hey, kid! How was your opening?" he asks.

"Hey! It was good!" I say. "How's D.C.? How's the President?"

"It's cold and full of politicians," he says. "But I'm a big fan of the President's, so that's been pretty cool. I'll be back in a few days."

"Good, we'll have to get together to celebrate your return."

"Definitely… hey, listen, I've been doing a lot of thinking and there's something I need to ask you…" his tone sounds serious.

"Audrey!" I hear a voice behind me.

"Jake, hold on one sec," I say, turning around to see Chace heading my way.

"Holding," says Jake.

"Oh! Hey, Chace, what's up?" I'm trying to sound casual, but my pulse is definitely quickened at the sight of him.

"You disappeared in there. Didn't give me a chance to say goodnight."

"Sorry," I say. "I have an early day tomorrow. Just heading home."

"Listen, I don't want to keep you," says Chace. "But I've wanted to ask you something and I keep missing my chance. Do you want to go out sometime? Like, just the two of us?"

"Seriously?" It comes out of my mouth before I can think of something smoother to say.

"Yeah." He smiles. "I think we'd have a good time together."

"Um, okay!" I know I must be blushing, but I'm hoping he'll think it's because I'm cold.

"Great!" He turns to walk back into the bar, and then he stops and turns around. "Oh, and Audrey…"

"Yeah?" I say.

"Hope you enjoyed the Macy's parade," he says with a wink.

"Aw man!" I'm instantly embarrassed. "I'm gonna strangle that child next week…"

"G'night!" he says chuckling. "I'll call you."

He walks back into the bar and it's several seconds before I can find the will to speak.

"Audrey?" I hear Jake's voice on the other end of the phone, still in my hand.

"Oh my God! Sorry, Jake! Are you still there?" I pull the phone back to my ear.

"Yeah, still here," he says.

"Did you hear that!? Chace asked me out!"

"Yeah…I heard," he says.

"I had no idea he even liked me! Holy crap, this is nuts!" Jake is silent on the other end of the phone. "Sorry, you wanted to ask me something… what's up?"

"Yeah… it's nothing important, kid. Don't worry about it," he says. "Listen, I'd better go. I have to be up early tomorrow. Congrats on the opening."

"Thanks!" My head is still spinning. "Night, buddy! See you when you get back."

Jake hangs up the phone without saying goodbye, but I hardly notice because I can't stop smiling. *Chace Campbell asked me out!*

Part III: Winter

"I think that you are very kind. I must confess that your goodness pleases me. I like you with your face better than those who, beneath a man's face, hide a false, corrupt and ungrateful heart."

- Beauty and the Beast
by Gabrielle-Suzanne Barbot de Villeneuve

From: Charlotte Brander <c.brander@googlemail.com>
Subject: Birthday Party?
Date: December 13, 09:15:01 am
To: Audrey Princeton <princeton.audrey@gmail.com>

Audrey!

Hope you are doing well, dear! I just wanted to say I'm sorry it didn't work out for an extended stay with us, but we so enjoyed meeting you during the summer.

I read about your company in Time Out, and I was so thrilled to see that you're doing Princess Parties!

I'd love to have you or one of your associates do Lily's birthday party, next month. She'll be turning four and... well, I guess cat's out of the bag, we're expecting our fourth in the spring, so I just can't even think about doing the party myself this year. (Pregnancy never gets easier!)

So if you have a minute, please let me know if you have any availability on January 16th. Thanks!

Kisses,
Charlotte

THIRTEEN

It's a frigid December morning, the day after the very first blizzard of the season. Logan has told me that having snow in early December is exceedingly rare and that usually, the first blizzard comes, conveniently, right before the holidays. I'm not sure if I should count myself lucky that I'll have a chance to get used to this before the inevitable Christmas blizzard? Or if it would have been nicer to have a couple more weeks without ice on the ground. Every part of me feels stiff as I'm still getting used to temperatures below forty degrees.

"Oh my God, it's freezing!" I say as I don my coat and walk out the door.

I'm heading out to perform a birthday party in the Bronx, which admittedly is not my favorite part of town to be traveling to. Most people who didn't grow up in New York City will tell you that Bronx is kind of a mystery. We transplants know that the Botanical Gardens and the Zoo are up there, and that Riverdale is supposedly a nice community, but other than that, it's basically the unknown.

The ground is slushy as the sun filters down, beginning to melt the snow that is piled high along 7th Avenue. Under my parka I have on the curly black Snow White wig, complete with red bow. I'm wearing a leotard, sweater and leggings.

Once on the Q train, I sit and collect my thoughts. It's been a few days since Chace expressed an interest in asking me out, but I haven't heard from him since then. I lean my head back against the wall of the train and close my eyes, daydreaming about his beautiful smile. Every time an image of him pops into my head, my stomach flips over.

My crush is starting to consume my waking hours and it's horribly inconvenient. He stars in my highly passionate dreams every night as well, and I wake up in the mornings feeling guilty, as if he will know how much he's been on my mind. It's that same sensation you get when you wake up hungover and worry that you texted someone you shouldn't have texted while drunk. Dream Audrey and Dream Chace are having a beautiful and loving, highly passionate relationship. But so far Real Audrey is practicing to become a nun, for all the action I'm getting.

At Times Square, I transfer to the 1 train and continue the next leg of my journey. *Why the hell hasn't he asked me out yet?* I wonder to myself as the train car bumps noisily along. Before our last encounter on opening night, I'd never in a million years have thought he would ask me out. But for some reason, now that he's expressed an interest, I can't help but feel impatient for him to make a move and back his words up with action.

I try to relax and listen to my music, getting myself into performance mode. I've got some birthday wishes to grant today! Gotta get my game face on.

When I exit the train at 238th Street, I proceeded to walk seven blocks, as instructed by this weekend's mom. When I arrive at the small duplex, I call to let her know I've arrived. She quietly lets me into the apartment and leads me directly to her bedroom where I can change.

"The girls have no idea you're coming. You look great!" she says excitedly. "Isabella is going to be thrilled!"

"Oh good! Okay, I'll be out in about five minutes," I say as I shut the door behind me.

After a few minutes of wrestling with a large amount of tulle and satin, I walk into the party in full royal regalia. I see the group of girls in their party dresses, the birthday girl clearly marked with a large pink tiara. I whisk myself into the room flaring out my gown as I walk. By this point in time, I've perfected my entrance. I kneel in front of the birthday girl, look up at her, smile and say, "Happy Birthday!" only to be met by a blank stare.

She quickly looks at her mother who chimes in with, "¡Feliz cumpleaños!" and then suddenly the little girl smiles at me and all her little friends start clapping.

Odd, I think to myself, so I try again. "Happy Birthday, Isabella, I'm Snow White!"

The mother jumps on top of my words with, "¡Feliz cumpleaños, Isabella! Me llamo Blancanieves!" And that's when it hits me. This isn't just some fun little exercise in Spanish...these girls don't really speak English.

Isabella's mom stands next to me and turns to the group of girls.

"Niñas. ¿Cómo se dice Blancanieves en Inglés?"

The little girls respond with a resounding cheer, "Snow Whi!"

"¡Bueno, muy bueno!" She praises them for properly translating the princess' name into English.

¡Ay dios mío! I think to myself. *Good lord.*

The rest of the party, I feel like the main speaker at the UN. Every craft needs to be explained in Spanish, every story I read needs to be echoed *en Español.* The only things they know in English are the songs from the movie, naturally. Let's just say it's a good thing I know how to sing 'Feliz Cumpleaños a ti.'

As the girls eat their cake, I walk around the room smiling at parents who chime in, asking me if I'd like cake and ice cream. "¡*Hola Snow Whi, Bueno, bueno!*" and "*¿Te gusta pastel y* *helado, Snow Whi?"*

I walk around the table and pose for pictures with the girls who are busily chatting away in Spanish. Every time I walk by one of them, they smile and wave and I reach down to give them a quick hug. They are very sweet girls, but my head is hurting from hearing certain Spanish clips and phrases I recognize, mixed in with so much I don't understand. My brain is automatically trying to catch up and interpret the bulk of what is being said. Every few minutes, I hear someone say something about *Blancanieves* and then roar with laughter. I'm starting to feel like I'm in the midst of a Comedy Central Roast that's been dubbed over, with the subtitles turned off.

By the time the maximally uncomfortable hour is over and I say *Adios,* I'm completely exhausted. I hadn't been prepared to deal with a language barrier and to be magical and enchanting at the same time.

I head back into the parents' room to change and breathe a sigh of relief as I sit down on the edge of the bed. Just taking off the awful black wig will be a treat.

"¿Snow Whi?"

I whip around to see the birthday girl staring at me in horror, as the wig sits half off my head, my long brown hair clearly visible.

"Oh no, no no, no!" I scramble to smash the wig back on my head as I usher a tearful Isabella out of the room as quickly as I can and close the door behind me.

I hear Isabella crying to her mother as I change back into my street clothes as quickly as possible. *Lo siento, Isabella.*

"Mija, ¿que pasa?" says the mom outside the door.

"¡Blanca Nieves, no es real! ¡NO ES REAL!"

I leave the party with a ten-dollar tip in my pocket, completely convinced that after all my hard work, albeit dubbed over, I have probably smashed Isabella's princess dreams forever.

When I get off the Q train at Prospect Park, I'm so frozen solid and tired that I decide to pop into a coffee shop on the corner to warm up before walking home. I'm about to log this day as complete crap when my phone buzzes in my bag and I pull it out to discover I have a text message from Chace!

> Hey you, wanna
> get a drink tonight?

My stomach flips over and a huge smile breaks out over my face. Just like that, my day is instantly awesome.

> Just had day from hell,
> would absolutely luv a drink.
> Need 2 change though,
> can we meet in a couple hrs?

I hold my breath as I wait for his reply.

> Sure! Meet at 7pm
> @ Columbus Circle?

A smile breaks out across my face as I text back.

> Done. See u then.

It's a quarter to seven when I exit the subway at 59th Street. The CNN sign reads thirty-nine degrees and I wrap my scarf around my neck a bit tighter as a cold burst of air whips past my face. I'm feeling pretty confident when I step toward the circle smoothing out my hair. My outfit is Logan-tested-Logan-approved.

I'm humming "I'm Too Sexy" to myself as I step up the last of the stairs.

Snap

I stop dead in my tracks and look down to see that the buckle on the side of my boot has just torn. *No, no, no, no, not tonight!* I'm instantly horrified. *Why did I buy the cheap boots instead of the ones that fit properly?*

In a panic, I hobble toward Duane Reade praying that they will have a sewing kit and that I'll make it back in fifteen minutes.

To my luck, there is one sewing kit left on the shelf. I scoop it up and then hobble toward the checkout counter.

"You want a plastic bag?" the cashier asks me as he rings up my three-dollar sewing kit.

"I don't need a bag. Thanks," I say. I extend my hand to grab the kit from him.

"Okay, you have a nice night ma'am. Happy Holidays," he says, sounding dead inside.

I'm trying to think fast, and figure out a place where I can sit down in a chair and sew my boot without my hands turning blue. Next door, thank goodness, is a Starbucks. I hobble frantically over, rush inside and sit down to fix the broken strap.

I carefully sew a stitch into the buckle that tightens the upper calf part of the boot, so it doesn't look enormous on my tiny legs. *Why did I have to be born with huge feet and small calves?* I curse the heavens silently. Just as I'm wrestling with the brown thread and needle, I feel my purse vibrate. It's Chace.

I'm in Columbus Circle.
Are you still coming?

I quickly text back.

On my way, 5 mins?

As I finish stitching my boot, my phone rings. *Oh my God, I said I'd be there in five minutes!* I think to myself as I reach for it. It's not Chace though; it's my mom. My finger reaches for the 'ignore button' but I push 'answer' instead. *Crap.*

"Hi Mom, I have to call you back tomorrow. I think I have a date and I'm running late," I say, slightly panic stricken.

"A date? With who?" she sounds crazed with curiosity.

"Too much to explain right now. Call you tomorrow," I shout as I hang up, tie the knot in the thread and prepare to run from 62nd Street down to Columbus Circle.

As I approach Columbus Circle, I slow down and see a figure standing on the center wall next to the statue of Columbus himself. He's in a leather jacket looking up at the giant man and I feel my stomach flip over. *How is this my life?* I silently will myself to stay calm, to play it cool, to not talk too much and to try and maintain eye contact without turning red.

As I approach, he spots me.

"There you are!" He smiles. "I was thinking you stood me up and was about to go party with the four British chicks that just asked me to take their picture."

"Sorry," I say. "Wardrobe malfunction."

"It's okay." He comes forward to give me a hug. *He's touching me!*

"Why didn't you wait inside the Time Warner Center?" I ask.

"Well, we said Columbus Circle and that's where I am," he says winking at me.

"Right," I reply.

"So, where do you want to go?" he asks.

"Honestly. I'm kind of hungry. I didn't eat much today," I say. "Do you want to eat?"

"Sure, I could eat," he says. "Let's walk and see what we come across."

He extends his arm and I link arms with him. My stomach is all butterflies. *He's still touching me!*

We stroll up Columbus Avenue and he tells me about his day.

"And then Tyler just said he needed to head back home and that he wasn't up for dinner, and I had been sort of planning to stay out later than five o'clock, so I figured I'd call you and see if you were up for hanging out. I went home and changed, then came to meet you."

"Sounds like a nice Saturday in the city," I say.

"Totally," he replies. "I love New York this time of year.

And even though everyone says this is kind of lame, I really want to go ice skating in Central Park."

"How seasonal," I say with a smile. "And not lame at all."

He smiles at me and I flush. "Would you ever wanna go ice skating with me?"

"Sure!" I clear my throat. "I'd be down for some ice skating. Sounds fun." *And super romantic!*

"Exactly. I think it would be fun."

"Definitely."

"So, I guess you want to know how I know about the parade?" He laughs.

"God…" I flush, embarrassed. "Don't remind me."

"It's alright," he says with a laugh. "It was a total coincidence that I saw the sign. I have friends who live in the West 60's and like to watch the parade over there."

"In my defense, the little girl I nanny took something I said out of context." I'm blushing like crazy now.

"Kids do that," he says. "Don't worry. I thought it was funny!"

"Glad I could amuse you," I giggle.

"Amuse you did," he says with a laugh. "What about sushi? This place looks decent."

"I'm game."

We sit at the restaurant for a leisurely two hours, trying different rolls, and sashimi and drinking sake. I don't think I've ever enjoyed such a long dinner in New York. Usually I'm in an out in an hour, but the time flies when you're on a freaking *date* with the most beautiful man in Manhattan!

Chace proceeds to tell me about his life since college and how he decided to come to the city.

"I'd just come off of a regional tour and my band was taking a break, so I figured screw it, time to make those Broadway boyhood dreams a reality," he says.

"Absolutely." I'm enchanted.

"So I packed up my stuff and drove here from St. Louis, crashed with a friend for a month, booked a commercial and that gave me the start-up cash I needed."

"Wow!" I marvel. "That's so cool. So what kind of music did your band play?"

"Indie rock," he says. "A couple of the guys moved to New York recently, so I'm thinking we might start a side project. You know, create a new sound. But, I'd only do it if I thought we could stand out amongst the huge wealth of bands from New York."

"I love Indie music," I say. "Did you produce any albums?"

"No," he says. "But I have some of our old stuff on my computer, I can send it to you sometime. Or you should come when we start gigging again!"

"I'd love to!"

We chat about music and compare our childhoods. His parents are still married, just like mine, something so rare these days. He grew up in St. Louis, went to Northwestern for school. Loves California, but says he'd miss the seasons if he lived there full-time.

Before I know it, it's nearly nine and the server informs us that they're closing for a private event. Chace and I fight for the bill, but he won't let me pay.

"Do you want to grab a drink?" he asks me. I guess he's as keen as I am to keep this date going.

"Sure. Keep walking? See what we see?" I ask.

"Sounds good."

We don our coats and scarves, he takes my hand and we head back out into the cold.

"So, what else do you have going on besides the reading?" I ask as we make our way west on 68th Street towards Amsterdam Avenue.

"Just working on my music, going to auditions for commercials and plays," he says. "Got a guest spot on SVU next week, which I'm pretty excited about."

We walk up Amsterdam Avenue and at 70th Street, I see a small bar that looks promising. It's a tiny little building, covered in twinkle lights, right next to the JCC.

"Over there?" I ask, pointing to my new discovery.

"That works," he says. He takes my hand and we cross the

street to enter the Amsterdam Alehouse.

"First round is mine," I say as I skip up to the bar and order us two Brooklyn Lagers.

"Thank you!" Chace calls after me.

I hand the bartender my card and he pours our beers and then hands them to me.

"Brooklyn's finest." I beam, returning to our table and setting the two pints down.

"So, what are *you* doing with your time these days? Other than our *wonderful* show," he asks me.

"Well, I'm actually nannying a few days a week," I say. "But I also started this princess party company and so far that's doing pretty well."

"I didn't know that," he says. "How cool!"

"Yeah!" I say. "I'm actually very proud of it. Today's party was a little rough though, I had a slight hair malfunction and might have crushed a little girl's dreams when I revealed I wasn't really Snow White."

He laughs. "We'll have to be sure we find some way for you to do penance."

"Seriously," I say.

"So, is it just you?" he asks.

"I've got a couple girls training with me now, which is great because I can book parties even when I can't do them and I still make a bit of money off of every booking. It's been so helpful in between gigs."

"I'm seriously impressed," he says as he reaches for my hand. "Baby, you're an entrepreneur."

Did he just call me 'baby'?

"Thank you," is all I can get out.

"Your hands are cold." He takes my palms and presses them around the warm candleholder sitting between us on the tiny wooden table.

"That's nice and warm." I smile.

"It is nice," he says, wrapping his hands around mine and holding them against the warmth.

For a moment we just sit there hand in hand. My gaze is

fixed on the candle because I don't dare look up into his eyes for fear that I'll blush like crazy.

"Miss Audrey, you are so unexpected," he says.

"I am?" I ask, sneaking a peak at his face.

"Yes, I didn't think much of you at first, but now I'm seeing you in this whole different light," he says. "You've surprised me."

"Oh," I murmur.

"Look at me for a minute?" he says.

I look up into his eyes.

"You have the biggest eyes I've ever seen," he says. "Beautiful."

A couple hours later, we arrive at the 72nd Street Subway station. It's nearly midnight.

"I have to take the A down to 42nd and transfer to the Q," I say, decently buzzed after three of Brooklyn's finest.

"42nd is my stop, so I'll ride with you and we'll figure it out," he says, taking my hand and leading me down the stairs toward the turnstile.

"I cannot believe how buzzed I am. I'm so glad I don't work tomorrow," I mumble as we walk down the stairs toward our track.

We sit down on the wooden divided benches, admiring the bizarre mosaic murals on the walls. I feel slightly dizzy and rest my head on his shoulder. *I wonder if he'll try to kiss me?* He's already held my hand. I tilt my head to look up at him and he smiles. I move my face an inch towards his before freezing. He holds my gaze for an instant, then moves his chin slowly toward mine. I close my eyes and wait for his lips, hoping I've read his body language correctly. As I feel the sweet, soft pressure of his kiss, my whole body starts to buzz with excitement. Inside my head, I'm doing a happy dance. *Chace Campbell is kissing me, people!*

Before I know it, we are full-on, savagely making out in the middle of a subway station. I feel his fingers running through my hair as he pulls me closer to him and the wind rushes into the tunnel as our train appears. *It's just like my dreams, actually, it's better.*

Somehow we board the train without separating our lips. We are still kissing as we zoom down the track toward the station at 59th Street. I hear gaggles of drunk, late-night passengers making comments and whistles, but they don't fully register with me. I just don't care. The doors open at 59th Street, and I hear the *ping-pong* as the doors close again, just before we start barreling toward 50th Street.

Chace pulls me onto his lap and his tongue caresses mine as he pulls my heavily-clad body towards his own. I don't even notice stopping at 50th Street.

It isn't until we hit 42nd Street that he pulls back, looks into my eyes, smiles and says, "Let's go."

I absolutely do not fight him, but take his hand and follow him willingly to wherever he is planning to take me, knowing full well that it isn't going to be to transfer to the Q.

FOURTEEN

The next day, Logan and I are in his kitchen making holiday treats for our friends and family. When I called him this morning and told him I was just getting home from my date with Chace, he demanded I come over immediately and give him every detail. I'm mildly hungover, but still riding the high of last night, so I don't care.

"Oh. My. God." he says. "You made out like a couple of teenagers on the C train?"

"Yup!" I laugh.

As we chat, we are busily making upscale versions of holiday classics. Gingerbread cookies with spiced rum, Swedish butter cookies with Macadamia nuts, peppermint bark made with actual Belgian chocolate; and after Jake's incessant begging, Logan has begrudgingly agreed to include white chocolate dipped Oreos.

"The C is the skankiest train," he says. "Even I know that... and I never ride them unless under duress."

"It was incredibly hot!" I giggle.

"Was he... ya know?"

"A lady never tells too much," I say.

"Prude!" he laughs.

"My lips were sealed with his kisses," I say.

"Okay, fine, tell me this," he says. "Am I safe in assuming you won't be going postal on a crowded street anytime in the near future?"

"I will not be going postal anytime soon." I giggle some more.

"Yes!" He laughs. "Okay, okay! Tell me this... if we're comparing Chace to say, Frosty the Snowman, is he sporting a nice carrot?"

"You did *not* just say that!" I squeal, my face turning red.

"You dirty little biz-natch!" he says. "Okay, last question."

"Oh my God, what?" I can still feel myself blushing.

"Which of these Christmas Carols would you equate to your experience with Chace? 'O *Come*, All Ye Faithful'? Or 'Silent Night'?"

"Logan!" I'm full-on laughing now. "The first one! Now, can we stop!?"

"Go girl!" he shouts. "Damn. I'm super jealous. That Chace is one fine piece of singing and dancing man candy. I was really hoping he'd turn out to be gay so I could snatch him away from you and leave you with Jake."

"Well, he's definitely not gay," I say. "I know someone who knows his ex and she's a girl."

"He hasn't met me yet," Logan mutters.

"Oh, and I have some gossip for you!" I say laughing. "You were right..."

"I always am, but what about this time?"

"I got an email from Charlotte Brander the other day..."

"Oh my God, what did she have to say for herself?"

"She said she read about the company in Time Out and asked if I'd do Lily's next birthday party..."

"Uh-huh..."

"...Because she's pregnant and can't possibly think about

doing it herself."

"Well, can't say I'm surprised," he says.

"I can't believe you actually called that one. What a piece of work she is."

"This town gets more and more predictable the longer you live here," he says.

"Clearly."

"Are you going to do her party?" he asks.

"Hell no!" I say. "As much as I would love to see Lily, I'm not giving Charlotte the satisfaction."

"I love your vengeful side," he says. "So, when are your parents getting into town? Are John and his wife coming too?"

"They're all flying in on the twenty-third."

"Whose idea was it to do the Princeton family Christmas in New York?" he asks.

"Honestly, I think my mom just wanted a break from having the entire family over," I say "She knew if they traveled, she'd be able to just relax and enjoy the holiday."

"Well, I'm glad we can give her a break. Do we have a final headcount for Christmas Eve?" he asks.

"Jake texted me yesterday and said his parents are traveling around Europe with some friends, so he's staying here."

"Will Mr. Hottie be joining us now that you've made sweet, sweet love?" he asks.

"I'm honestly not sure how much we'll see each other until we start the reading up again after the holidays," I say "We've only had one date."

"Guess we'll find out," he says.

"Guess so," I say. "Is your mom going to fly out?"

"My mom is staying in Marin," he says.

"Really? She's not going to see you on Christmas?"

"Well, my sister just had a baby," he says. "And my mom is sort of helping her right now because her husband travels a lot. She doesn't feel right leaving."

"I didn't know Corrine had a baby!" I say. "Why didn't you tell me?"

"Um… I hate children?" he says.

"You can't hate your own niece or nephew!" I protest.

"Ugh. I'll fly home in February and see it then," he says. "Newborns freak me out. I'm worried I'll get drunk and poke that soft spot and ruin its brain or something."

Logan and I finish making our treats and then I give him a kiss on the cheek and head out into the frigid afternoon. I'm meeting Em for our first party together, one for a family downtown. She and Kay have observed a couple parties I've done since Thanksgiving and now I feel confident that they're ready to get started.

Just before two o'clock I arrive at a building in Chelsea and see Em standing outside in the cold. I walk up and give her a hug.

"Ready for your first party?" I ask.

"Yes ma'am, boss lady." She salutes me.

"Okay, let me call the mom and tell her we're ready to change." I pick up the phone and dial the mom's number. She answers after three rings. "Hi, is this Kelly? We're here to change."

"Hi! Oh good," she says. "I'll send my husband right down to let you in!"

After a minute the dad comes down and lets us into the building.

"Hi ladies," he says. "Thanks so much for coming!"

"No problem." I smile. "We just need a place to change."

"Well, there's a mail room over here," he says. "You can change in there and I'll watch the door."

"Great!" I say.

We follow the dad toward the mailroom. He walks inside with us and closes the door behind him, turning his back to us.

What the hell? I give Em a look that conveys my confusion and she shrugs her shoulders slightly.

"Um…sir, do you think we could have some privacy?"

"Oh… sure," he says, walking out of the mailroom and closing the door behind him.

"So awkward!" Em whispers to me.

"So, how long have you ladies been doing princess parties?" the dad asks from the other side of the door.

"We just started the company in the fall," I say as I wrestle with the giant ball gown as quickly as I can.

"Bet you meet a lot of strange parents, huh?" He laughs.

"Uh… yeah, you could say that." I slip my gown over my head and tighten the corset strings.

"My wife used to work as a nanny here before we got married and had the kids," he says. "She has some stories."

"I'll bet," I reply.

Em looks at me and mouths, "Oh my God," as she puts her wig on. I just shake my head, laughing silently.

After that torturously awkward five minutes is over, Em and I walk upstairs with the dad into the party.

The room of their giant loft is covered in billowing pink, silken fabric that has been draped along the ceiling and down the walls giving the illusion that we have just walked into a huge pink cloud. Dozens of purple, glittering stars hang down from the pipes above our heads on fishing line. The living room rug is covered in large purple and pink satin pillows, which will provide a perfect place for us to perform circle time. And in the corner of the room, a vanity table and two chairs that have been generously set up for us to do makeovers on the girls. Kelly has truly outdone herself, or hired someone amazing. It's a shame her husband is such a weirdo.

"Kelly did this all herself," says the dad, as if he's reading my thoughts. "She's the creative one in the family, an interior designer."

"Really stunning," I say in awe.

"This way, the girls are in the play room," he says.

"Ladies! Hi!" shouts a lovely slender blonde woman. She saunters over and takes both Em and I into a friendly embrace as we near the party room.

"Hi!" I say. "You must be Kelly."

"That's me," she says. "We are so excited to have you here! The girls are all a twitter."

"We're very excited too!" Em chimes in.

"I'm going to have the adults in the kitchen so you won't be interrupted," she says. "And I'm sure you saw that everything you need is located in the living room."

"It looks fabulous," I say as we walk into the playroom to meet a gaggle of giggling girls who scream in unison the second they see us.

In spite of the strange changing experience we had upon arrival, the party goes really well. Kelly's daughter Stephanie and her friends could not be any sweeter. They're all about three years old, some are shy, some are precocious, and all of them are adorable. We perform makeovers on the girls, we make necklaces, and finally we finish up on the pillow-laden floor with some games. We play princess trivia and each girl gets tossed a candy when she gets a right answer. The game is going so smoothly, and the girls are having a blast.

"Who can name this princess tune?" I shout as I begin to hum a popular princess favorite.

"Cinderella!" shouts a little girl named Piper.

"Very good, Piper!" I say as I toss her a candy.

Em looks lovely in her costume and she's having a ball. She's as excited about all the games and activities as the girls are. I'm about to have the girls stand up and perform the Princess Pokey when I see Piper fiddling with the wrapper on her candy and I realize in a moment of pure, unadulterated horror, that Jolly Ranchers are a choking hazard for three-year-olds. *Holy shit.*

"Oh no…" I say.

"What?" Em asks.

"These candies are too small for them," I mutter in a panicked whisper. "I usually bring lollipops, but they ran out at the store, and I was up really late last night drinking. They could choke on these!"

I'm seeing lawsuit paperwork flying at my face, hearing jail bars crashing closed in my mind. I'm about to have a full-blown anxiety attack when Em jumps in.

"Ladies!" she begins. "Does everyone have their candies?"

"YES!" shout the girls together.

"I want you all to hold out your candies in one hand and raise your other hand to the sky," she says and the girls oblige. I watch her closely. "Repeat after me! I promise…"

"I promise," they repeat.

"I princess promise!" she says.

"I princess promise!" they say, giggling.

"That I will wait until after the party," she says.

"That I will wait until after the party," they repeat.

"To eat my candy with my mom and dad!" she says.

"To eat my candy with my mom and dad!" they say.

"Very good Princess Promise!" she says. "Now will everyone please go put their candies on the table and we'll sort them out after we're all done with our games, alright?"

I watch stunned as all fourteen girls stand up and walk over to the table and set their Jolly Ranchers down.

"Now! Let's do the Princess Pokey!" Em shouts and all the girls jump up.

"Oh my God," I say. "That was amazing!"

"I got your back my princess sista, don't worry," she says.

"Can I quote *Casablanca* and say I think this is the beginning of a beautiful friendship?"

FIFTEEN

There are several words and phrases you never want to hear from your partner when you're about to perform a high profile birthday party. One of those is the phrase, "Oh shit!"

"Oh shit, what?" I ask in a panic.

"I just zipped up my dress and the zipper broke off!" says Kay.

"Oh shit," I say.

"Oh my God, I've just ruined my first party!" she says frantically.

We're standing in the back room at FAO Schwarz, the most famous toy store in all of Manhattan, and the most prestigious place to host a children's party. The zipper on Kay's dress has just broken and we only have one Sleeping Beauty gown.

A woman named Wendy has hired us to perform at her daughter's third birthday party. We had to go through several interviews just to be booked for this gig.

The team here has done an amazing job with the décor. The party room is decked out like it's prom night. There are balloons everywhere, two giant castle cakes, bubble machines going, and a stereo playing princess-themed music in the background.

Each child gets to choose a costume of their favorite princess or superhero to wear during the party and then take home. On top of that, each child will also get a bucket filled with expensive toys and candy all purchased in store. This party easily costs what my brother and his wife spent on their wedding. In other words, we can't screw this up.

"Okay, let's not panic," I say.

"I've just ruined this entire party!" says Kay, near tears.

"Maybe I can duck out and go buy some safety pins?" suggests Em.

"We have to perform in fifteen minutes," I say. "And you're already dressed."

"Holy crap-fire-balls-why!?" shouts Kay. "I'm sweating, Audrey, I'm starting to sweat."

"Kay, pull it together!" shouts Em. "This isn't hopeless. Audrey and I can start the party; we just need to figure something out for you."

"I don't know," I say. "I have other gowns, but they're in Brooklyn. By the time Kay could get there and back, the party will be over."

"Are you going to fire me over this?" asks Kay.

"No! Calm down," I say. "Maybe I could call Jake...Or Logan!"

I pick up my phone and frantically dial Logan's number.

"Oh my God, what?" he answers.

"Doll, it's me!" I say. "I need your quick brain right now. It's a bit of an emergency."

"I'm here, what's going on?" he says.

"Kay's zipper broke and we go on in fifteen minutes."

"Where are you?" he says.

"FAO Schwarz," I say.

"Oh dear God," he says. "The mother of all children's

party locations."

"I know," I say. "It's bad. They're expecting three of us; we can't just do the party without her."

"What's her character?" he asks. I hear a door close on his end of the call and then the honk of cars on the street.

"Why does that matter?" I say confused.

"Just answer the question," he says to me, then calls out, "Taxi!"

"Sleeping Beauty," I say. "Where are you?"

"Perfect. Okay, here's what you're gonna do. You and the other girl go on. I'm getting in a cab right now with my sewing kit. You're twenty minutes away, but I think my new friend Emile here can get us there in fifteen. He looks sturdy."

"What are you, Winston Wolfe?" I say.

"No *Pulp Fiction* references right now, Holly," he says. "Listen to me. Tell the kids that Sleeping Beauty is still asleep and that you'll need everyone to believe in magic or some shit to wake her up."

"Isn't that from Peter Pan?" I ask.

"Holly, sense the tone," he says.

"Right." I laugh. "Okay! Got it!"

"I can get her sewn into her gown in about five minutes, so you'll need to stall a bit," he says. "Whatever you do, don't let on that anything is wrong. This is just part of the act."

"Okay," I say.

"Trust me, any parents hosting a party at FAO consider slouching to be unprofessional, so don't let on that you're having any kind of problem. Ham it up as much as you can with some, 'I can't hear you!' nonsense."

"Alright," I say. "You're amazing!"

"I'll be there soon!"

I turn to the girls and tell them the new plan. The color returns to Kay's face and Em and I start to scheme our stalling tactic.

Within fifteen minutes, Logan has appeared at our side.

"Your fairy-fucking-godmother has arrived," he says dryly, entering the room. "You don't even want to know what I had to do to get here. Emile might have driven on the sidewalk for a portion of 8th Avenue, and we might have knocked down some Christmas decorations on 58th Street."

"Logan, thank you a million times over," I say.

He sets his sewing kit down on the table with a thud. "Where's the garment?"

"Right here," says Kay, meekly holding up the skirt around her waist. She still looks a bit ashen and panicked.

"Chin up, your highness, we're gonna get you in there," says Logan with a tender smile. In spite of all of his sass and sarcasm, he shines in an emergency - especially a fashion emergency. "I can work faster than fifteen magic mice! This is kid's stuff. No pun intended."

Kay starts to laugh, and I see her relax.

"This is one hell of a save," says Em beaming.

"Alright, Cindy and Snow," says Logan. "Get the hell out of my way and go entertain some children. Mama is working here."

"I love you," I say. I kiss Logan on the cheek and Em and I dash out into the party.

Logan's idea is a complete success. The children shriek with delight every time they all yell, "I believe in magic!" and we shout back "I can't hear you!"

Parents are snapping photos and laughing with each other as they watch their kids so fully enthralled. As predicted, within five minutes, Kay enters the party yawning and the crowed erupts into fits of giggles and screams.

"Is someone having a party?" she says emphatically, and the children squeal with delight. I look in the direction of the back room and see Logan leaning against the wall, half-hidden by the doorway. He gives me a wink and a smile before disappearing, as if by magic.

The rest of the hour goes flawlessly. Kay's dress holds up like it's brand new. Logan has not only sewn her back in, but removed the zipper entirely, punched holes in the back of the bodice and laced it up with pink ribbon. I think it is safe to assume he had that on him when he arrived. The parents are overjoyed with our performance.

By the end of the party, Juliet, the birthday girl, is being carried around by Kay, whispering secrets in her ear every few seconds. I'm so glad that Kay was able to perform the party since we came to learn that Sleeping Beauty is Juliet's favorite princess.

"Ladies, you were wonderful!" says Wendy as we prepare to exit the party. She hands me an envelope. "A token of our appreciation."

We wave goodbye to the kids. Kay gives Juliet one final birthday hug and the three of us head to the back room, completely and totally unscathed.

"That. Was. So much fun!" says Kay.

"You did great, girl." I smile at her.

"A smashing success." Em chimes in.

We help Kay out of her dress and put our costumes back into our garment bags. As the girls pack up their wigs and brush out their crumpled hair, I tear open the gratuity envelope from Wendy and count the bills. Inside sits six-hundred dollars.

"Ladies?" I say, holding up the bills for them to see.

They both turn around to face me. Em's eyes double in size and Kay claps her hand to her mouth as she gasps.

"Champagne tonight?" I say.

"Only if Logan joins us!" Kay insists. "My treat."

It's a Monday night, just three days before Christmas and I'm sitting at Amelia's Holiday recital at a church on the Upper East Side. I'm not required to attend the concert, but I wanted to be here to see her perform.

Evan, sits in the pew next to me playing math games on his hand-held device. I've told him several times that when he's older, he'll want to know some of Amelia's friends and make a good impression on them, but his only interests seem to be basketball and his Wii for now. The girls finish singing "Silver Bells" just as my phone buzzes with a text.

Hey cutie!
What r u up to?

It's Chace. It's his first contact since our date nine days ago. Yes, I've kept count. The minute I see his name appear on my phone, my heart starts racing. I time exactly four minutes before I respond.

Kid's recital on
the UES. U?

Another minute passes before he replies.

Just finished an audition.
Wanna meet for dinner?

I reply, holding my breath.

Not sure.
Where? When?

About thirty seconds later his text beeps through.

Doesn't Matter.
I can come to you.

I reply.

No that's silly, I need to
head west anyway.
I left some stuff at my
Work. Meet on UWS in 30?
Lincoln Sq?

He replies.

Sounds good.
See you then.

When the concert ends, I give Amelia a big hug, bid a quick farewell to the family, wishing them a safe trip to Bermuda, and duck out towards Park Avenue before the entire congregation is out there fighting me for cabs in the frigid evening air.

Within five minutes, I've successfully hailed a cab and I'm speeding toward the Westside to meet Chace. My heart is beating a million beats per second and I almost feel ashamed for being so excited to see him.

"Audrey, you get too excited too soon," I mutter to myself. "Just be cool."

The cab drops me off at 66th and Central Park West and I quickly grab my bag from my work building before walking along the icy street, toward Broadway. When I hit the corner of 63rd and Broadway, I text him my location and then stand next to my usual sushi take-out place.

After a few minutes, I can't help myself. I look around, anxiously searching the crowd for anyone who looks like him, but I don't see anything. It's hard to pick out hair color in a crowd of people wearing hats and scarves.

Eventually, I turn and lean up against one of the cement columns of the building and check my phone.

"Hello, beautiful." I hear his voice and jump.

"Chace! You scared me!" I giggle. He pulls me into a tight embrace and kisses me firmly. My knees buckle.

"I'm glad to see you," he says, looking at me, his blue eyes shining. "How was your day?"

"It was good." I smile dreamily up at him. "How was yours?"

"Better now," he says. "C'mon, we have a reservation."

We walk up Columbus Avenue, which looks like a winter wonderland with all the holiday twinkle lights in the trees.

"New York at Christmas time is really something wonderful," I say, beaming at our surroundings.

"Sure is!" he agrees.

As we walk, we see vendors selling Christmas trees, and the smell of the pines fills me with what some might call Christmas Cheer.

We turn the corner onto 73rd Street and duck into a tiny Italian restaurant. The railing along the stairs is adorned with festive pine boughs and tinkle lights, and a holiday wreath hangs in the window.

"Buona sera, signiore," says the host in a suit and tie. I hope that he's a real Italian and not just putting it on to create ambiance, but the effect is still the same, completely charming.

"Hello," says Chace. "We have a reservation for two under Campbell."

"Molto bene!" he says, and turns to me. "Right this way, Bella."

We are seated at a tiny table near the window. The restaurant is set down a bit from the sidewalk, so we watch people's feet go by as we wait for our water.

"How is the princess-ing going?" he asks.

"Oh my goodness, we had the most epic save ever the other day…"

As I regale Chace with the story of FAO Schwartz and Logan's dramatic rescue, the waiter comes and brings us bread and sparkling water. Chace hangs on to my every word, smiling, his eyes twinkling. He has this ability to make me feel like the most important person in the world when he listens to me.

"Have we decided on a wine?" asks our waiter.

"Yes, two glasses of the house Chianti," says Chace smoothly. "Oh, sorry, do you like Chianti, Audrey?"

"Sounds lovely," I say.

"Great, that'll be perfect," he says to our waiter. "So, finish your story."

"Well, the parents were so excited, and the birthday girl loved Kay, I mean it was just too perfect. And then the mom ended up tipping us two hundred dollars each. I made rent with just three parties last weekend!"

"I'm thrilled for you, babe." He beams. "You're doing so well! New York is not easy your first year, and you've only been here six months."

"I finally feel like everything is falling into place," I say. "I just need to keep pushing for auditions."

"You'll get there," he smiles.

"Chace, can I ask you something?" I say.

"Of course," he says.

"I don't want to be the 'where's this going?' girl, but are you seeing other people?"

"You mean tonight?" He winks.

"No," I laugh. "Just in general, like do you see lots of girls?"

"Why would you ask me that, doll?" he says. "I'm here with you."

"I know, but I just feel sometimes like I'm so out of your league." I admit shyly. "That first night... I sort of thought it was a one-time thing. I might have been a bit more...reserved had I known..."

"Audrey, I don't date more than one girl at a time. I think you date someone because you feel something, right?" He grins and takes my hand just as the waiter brings our wine.

Chace gives it a swirl and a sniff before taking a sip.

"Perfect," he says.

"Very good, signiore," says the waiter, before walking away.

"And, I don't mind that things got physical the first night." He intimates to me, lowering his voice. "We had a lot of beer and I already knew how I felt about you anyway, so it didn't turn me off or anything."

"Okay," I say, feeling rosy after hearing him talking about his feelings. "So... new subject. Are you going home this week for Christmas?"

"I'm not sure," he says. "My parents are talking about visiting my sister's family in Florida this year and truth be told, I'm not crazy about her in-laws. I have a flight booked to fly down Thursday for Christmas day just for a quick trip, but I'm not sure if I'm going to go."

"Well, Logan and I are hosting a dinner on Wednesday for Christmas Eve, if you'd like to join," I say, not daring to mention just yet that my parents will be there.

"I might just take you up on that," he says.

Chace and I sit at the table drinking wine and nibbling on olive focaccia bread. When our waiter comes back to take our order, Chace and I both order Spaghetti Carbonara. Chace decides we must try something else too, so we order the spaghetti and a Gnocchi Siciliano as well.

We fall as easily into conversation as we did the night of our first date. He smiles at me and laughs when I say something funny. He looks totally enchanted with me. I find myself staring dreamily into his eyes as he talks about the past gigs he's done, tours and shows. It's so wonderful to be on a date with someone who shares my love for the theatre, but isn't gay.

We talk about our favorite plays, and the productions we did in high school and college. He tells me about his family in St. Louis and why he's a die-hard Cardinals fan.

"What's your family like?" he asks. "You mentioned them a bit the other night."

"They live in Pasadena," I start.

"Is that where the Rose Bowl is?" he asks."

"Yeah! I grew up there. It's pretty different from the rest of L.A. Kind of like growing up in a small town outside a big city."

"Siblings?" he asks.

"I have an older brother, John," I say. "He and his wife, Sophie live in Palo Alto. He's teaching at Stanford and she is a kindergarten teacher."

"Nieces and Nephews?" he asks.

"Actually no," I say. "They've been trying to have a baby for over a year, but they're not having any luck."

"I'm sorry to hear that," he says.

"Yeah, they're pretty discouraged that it hasn't been as easy to start a family as they always thought it would be."

"I can imagine," he says.

"But let's talk about something less depressing!" I shift gears.

We talk about how much we both love New York and the places in New England that we want to visit, but haven't had the chance to yet. Chace has always wanted to go skiing in Vermont and we are both dying to visit Cape Cod and Nantucket in the summer.

We finish our tiramisu, Chance signs the bill, and we pile all of our layers back on and walk out into the chilly night.

"Hey, you know what we should do?" he says.

"What? I ask.

"You'll see." He smiles. We walk over to Columbus Avenue and he hails a cab. "49th and Park, please."

The cab zooms us down Columbus Avenue before turning on to the 66th Street transverse. As we fly through the park, Chace reaches for my hand. I keep trying to figure out where we're going, but I'm not quite sure.

As we near 49th and Park Avenue, I realize he's taking me to see the holiday decorations at the Waldorf Astoria.

He pays for the cab and climbs out of the car first, taking my hand to help be back out onto the icy sidewalk.

"Oh my goodness," I say as we walk into the lobby and see several humongous Christmas trees covered in the most beautiful decorations I've ever seen. We walk hand in hand, admiring each one and all the smaller decorations around the room. And when we've gotten our fill, Chace takes my gloved hand and leads me back out onto the street and then two blocks west to Rockefeller Center.

"What do you think?" he says. "Wanna try our luck on the ice?"

"I'm so terrible, but I'm willing!" I say. "Don't forget I grew up in Los Angeles. We don't have winter there."

"Well, surely you must have gone rollerblading as a kid, no?" he asks.

"That was many moons ago, sir," I tease.

As we head down to the rink area, I snap a quick photo and text it to Logan, telling him Chace is taking me ice-skating.

I hate you.
Wait, R U sure
he's not gay?

Chace and I tie up our skates and set out on the ice. I feel like I'm in a scene from a movie like *Elf* or *Serendipity*. It's the perfectly stereotypical, dorky, romantic thing to do on a second date in New York City during the holidays.

As we skate hand in hand, with Christmas carols playing in the background, my heart is bursting with excitement. I can't stop smiling. I don't know if I was ever in love with Brent, but I'm pretty sure that I'm falling in love with Chace.

SIXTEEN

Is there any better aroma than that of a holiday meal cooking? There is something about the combined scent of onions sautéing in butter, the turkey roasting in the oven and cinnamon and cranberries bubbling away on the stovetop.

It's Christmas Eve, and Logan and I have been cooking in his kitchen all day. My whole family is in town and I couldn't be happier to be hosting this dinner tonight.

"Baste, Holly, Baste!" Logan calls to me as he works on peeling potatoes.

"I'm on it!" I call as I open the oven, pull the rack out slightly and begin basting our bird. Jake and Chace will be here in an hour. It will be the first time Chace will be meeting, well… everyone.

While he says he's totally cool with meeting my family, I think he must be a bit nervous. But I have gotten him the best Christmas gift and I cannot wait to give it to him.

"Audrey, do you need help?" My mom calls from the living

room.

"No, Mom!" I call back "You just keep relaxing and enjoying yourself!"

"She can't help herself, can she?" says Logan.

"Nope," I say. "She's dying to get in here and get her hands dirty."

"Not gonna happen, Linda!" Logan calls out. "Your job tonight is to drink plenty of that fine Napa wine that you guys brought with you!"

Logan has designed the perfect holiday feast. Our turkey is stuffed with an apple, walnut and cranberry dressing and was marinated in what he describes as a "delicate sage and citrus marinade." The potatoes will be served au gratin with Gruyere cheese and a drizzle of truffle oil. The sweet potatoes are being brûléed with maple, pecan, brown sugar and his industrial strength blowtorch. He's also got a prime rib cooking in tandem with the turkey and an assortment of roasted vegetables in the oven.

My parents, freshly back from a wine country trip up and down the California coast, have brought several bottles of excellent wine from Napa and Paso Robles, including my dad's absolute favorite, Justin Cabernet. To make things even better, the doctor has told my father that he can curb his vegetarianism for the holiday, as long as he eats plenty of vegetables and limits his meat intake to poultry and fish.

I finish basting the bird and close the oven. I'm about to ask Logan what else I can do when the buzzer to the apartment rings and Baxter starts barking and turning in circles.

"Go ahead and get that," he says. "I'm in the zone right now."

I prance out into the living room and hit the intercom.

"Yeeeess?" I say.

"Hi kid, it's me," says Jake.

"C'mon up!" I buzz the door open.

After a moment I hear Jake's footsteps in the hallway and open the door. Baxter goes running out to Jake and jumps on his legs.

"Hey Bax," he says. "Merry Christmas."

"Merry Christmas to you too, Jake!" I say in my Baxter voice.

Jake rounds the corner and walks toward the door. He's holding a few gift bags, his camera bag and a bouquet of red roses. He's wearing a shirt and tie under his coat, and his winter beard is nicely trimmed and shaven. He looks very handsome.

"Merry Christmas!" He gives me a big hug. "The roses are for Logan."

I laugh. "Merry Christmas to you too, Jake! Man, you clean up well!"

"You look perfectly lovely yourself, kid. But don't let it go to your head. I'm just trying to impress your family."

We walk inside and I introduce Jake to my parents. He turns to my mother and then me. "Well, now I know where you get it from," he says with a wink.

"Oh, I love this boy already!" says my mom, giving him a big hug.

Jake shakes my father's hand, meets my brother and Sophie, and then walks into the kitchen where he gives Logan the roses.

"Really, Jake? Red roses?" Logan teases. "Are you proposing to me after dinner?"

"Hey, I thought they were seasonal," says Jake. "Christmas is a red and green holiday!"

"Come here." Logan teases as he gives Jake a big hug. "I'll just take out the baby's breath and they're fine."

"I also brought a bottle of bourbon for the eggnog," says Jake. "The good stuff."

"Lovely," says Logan. "Now there's a gift I can get behind."

"Do you *ever* have a problem getting behind anything, Logan?" I tease.

"Well played," says Jake, raising his hand to high-five me.

"Too easy," I say, slapping his palm.

"Both of you, out of my kitchen!" says Logan.

"I'm going to go put on some Nat King Cole," I say as I walk out into the living room. "Everyone enjoying themselves?"

My parents could not be happier sitting on Logan's comfortable couch listening to Christmas music and sipping wine. As I change the music, the door buzzes again and my heart nearly stops before it kicks into hyper-drive. "That's Chace!" I whisper to my family, as if he can hear me.

"Hi!" I call into the intercom.

"It's me," he says. I buzz the door and walk out into the hallway to greet him. He walks up the stairs toward the door and gives me a smile.

"Hey you," I say, smiling. "Merry Christmas!"

"Merry Christmas, doll." He gives me a big hug and quick kiss on the lips. "Don't want to mess up your lipstick."

He's dressed in a dark green shirt and black tie, fitted blazer and black slacks. His hair is perfectly coiffed and his shoes could have been shined today. In other words, he looks like a perfect gentleman. *My perfect gentleman.*

"C'mon in and you'll meet everyone," I say.

"No pressure." He smiles.

I open the door. "Everyone, this is Chace."

"Hi Chace, we've heard so much about you!" says my mom, the first one to step forward and give him a hug. "I'm Linda, Audrey's mom."

"Oh wow, a hug," says Chace. "Nice to meet you, Linda."

"And this is my dad, Howard," I say.

"Nice to meet you, Chace," says my dad shaking his hand. "Is that short for something?"

"No, it's just Chace," he says.

"Oh, okay then," says my dad.

John and Sophie introduce themselves and then Jake and Logan walk in to say hello.

"Hey man, nice to meet you," says Jake, shaking Chace's hand. "Audrey's talked a lot about you."

"Thanks," says Chace.

"Hello, handsome," says Logan. "We met briefly at your opening for the reading."

"Yeah, of course, Logan a pleasure to see you again," Chace says, shaking his hand.

"Ooh! Enchanté," says Logan with a giggle. "Now, if you'll excuse me, I have to finish our supper."

We sit in the living room with my parents and Chace asks them about their trip, how the weather is in California this time of year, what airline they flew, how they're enjoying New York so far. He's being so polite and charming and my parents seem to really like him.

"Before we eat," says Jake. "I brought my camera and I thought it would be nice to take a picture of the whole Princeton fam in front of the tree."

"What a nice idea, Jake!" says my mother. "Let's take that photo before I eat too much of Logan's delicious food and start looking like Mrs. Claus."

My family and I stand in front of the tree and I hold Baxter in my arms while Jake snaps a few photos.

"Alright, let's get one of Logan and Audrey," says Jake.

"I can't! I'm brûléeing!" shouts Logan from the kitchen. "Later!"

"Okay, how about Chace and Audrey?" says Jake.

Chace and I stand by the tree and pose for a photo.

"Watch out, Barbie and Ken!" says Sophie with a giggle.

"Alright now, Jake, you go stand with Audrey and I'll take one of you two," says my mom.

"Oh, that's okay, Linda. I usually stand on this side of the lens," he says.

"Don't be silly, you get a photo too!" she chides him.

"Alright." Jake concedes. He walks over to me, wraps his arm around my waist, and we stand and pose for a photo.

"Another handsome duo!" Sophie teases. "Watch out, Chace!"

My eyes dart over to Chace nervously, but he chuckles.

After we finish photos, Logan calls us over to the table for dinner. Jake carves the turkey, my father refills everyone's wine glasses, Sophie and my mom and I help organize serving spoons, and finally, we all sit down together.

After everyone is served, my father picks up his fork and taps his wine glass a few times.

"I'd like to propose a toast," he says, raising his glass. "To my baby girl, Audrey. We're so proud of you, princess! You're literally a princess now."

Everyone chuckles. "Thanks daddy," I say.

"And you're making great strides toward achieving your dreams. You're surrounded by good friends, two very nice gentlemen that we're just meeting this evening, and of course to our host, Logan. Thank you for having us. This may be the fanciest Christmas dinner we've had in years!"

"Yes, I'm not even sure what truffle oil is!" says my mother, raising her glass. "Thank you, Logan, for giving me the year off. I am much obliged."

"Cheers!" we all say, and clink glasses.

"This is some great wine," says Chace, taking a sip.

"Thank you," says my dad. "Justin is our favorite."

"When Audrey and I were in high school, Howard and Linda never drank," says Logan. "I think they were trying to be a good influence, is that right?"

"You're damn right," says my dad playfully. "We didn't want a bunch of alcohol in the house with impressionable teenagers around."

"Especially a gay one," Logan says with a wink. "Quick! Hide the rosé! Am I right Chace?"

"Oh, I do enjoy a nice rosé for an outdoor party," says Chace.

Jake starts to laugh and I kick him under the table.

"Yeah, but then as soon as Audrey left for college, their true lush-personalities came out!" says John. "They went on one wine tasting trip with some friends, and now they can't be stopped!"

"John," says my mother. "We drink very responsibly and only over-indulge on certain special occasions."

"Like a Saturday?" Logan chimes in.

"Oh, Logan, hush your mouth!" says my mother with reproach. "You've been drinking since that turkey went into the oven."

"Linda, you and I both know that that's the only way to spend hours cooking," says Logan. "Gotta get a little chef's buzz going."

"I hate to admit it, but that's true." My mother laughs.

"Well, both Linda and Howard's palates are very refined now and they only come back with the good stuff," Sophie says. "And we're grateful. We work long hours!"

"That's right!" says my dad. "And as I recall, we helped choose some excellent wines for your wedding."

"You did," says Sophie.

"It was a really beautiful wedding," says my mother tenderly.

"This food is wonderful Logan," says Jake. "The turkey is so moist."

"Oh, don't say moist!" I say. "Worst word ever."

"The turkey is divine," says my mother. "I need to get your sweet potato recipe, honey."

"We'll talk before you go," says Logan.

"What about you Jake?" says John. "Anyone special in your life? Think you'll ever take the plunge?"

"Oh wow, put me on the spot there, John." Jake looks a bit self-conscious. "Well...I'd love to get married someday, just haven't managed to woo the right girl yet."

"Do us all a favor and stop dating models," Logan teases. "It's very hard to have a fabulous wedding if you marry a girl who won't eat the cake."

The table erupts into laughter.

"Touché, Logan," says Jake as he takes another mouthful of turkey.

"Oh, to cake!" I say raising my glass. "May I never be the kind of girl who won't eat cake!"

"I'll drink to that!" says Jake.

"What's in this stuffing?" asks my dad.

"Apples, walnuts and cranberries," says Logan. "And a little bit of herb butter."

"How about you, Chace? Are you the marrying kind?" asks Jake abruptly.

"Jake," I whisper under my breath.

"I'm just asking the same question your brother asked me," says Jake. "I hope that wasn't offensive?"

"Oh, no," says Chace amicably. He pauses for a few moments before answering. My stomach tightens with nerves. "Well, my parents have been married for a long time and they're very happy. I like the idea of marriage for sure, just want to make sure I have all my professional ducks in a row first. I'd really like to accept that Tony award before I accept a girl's hand in marriage."

"Wow, a Tony," says John. "That's pretty ambitious."

"That's why I moved here," he says. "That, and maybe starting a new band project. But I've seen a lot of my friends win Tony's and I'd like the chance to stand up on that stage graced with an award from my peers. Wouldn't mind a Grammy either."

"I think that's a noble ambition," says my mom. "I'm sure Audrey will be up there too someday!"

"Actually, one of the things I like about Audrey is that it seems that her passion has evolved into wanting to be a part of an artistic community, not just winning an award," says Jake with an edge to his voice.

"Well, I guess my goals are a bit different," says Chace.

"We all have to have certain goals in mind!" I jump in, defending Chace. "I'm sure lots of famous Hollywood actors have practiced their Oscar speech with a bottle of conditioner or something."

I look to my brother to back me up and he quickly changes the subject. "How are the parties going, Audrey?"

"Oh, they're going well!" I say. "It's kind of a well-oiled machine now. We've had a few missteps along the way and a few spectacular saves, but for the most part, it's been great!"

"Yes, someone had to race up to the East Side a few days ago to sew one of the girls back into her dress," says Logan.

"And was that you?" asks my mother.

"Linda, who else would have an industrial strength sewing kit and extra satin ribbons lying around?" says Logan.

"I'm sorry I doubted you, honey," my mother teases.

"Otherwise, our girl is the talk of the town a far as birthdays are concerned," says Logan.

"And we're all real proud of ya, kid," says Jake, raising his glass.

"Here, here!" says my mother. "Always knew our girl had a mind for business and creativity. I think it was that Montessori school she attended as a child."

After dinner we move into the living room where Logan puts out an assortment of cookies and a pumpkin pie. Baxter is asleep under the Christmas tree and the rest of us curl up on the sofa and surrounding chairs with cups of hot cider.

"Well, I have some stocking stuffers," says my mom, opening a big bag that she had stashed under the tree.

"Oh, are we doing presents now?" I say. "I have some as well!"

"Apple doesn't fall far from the tree," says my dad to Chace.

My mom presents us all with hand knitted-scarves made from the softest yarn I think I've ever felt. She's even made one last minute for Chace.

John, Sophie and I give her a big hug and we all wrap our scarves around our necks. We know the drill.

"Wow, thank you so much Linda!" says Jake as he gets up to hug her. "I just lost my favorite scarf yesterday. How did you know?"

"Oh a mother always knows," she says smiling.

"This is a very nice gesture, thank you!" says Chace.

"Linda, I don't usually enjoy handmade things," says Logan candidly. "And you *know* how I feel about craft fairs… but I have to say, your craftsmanship is exquisite. I think I will actually wear this."

"Well, thank you dear, that's quite a compliment."

"I have a few of my own gifts now!" I say, ducking under the tree. "I hope you all don't mind, but I'm so excited to give Chace his gift. Could he go first?"

"Oh, Audrey, I didn't know we were doing gifts tonight," says Chace, visibly uncomfortable. "I was going to give you your gift next week on our date night."

"Oh, that's okay! I really don't mind. I'm just excited for you to see what I got!" I hand him a small red box. My heart is pounding as he opens it.

"Oh my gosh, are these lift tickets?"

"Yep!" I say excitedly. "We can finally go to Vermont!"

"Audrey, that's quite a gift!" says John.

"Don't get too excited everyone. It was a Groupon," I say in response to their shocked expressions. "There's a resort near Mount Snow, so we're staying there for a night and then we have lift tickets for a day on the slopes!" I grin. "Chace has always wanted to go to Vermont, so now we're gonna do it next month. Jake, you won't mind watching Baxter, will you?"

"That's fine," Jake says, standing up. "I think it's time to open that bourbon, what do you think Logan?"

"Sounds about right," says Logan. "I'll help pour."

"Audrey, this is such a sweet gift. Thank you so much!" Chace gets up and gives me a big hug. As his arms encircle me, I bask in the utter joy I'm feeling. My best friends, my family and my new boyfriend are all under one roof celebrating the holidays. It just doesn't get much better.

Jake and Logan return from the kitchen with eggnog for everyone. Jake is drinking his bourbon neat, as always.

We finish exchanging our gifts, and then as we do every year, we turn on *It's a Wonderful Life* in black and white.

After the movie, my family goes back to their hotel to catch some sleep. Chace, Jake and I sit on the couch sipping our drinks as Logan retreats to the kitchen to wash the dishes.

"Do you want help?" I call.

"No, no! I work faster alone!" he calls back.

"I should actually head out myself," says Chace. "I'm going to catch that morning flight down to Florida after all."

"Oh good," I say. "I'm sure your family will be glad to see you."

"Jake, it was nice to meet you, man," says Chace.

"Yeah, you too," says Jake.

"Do you want me to walk you out?" I ask Chace.

"No, you're fine." He kisses me softly. "Merry Christmas, doll. I'll see you for New Year's."

He walks out the door and I close it behind him, returning to the couch to sit with Jake.

"What's happening on New Year's?" he asks, slurring slightly.

"Oh, some party he wants to take me to," I say.

"Well, I'm glad you're happy…"

"Jake, are you alright? You seem a little weird since dinner."

"Oh I'm fine," he says. "I'm feeling full-a-holiday cheer."

"That code for bourbon?" I ask.

"Very good," he says.

"What are you going to do for New Years?" I ask.

"Oh, I dunno," he says. "There's some party some people in my office are throwing, but I'm not sure I wanna go."

"Could be fun," I say.

"I think I wanna kiss this girl then, but I don't think it's gonna happen. Don't think it's meant to be."

"Oh yeah? Who's the girl?" I ask.

"Jus-some-girl," he says. "I'm gonna go take a whiz, kid. I'll be back."

Jake stumbles into the bathroom humming "Auld Lang Syne." After a few minutes I hear the sound of him vomiting into the toilet.

Logan comes rushing out of the kitchen holding a spray bottle of Tilex.

"I heard that," he says. "If he wipes his vomit-stained-mouth on my new hand towels, SO HELP ME!"

"I'll take care of him," I say. "Can I set him up on the sofa? I've never seen him like this."

"Yeah, I'll grab a blanket and pillow," he says.

After a few minutes Jake emerges from the bathroom,

looking pale. "I lost my holiday cheer," he says to me. "It's all gone."

"Let's get you set up on the sofa," I say.

"No, no, no, no....not you," he says. "You should go be with your boyfriend...because I'm fine."

"Here, Jake," says Logan, holding out a blanket and pillow.

"Thanks, buddy," says Jake.

He grabs the blanket and pillow and flops down on the sofa, fully clothed.

Dear Ms. Princeton

We are looking forward to having you and Mr. Campbell as our guests this upcoming weekend!

Here at Mt. Snow, customer satisfaction is of the utmost importance to us so we are sending this email to confirm the upcoming details of your all-inclusive stay with us!

We have confirmed your request for a bottle of Veuve Cliquot and two glasses for your in-room sunset cocktail hour. Your room has spectacular views of the mountains, so we expect you will be fully satisfied by the ambiance. Also your dinner reservations at Çava have been confirmed for 7pm that same evening.

Your lift passes are attached here as PDF's or you can pick them up at the Ticket Office upon your arrival at Mount Snow. Please be advised that daytime temperatures at the summit have been ranging from 5*-10*F during the day. We ask that you prepare accordingly as a safety precaution.

Again, thank you for booking with us and please let us know if we can do anything to make your stay more comfortable.

Kindest Regards,
Steven Klein
Mount Snow Cabin Rentals Reservation Specialist

SEVENTEEN

The first time you go away for a weekend in a new relationship is pretty special. For some couples, it's the first time they realize that the relationship has taken a more serious turn. For others, it can be the first time they are alone together without roommates in the next room.

For me, it's definitely the former. Chace and I have been in Vermont for twelve hours and it's been delightful. We arrived this morning to fresh powder on the mountains. I haven't skied since I was a teenager, when our family took a ski trip to Mammoth Mountain, but I held my own. Chace is a much more expert skier, having taken many trips to Vail. We skied a half day and then came back to the cabin to refresh before leaving for dinner. Now that we're back, I'm looking forward to opening a bottle of wine and relaxing by the fire in our cabin.

"Wow, that was a great dinner. Really well seasoned," says Chase, as we walk into the living room of the cabin. "Perfect and hardy after a day of skiing."

"It was." I walk over to him, wrap my arms around his neck and give him a kiss just below his earlobe. "I brought a little something for you."

"What is it?" he asks.

"Dessert," I say coyly.

"What kind of dessert?" he asks.

"Just a little something black and lacy. Thought my boyfriend deserved a little treat on our first couple's getaway together," I say, nibbling his ear.

"Boyfriend…"

"Well, yeah. It's been a month since our first date…"

"I actually wanted to talk to you about that," he says.

"About what?" I whisper into his ear.

"I just wanted to make sure that we aren't getting ahead of ourselves."

"Chace, we've already slept together several times." I look up at him and laugh, but his face is serious.

"No, I mean… I wanted to make sure that you knew that I'm not looking for a serious relationship," he says.

"What?" I'm confused.

"Well, you know, this weekend was about us having fun, right?" he says. "Just us spending time together and having a great time."

"Of course," I say. "But…"

"But beyond that, you know, we should play it by ear."

"I'm sorry but…what exactly does that mean?" I step away from him and sit down on the sofa.

"I'm just really consumed with my career, Audrey. And while I really like spending time with you, my focus kind of needs to be on auditions," he says. "I thought maybe we'd talk about that when we got back, but since you brought up the whole boyfriend thing… maybe now is as good a time as any."

"Are you serious?" I'm stunned.

"I really like you, Audrey," he says. "But I just need to make myself clear. My goals are a bit uni-focused right now."

"So, wait… when you were telling me that you don't date

more than one girl at a time because you should feel something, that was not true?"

"I actually think I heard that in a movie once, but I wasn't lying about feeling something for you," he says.

"You heard that in a movie once?"

"I think so," he says. "But it seemed like the right thing to say at the time. I said what I meant."

"So, just so I'm clear," I say. "You don't want to take responsibility for this. You don't want to have the commitment. Is that it? Why are you even here?"

"Audrey, you gave me this trip for Christmas. I wasn't going to not take it with you!" he says. "Look, I just didn't move to New York to find a girlfriend...I'm not looking to be tied down right now. I'm married to my work. I came here to be an actor on Broadway. I really like you, but I'm just not sure I can be what you need right now. I'm sorry."

"Wait, what makes you think you're an expert on what I need?" I say, standing up from the sofa and beginning to pace the length of the room.

"I just think you want a serious, full-time relationship. And I'm not sure I can give you that. I'm just really independent," he says.

"You met my parents..."

"You invited me to Christmas dinner and you didn't even tell me they were coming until the day before."

"You just want to end this because you need more time to audition?" I say. "There is good stuff here, Chace! You're just going to run away the second it starts to get real?"

"I just don't think it's a good idea for us to get too intimate when I know I can't give you what you want."

"Too intimate?" I say, astounded. "You're worried about us getting too intimate? After we've been sleeping together for a month? *Now*, you're worried about getting too intimate! You're making excuses!"

"I'm not, I'm just trying to be real with you before this gets any more complicated. I think I mentioned at Christmas dinner that I didn't want to be tied down yet, that I'm focused on my career."

"You just said that you 'said what you meant,' about feeling something for me. Now you're saying you need to spend more time to focus on your career and you don't think it's a good idea for us to get too intimate. So what's really going on? Is it that you're too chicken to actually do this for real, or you got what you wanted out of me and now you want to run away and act like I misunderstood you?"

"Can we just pump the brakes a little and let things play out at a bit more of a natural pace? I was really hoping to have a nice weekend with you."

"The nice weekend is over, Chace," I say as I as I grab my clothes and shove them into my overnight bag and then march into the bathroom for my toiletry bag.

"Audrey...I'm sorry," he says.

"It's fine. I get it. I've heard it all before. It was fun while it lasted." I zip my overnight bag, grab my purse and start to walk towards the front door of the cabin.

"Where are you going? Don't you think you're overreacting a bit?"

"I'm overreacting?" I say. "How's this for an overreaction? That car outside is rented in my name, so you can find a bus back to the city."

"You can't be serious," he says. "It's twenty-five degrees outside and it's starting to snow!"

"You're really independent, Chace... you'll figure it out." I don't even hesitate as I walk out of the cabin and slam the door behind me.

It's well after midnight when I get back into the city. For some reason, I can't swallow the thought of going back to Brooklyn. I call Logan, but when he answers all I hear is loud club music in the background, so I drop the car off in Midtown and then take the subway down to Jake's apartment, hoping he's home.

I walk up to the front door, remove my gloves and press the button on his intercom. As it buzzes I can hear Baxter barking upstairs, but Jake doesn't answer the intercom.

I pull out my cell phone and dial his number.

"Hello?"

"Jake, it's me." Suddenly I am fighting back the tears that are welling up in my eyes.

"Hey kid! How's Vermont?" he says. "You okay?"

"I'm outside your apartment." I can't help it. My voice is shaking. He must know something has happened.

"I'm three blocks away. I'll be there in five minutes," he says.

I stand, huddled in the doorway of Jake's building, bouncing around to keep warm, snow falling all around me.

Exactly four minutes later I see a figure running down the block through the snow. I know it's him before I can even make out his face. As Jake approaches me with a concerned look, I can feel the hot sting of tears behind my eyes.

"What happened?" he asks, offering me a hug. But I can't answer.

The entire five-hour drive home from Vermont, I had been fuming mad. By the time I crossed the George Washington Bridge, I was exhausted, but hadn't shed a single tear. Now though, I feel myself break in Jake's strong arms.

"He turn out to be a prick?" Jake asks. I nod my head into his chest, still sobbing. He tightens his arms around me and kisses the top of my head. "Come on inside. I'll pour you a drink and we'll talk it out." He unlocks his door and we walk inside.

"I'm sorry, Jake," I stammer as I wipe the mascara tears off my face and enter his apartment. "I should have known it was too good to be true."

"Well, I never liked Chace." He walks into the kitchen. "I've always thought you could do better."

Baxter runs in from the bedroom, jumping on my legs to greet me.

"Baxter is the longest relationship I've ever had with a boy," I say, as I reach down to pet him. "Hi, buddy."

I sit down on the couch and Jake walks back into the living

room with two glasses and a bottle of something amber-colored.

"Explain to me who goes away for the weekend to dump your girlfriend?" he says. "Even the biggest douchebags I know would never do that. Total low blow."

"It started out him wanting to talk about taking things slow, but then he just started making excuses saying he couldn't give me what I want and thought it would be wise for us not to get too intimate."

"Wow…"

"But then I sort of flipped out and left," I admit. "It's definitely over."

"Sorry, kid."

"Ugh, I can't believe I got a bikini wax and a haircut for this. I'm an idiot."

"Audrey, c'mon." Jake hands me a glass with a bit of the liquor inside.

I take a sip. The warmth that fills my throat and chest immediately, makes me feel calmer than before. "This is good. What is it?"

"A little Four Roses single barrel bourbon," he replies as he sits down beside me on the couch, Baxter having already jumped up and laid down in Jake's usual chair.

"No idea," I say. "But I like it."

"Listen, kid. You're not an idiot. You just picked the wrong guy. Not all guys are assholes, but Chace… may I speak candidly? Or is it too soon?" he asks.

"By all means," I say with a half-smile as I down the rest of the glass and place it firmly on the coffee table theatrically. Jake laughs and pours a second glass before handing it to me.

"Chace is a self-absorbed kind of guy. I don't think he means any harm, but he lives in his own world where the only thing that's important to him is his acting career, his band and his own vision of what happiness means. I don't really think he thinks much about who he takes down in the process."

"Jake, you got all that from having met him once?" I ask, feeling bewildered.

"I only needed to listen to him talk for half a minute about how he moved to New York to simultaneously win a Tony and Grammy award to get his number, kid." He sighs. "But you seemed to really like him, so I didn't want to rain on your parade."

"See, how did you pick all that up and I didn't?" I ask.

"Love is blind?" he hedges. "Or maybe because he's in a band? What is it with girls and musicians anyway?"

"You know what I think?" I say.

"What?" he asks.

"Humans are addicted to unrequited love. We always want what we can't have and what we know on some level is bad for us."

"That's pretty deep," he laughs. "And about fifty percent bullshit."

"I mean it, Jake. I knew on some level that Chace was too good for me. Or maybe not too good for me, but that I liked him too much and there was no way he'd be into that for very long. Ya know who the guys are that fall desperately in love with me?"

"I haven't the faintest idea," he says.

"The ones I could give two shits about," I say, defiantly. "That's always how it happens. The ones that want me bore me to tears, and the ones I want are threatened or intimidated by me."

"Well... I don't even know how to respond to that, but I think maybe you're slightly off base," he says.

"I dunno. I think I'm onto something."

"Wait a minute... Did you drive all the way back from Vermont with him?"

"Are you kidding? I left him at the cabin and told him to catch the bus."

Jake bursts out laughing. "You left him in middle of nowhere, Vermont with no way to get back?"

"Yep," I say.

"That's ballsy, kid! I'm kind of impressed."

"Thank you!" I let out a giggle and reach for the bottle.

"More? Why don't you finish what you've got first?"

"Do you want some more?" I ask.

"I'm okay," he says. "I already had a few at the bar before you called me."

Now that he mentions it, he does look a bit rosy in the cheeks. "Guess I gotta catch up then," I say as I down the rest of my second pour. I'm definitely feeling sunnier on the inside. "Jake, is there something wrong with me? Every time I meet a nice guy, he turns out to be a jerk. Is it me? Do I just turn men off?"

"It's absolutely not you, kid. You're a fantastic girl. And the right guy is out there."

"Ugh. He seemed so perfect," I whine.

"Audrey, can I let you in on a little secret? No guy is perfect. But with that being said, some of us are better than others."

"Let's hope so," I say.

"I know so." Jake smiles. "Music?"

"Why not!" I say.

Jake sets his drink down, gets up and walks over to his record player and vinyl collection while I pour a tiny bit more bourbon into our glasses.

"Music is always good. Should be something that goes nicely with this yummy bourbon!" I say.

I love Jake's record collection. He has flawless taste in music and we love all the same albums.

He reaches for a cover with bright colors on it and pulls out the beautiful black disc.

"How about a little Jimi Hendrix Blues? That seems appropriate."

"Works for me," I say, as he places it on the player and the needle hits the record with the comforting crackle and pop sound that will always remind me of Jake's living room.

The music swells and fills the room with its bluesy, vintage sound. Jake returns to the couch and smiles. "Feeling any better?"

"So much!" I say, my head starting to buzz. "I love Jimi

Hendrix. This album is totally underrated. Why is that?"

"I'm not sure. But it's pretty damn sexy." He smiles. "The man basically made love to his guitar."

"Which is the song I like?" I ask.

"You like 'Red House,' " he replies. "Last time you were wasted and crashed here, I played it and you said it made you feel like a 'real woman' to listen to it."

"I did not! Did I really?" I ask, embarrassed. "Good lord, why do you put up with me?"

"It was pretty funny, kid. I'm a big fan of drunk you," he says as he reaches over to clink glasses with me.

"I'm not sure we should be drinking to that, how about to me offering you rent for crashing on your couch."

"You know you're welcome here anytime."

Jake and I sit on the couch listening to records and sipping bourbon for another hour. I feel completely warm and relaxed. Jake is making me laugh with his impressions from Saturday Night Live, and we're enjoying watching the snowfall outside his large bay window.

After a while, Jake stands up from the couch and walks out of the room. He returns with a throw blanket for me and plops back down on the couch. We've both been drinking, but he somehow seems to be more together than I am.

"You're such a good guy, Jake," I say as I accept the blanket and spread it over my legs. "Hey, whatever happened with that girl you told me you liked?" I lean against the armrest of the couch, propping my feet in Jake's lap.

"What girl?" he asks, looking perplexed.

"That girl you told me about on Christmas? You said there was a girl you liked who you wanted to kiss on New Year's."

"I said that?"

"You were pretty hammered," I laugh.

"Yeah, I'm sorry about that. I definitely had a bit more of the Christmas Cheer than I can normally handle." He chuckles. "But I'm not sure about that girl...I don't know if she feels the same way, and we didn't kiss on New Year's."

"Well, you should find out," I say.

"It's not that simple, kid. The situation is kind of delicate."

"How so?"

He hesitates. "It's hard to explain."

"How come I've never met her?"

"She… lives in Boston," he says.

"Oh."

"Can we talk about something else?" he asks, visibly uncomfortable.

"Sure. Sorry, I didn't mean to pry."

"No, it's alright. You're fine," he says.

"Well, thank you for being so sweet tonight and for dog-sitting Baxter, even though you hate Chace."

"Don't mention it. I love Bax and I don't hate Chace. I just don't exactly care for him."

"I know you're not a fan, but do you dislike him because you're both so different, or because you're being protective of me?" I ask.

"Honestly, a little bit of both," he says candidly. "I just think you can do so much better. I think you deserve more than him."

"You are far too kind, sir," I say.

"You're a good person, Audrey, and you deserve a guy who can see everything that you are, not a guy who just wants you in his bed," Jake says, looking me square in the eye.

His words hover in the air for a second before I can think of a response.

"Well, Jimi isn't the only sexy person in this room. I can be pretty damn sexy when I want to be," I joke, attempting to ease the tension I feel.

"I know you can." Jake laughs.

"You think I'm sexy?" I smile, sitting up straight, legs folded. Jake laughs again, but he looks a little bit self-conscious this time. "You think I'm sexy, don't you! Are you blushing, mister?"

"C'mon! Any person with a decent head on their shoulders can see that you're smart, funny and semi-attractive." He smiles a sly smile.

"Hey!" I say, playfully smacking his leg.

"Okay, maybe more on the side of beautiful."

"You think I'm totally hot and sexy!" The bourbon is making me bold.

"Fine then, I do," he says with resignation.

"You're drunk, Jake."

"Not *that* drunk."

"Fine then, maybe I think you're sexy too," I say, adding to the banter.

"No you don't!" he says.

"Sure I do!" I exclaim. "You're an incredibly talented photographer. You're sweet and kind. You are totally selfless, maybe to a fault. Plus, you've got the whole tall, dark and handsome thing working for you!"

"Oh c'mon," he says.

"I'm serious, Jake. I mean, I'd make out with you," I say.

"Okay, *you're* drunk, kid."

"Not *that* drunk," I say sincerely.

Jake locks eyes with me and I feel something tighten in the pit of my stomach before I have to look away, suddenly feeling warm. We both fall silent and as the song ends, and the room fills with a tense electricity.

After a moment, the next song begins and Jake breaks our silence.

"If something were ever to happen between us, I wouldn't want it to be a drunken mistake."

There's a sweetness behind his eyes that I hadn't noticed before.

"Jake… I'm not that drunk," I say.

I can't tell if it's the warmth of the bourbon, or the fact that I'm finally feeling relaxed after a supremely awful day, but in this moment, Jake looks different to me. He doesn't look like my buddy who teases me mercilessly. He doesn't look like a brother. He looks like something else altogether. I feel my stomach tighten with an unfamiliar longing.

"You just broke up with Chace," he says. "You're

vulnerable and you've been drinking."

"Jake, today has been awful," I say. "I just want to forget about it. I just want to forget it happened. Please... help me forget?"

I lean towards him, placing my hand on his chest.

"No, kid," he says softly, lifting my hand off his body and placing it on the couch in between us.

I suddenly feel hot with shame. "Is it me?"

"What? No!" he says. "That's not it at all. You're beautiful. You're amazing. I just don't think it's a good idea."

"I don't understand," I say, feeling my face burn with humiliation as the tears well up in my eyes.

"I just don't think it's a good idea right now," he says.

"Nobody wants me," I whisper, half to myself as the hot tears roll down my cheeks.

"Jesus... Audrey, don't cry, I just..."

"I'm gonna go." I start to get up from the couch. "I think I need to go home now."

"That's ridiculous!" Jake protests. "It's two-thirty in the morning and we're in the middle of a goddamn blizzard."

"I'll be fine," I mutter.

"I don't want you taking the subway right now," Jake says, his voice starting to sound panicked. "They're probably not even running with this weather."

"I said I'll be fine. I'll take a cab!" I snap. "Where's Baxter's carrier?"

I pace around the living room, angrily gathering Baxter's things.

"Shit..." he says.

"Baxter, time to go," I say, as I grab my parka, my bag and his leash from the coffee table.

"Shit." Jake says again.

"Goodnight, Jake," I say, heading for the door.

"Dammit, Audrey. No! I'm not letting you leave. It's late and you could get hurt!" he says firmly. He comes up behind me and grips my shoulders, bringing me to a halt.

I freeze. He softens his grip on my shoulders and pulls me

back against his chest, leaning his face toward my neck.

"I need to go," I murmur.

"Don't go, kid." He breathes softly as he touches my skin with his lips.

My breath catches in my chest and I drop my bag; it hits the floor with a soft thump. I don't move an inch as he tilts his face forward and kisses me softly on the nape of my neck. My eyelids flutter closed and I feel goose bumps raise on my arm.

"Don't just do that because you feel sorry for me," I whisper. "I don't want you to kiss me out of pity."

"I'm not," he breathes. "I'm kissing you because I want to. I've wanted to for a long time."

I can't think of anything to say, so I stay quiet, every nerve in my body buzzing.

"Audrey, don't you understand? There is no girl in Boston," he whispers against my neck. "It's you…"

I turn around slowly and look at him, understanding washing over me.

Jake looks me in the eye as if he's trying to decipher my feelings. I feel my stomach tighten again at his gaze. He brushes a strand of hair out of my face and rests his hand on my cheek, stroking my skin with his thumb. The warmth spreads throughout me as I lean toward him on tiptoes and kiss his lips softly, tentatively.

I feel his fingers intertwine in my hair as he bites softly on my bottom lip. After a moment, I pull away looking into his eyes. "Jake, I want you."

"I want you too, kid… But I don't want to take advantage of you when you're in this place and we've both been drinking. I don't want you to regret this tomorrow."

"I don't care about tomorrow," I say firmly.

"Audrey…" he says. His gaze is hard and his forehead is screwed up in thought as he visibly wrestles with his morals and desires.

"Please," I say gently.

His face softens with resignation.

"Fuck it," he says as he wraps his arms tightly around me

and pulls me toward him.

Our lips meet with a hungry ferocity and all familiarity is lost as I melt into his kiss and his embrace. He isn't the Jake I've known. He isn't my best friend. He is just someone I want. Someone I want badly. His tongue softly caresses mine and his strong arms pull me closer.

I'm barely registering anything except for the taste of his mouth and the feel of his arms. He lifts me up and I wrap my legs around his waist. He carries me into his bedroom where we crash down on the bed, our fate already sealed.

EIGHTEEN

I wake up with my contacts still in my eyes. I pull them out and rub the sticky gunk out of the corners. It only takes a split second for the searing pain of my head to hit me like a wrecking ball. I close my eyes tightly and fall back against the pillow groaning. Another few seconds pass before I realize that I'm not in my own bed. I squint around the bright room, making out my surroundings. I'm alone in Jake's bedroom.

"What happened last night?" I wonder aloud as I cover my face with my hands. "OH MY GOD!"

I bolt upright and the room spins. I look down, realizing I'm naked, and pull the sheet tightly around my chest. I look over to the nightstand where my phone sits. It's ten-thirty. I grab my phone and see that I have a text from Jake and eight missed calls from Chace.

"Oh my God, why did I do this? What is wrong with me!?" I shout to myself.

I open the text from Jake, sent fifteen minutes ago.

Hey kid, gone to get bagels
and coffee. Back soon!

"Audrey, you're such an idiot!" I say aloud, as the scene from last night floods my memory. Jake and I drinking, Jake and I fighting. Jake stopping me from leaving, us kissing. Jake and I lying in bed, tangled in a passionate embrace. I remember the way I felt, that I wanted it to happen; I had wanted him. But in the light of day, the memory makes my stomach churn with nerves.

What have I done? I lament to myself. *I'm a horrible person!*

My phone rings and I jump, thinking it must be Jake, but I look down and see that Chace is calling again. I decide to answer it.

"Chace…"

"Babe? Oh thank God! I was so worried!" he says.

"Why would you be worried?" I say.

"I never heard from you last night. I was worried something happened. It started snowing pretty hard up here."

"Oh," I say. "No, I'm fine. I got back into the city before the storm."

"Baby, I've been up all night thinking. I feel terrible about what I said. I just got scared. Things have been moving so fast with us. I just… I do care about you, I really care about you. Can we compromise?"

"What do you mean?" I ask, feeling a bit softer toward him.

"What if we spend Wednesdays and Fridays together, then we can see each other consistently and I'll spend the other days focusing on auditions? You're my girl. I love having you in my life," he says, and I freeze at the sound of his words, tongue-tied.

"Yesterday you said you couldn't give me what I want," I stammer.

"I was being an idiot. I couldn't stop thinking about you last night, and when you didn't answer I was sick worrying that something had happened to you. I don't want to lose you, babe."

"Chace, I don't know. I mean, I feel really confused. I need to think about this." My head is spinning.

"Of course, take all the time you need. Let's meet for dinner on Wednesday and we can decide. Okay?"

"Yeah, alright... Wednesday would probably be OK."

"Hey, kid, I'm back!" I hear Jake's voice as the door to the apartment opens. *Shit.*

"Is that Jake?" Chace asks.

"Yeah..." I say hesitantly.

"Shoulda known you'd have gone there. Does he think I'm a complete douchebag?"

"Umm..." I say.

"Audrey?" Jake walks into the bedroom holding coffee and bagels. I feel my cheeks flush with embarrassment when I see him.

"Tell him I'm sorry for being such a tool," Chace says. "Listen baby, I'm getting on a bus. I'll be back in the city this afternoon and I'll see you on Wednesday, okay?"

Jake looks at the phone and I can tell from his expression that he knows who's on the other line.

"Okay, talk to you later, bye," I say, as I end the call.

"What does he want?" Jake asks with forced casualty as he sits down on the bed beside me.

"He wants to talk," I say weakly. "Apparently he's come to his senses."

"Wow...You're not seriously thinking of giving him another chance are you?"

"I don't know, Jake. I feel so confused. Last night was..."

"I knew it! I knew you'd regret it. I tried to stop it, but you were begging me for it," Jake says, looking frustrated and hurt.

"I know. I know. I'm so, so sorry Jake. I was so drunk." My head falls into my hands. "I feel like a complete asshole."

"Are you actually going to see him? After what happened last night? I thought that we..." he trails off.

"I don't know...maybe," I say, head still in my hands.

Jake is silent for a long while before I feel the bed rise as he stands up. "I need to go for a walk," he says. "There's coffee and bagels. Take whatever you want. I'll see you later."

"Jake, please! Don't be like that. I just need some time to think."

"Don't bother, kid. It was a drunken mistake. Forget it ever happened."

I sit on the bed feeling stunned as Jake walks out into the hall and slams the door behind him.

The ride home on the Q train is terrible. My head is pounding and my stomach is in knots. Baxter sits in his carrier at my feet as I lean my head against the wall of the train and try to tune out the loud noises and bumps of the un-even track.

I keep trying to clear my head from the night before, but each time I close my eyes, I'm seeing visions of Jake and I together, and my stomach aches. Jake cares about me, he protects me, but Chace makes me weak in the knees with his eyes. Chace melts me with his kisses and sends a shiver down my spine with a smile. It's a completely different kind of feeling. And maybe he was just scared? Lots of guys get scared when they're falling in love. And I love him too. I'm so in love with him. He's perfect for me. He wants to try and work things out with me. He wants to prioritize us and that's all I wanted, wasn't it? I just wanted him to make me a priority.

The more I think about it, the more I feel awful for sleeping with Jake. I know that I thought things were over with Chace last night. I know that we essentially broke up when I left Vermont. But why would I cross that line with Jake? He's my best friend! I've spent the night at his apartment a zillion times before and nothing has ever happened. Nothing has even been close to happening... But then I think back to his words: *"Audrey, don't you understand? There is no girl in Boston. It's you."*

How long has he liked me? How long has he had feelings for me without saying anything? He was with Chloe for so long! They lived together! And how do I tell Chace that I slept with Jake? He will never forgive me. I'll lose him.

I get off the train at the Parkside stop, letting Baxter out of his carrier so that we can walk back to our apartment. When we get inside, I crawl into my bed, not bothering to remove my shoes or coat. I just pull the covers over my head and drift off into a restless slumber.

The next evening I sit at dinner with Logan. The guilt I was feeling initially has tripled now that I've sobered up completely. My stomach is in knots every time I think about what I've done.

"Paulie, say something," I plead miserably.

"I can't seem to find the words," he says.

"I'm a terrible person..." I mutter. "I feel like I cheated. Did I cheat on Chace?"

"Absolutely not," he says definitively. "You and Chace broke up a good... six hours before you slept with Jake...so that's not cheating."

"A very minor technicality," I say, head in my hands.

"But if you decide to try and work things out with Chace, you absolutely cannot tell him you slept with Jake."

"I know," I mutter. "I feel awful!"

"If you tell Chace, he'll get territorial. Then he either won't trust you, even though you clearly ended things with him before it happened, or he won't want you to be friends with Jake anymore, and we cannot let that happen."

"You really like him now, huh?"

"Jake? Of course! He's part of the family now," he says. "We can't lose him."

"Paulie, he won't take my calls," I say. "I've called him seven times this morning, and he won't answer. And I've sent him an obscene amount of 'I'm sorry' texts, but he won't reply. Maybe I should write him an email?"

"Holly, I say this with love, but you need to go ahead and give Jake some space," he says. "Going all psycho-girl-who-won't-stop-calling is not going to help your cause."

"I know, I know," I mutter.

"And don't even get me started on your novel-length emails about your feelings," he says. "Guys hate those. I'm gay and I hate them. Sometimes you just say more than you need to, my love."

"What am I just not allowed to express my feelings?" Now I'm perturbed. "I usually only write those when I'm PMS-ing, and…"

"Holly, in this instance, it's not about your hurt feelings. Jake has liked you for a while now, and he opened himself up to you the other night and made himself vulnerable. And I'm sorry, love, but you kind of, well… you shit all over that. So you need to give him whatever time he needs right now."

"You knew that he liked me?" I ask.

"Didn't you?" He raises an eyebrow.

I must give him a blank stare in return, because he sighs and then continues. "I guessed it a while ago, but I knew for sure at Christmas. I saw the look on his face when you gave Chace the Vermont trip and then asked him if he'd dog sit while you two were away. He switched to straight bourbon after that."

"Oh my God, I'm a terrible person! I'm awful. I'm the worst!" I thump my head against the table. "I've just broken my best friend's heart and semi-betrayed my boyfriend all in an eight hour period! I'm the anti-cupid. I ruin love!"

"Holly, if you want my advice, I think it would be wise for you to call Chace and tell him you need another week to think about things."

"You think so?" I ask.

"Yes, I do," he says. "You have too many emotions and too much guilt swirling around in your pretty little head right now and you're not going to make any coherent decisions in two days."

"You're right," I say. "Good thinking."

As Logan and I say goodbye and I begin trudging through the snow towards the train, I'm resolved that I'll give it another week before I decide anything. I do feel confused. I do feel guilty. It would be smart to give myself some time to really think about things before I decide what to do.

But when I walk into my building, I find a box in the mailing room addressed to me, containing a dozen yellow roses and a card that reads, "Can't wait for our date!" As I place the card back into its tiny envelope, I feel my resolve break, and I know there's no way I won't be in Chace's arms by Wednesday night.

NINETEEN

It turns out that there really is no way to get around sex complicating friendships. I guess I should have known that, but I was sort of hoping that it wouldn't be an issue for Jake and me, since we were so close before anything happened. As much as I would have loved to believe that you can intellectualize a drunken hook up and move past it quickly, it seems it can't be done. Particularly when one person has feelings and the other does not share the intensity of those feelings. It doesn't really matter how close we were before. Now… everything is just a mess.

"Do you have that last box, babe?" Chace asks, as I carry in my last box of DVDs.

"I've got it." I set it down on the coffee table.

In spite of my angst about what happened between Jake and me, I've chosen to stay positive and spend my time devoted to the relationship in my life that is working.

Chace and I have only been living together for four hours,

but I'm already over the moon about it.

The night that we reunited was one of those unbelievably cold and clear winter nights, where you can see a million stars, even in spite of the light pollution from the city. It felt like the kind of night where you just need to pause and reflect. I insisted that Chace and I spend the evening working things out, instead of going out to dinner. It seemed more logical to really talk through our issues before doing anything date-like, and we ended up sitting on his couch for several hours communicating in what felt like a very grown-up way.

"I just got scared," he said.

I apologized for jumping the gun a bit with the commitment and he then admitted that he had indeed over-reacted and handled the situation in Vermont badly. I then conceded that I might have gotten a bit dramatic myself – I mean, I left the guy in Vermont with no transportation. He said he couldn't stand to be away from me, and that after coming so close to losing me, he wanted to be better. He told me he wanted to be the kind of man I deserved. I have to admit, I melted again into being wanted. As much as I felt like I should confess to him what happened with Jake, I took Logan's advice and opted to keep that detail out of our conversation. It just didn't seem like we needed any more obstacles to overcome.

After that night, we kept up our plan to spend every Wednesday and Friday together, but that quickly evolved into us spending nearly every night together. As soon as I started leaving several changes of clothes in his closet and having Baxter stay at his place while I worked, Chace decided that we might as well move in together. We found a little place in Chelsea, which is perfect for auditions for him and an easy commute to work for me. I know that even Logan was a bit surprised that we chose to make this kind of commitment so quickly, but when you know you know, right?

"Is Jake coming to our housewarming party?" asks Chace. "I haven't seen him in a while."

"Um, I don't think so," I say. "He's been really busy with

work."

"Oh, okay," he says.

I've been avoiding telling Chace that Jake and I are on the outs. I'm hoping that we can work things out before I'll really have to explain his absence in my life. I tried to take Logan's advice and give Jake space, but of course the temptation to write him a huge email, apologizing and trying to explain my feelings, was too great. Jake hasn't responded to any of my emails, and he won't answer my texts, so I've officially decided to just let it go... at least for now.

I've been really good about giving Chace space to focus on auditions, but he's had a tough month. Since our reading closed, he hasn't booked anything. He seems frustrated with his career and I've found myself worrying that if I book a gig before he does, he will be threatened by my success and won't want to be with me anymore. I've kind of been taking a break from auditioning, but not exactly because of him. It's just that, I really do need to spend some time brushing up on my skills before I keep auditioning, so I've been filling my free time with dance classes and voice lessons instead. I added a couple more seminars at Actors Access as well. I figure by the time my skills are super sharp, Chace will book something and then we will be back on an even playing field, which will be better for our relationship anyway. He's been very supportive of my business though, allowing me to turn one of our small closets into a storage facility for costumes and party materials.

After we unpack all of our boxes, we order take-out from the corner Chinese restaurant and sit on our couch relaxing.

"Gosh, I didn't realize how hungry I was," I say, nibbling on the last egg roll. Neither of us has eaten since breakfast.

"Moving takes it out of ya," he says sipping a cold beer.

"Well, we're in," I say surveying the room.

"We are in, indeed," he says, exhaling. "Pretty crazy."

"Got a lot of unpacking to do tomorrow," I say.

"Definitely a lot of boxes." He smiles and reaches over to take my hand and kiss it.

"I know," I say. "I still can't believe your Midwestern

Republican parents are okay with this."

"It was a bit of a risk. Have you told your parents?" he asks.

"Oh yeah, they are so progressive, they don't care."

"I just reminded my parents that I'm over twenty-five and I'm a responsible adult. I think in truth they prefer a 'don't ask don't tell' policy when it comes to my sex life."

"Understandable," I say. "Well, I'm going to take a shower."

"A shower sounds like a good idea, indeed," he says. "Want some company?"

"Um, I love living with you!" I blurt out. "We can just walk around naked like it ain't no thang!"

"We can," he laughs.

"I could cook you dinner in nothing but an apron," I say.

"Long as you don't burn yourself," he teases. "I'll be in in a few."

I'm walking down the street following Jake. It's a stormy afternoon and the rain is coming down in sheets, making it difficult for me to see as I walk.

"Audrey, you need to stop contacting me," he says, walking faster away from me. *"There's nothing else to say."*

"Jake, please! You have to know I feel terrible." I try to walk after him, but can't move fast enough to catch him.

"I honestly don't care. I told you I had feelings for you, we slept together, and you went back to him!" He's angry, and his words feel like knives being thrown my way.

"Jake, you're my best friend, I don't want to lose you!" I call.

"You're just another crazy girl out to hurt me!" he yells. *"Stop calling me! Stop texting me! Stop emailing me! You can't fix this."*

"Jake, please!"

"No, Audrey! Our friendship is over and I never want to see you again! You're a bitch!"

"Jake!" I jolt awake, gasping for air.

As my heartbeat steadies, I reach over in the dark to cuddle with Chace, but my hand lands on an empty spot in the bed and I realize he's not there.

I squint in the dark to grab my cell phone so that I can see what time it is. It is nearly four in the morning.

I crawl out of bed, grabbing my warm robe, and shuffle sleepily into the living room. Chace is sitting on the couch writing in a notebook by the light of a single lamp.

"Hey, are you alright?" I ask.

"Jesus, babe!" He jumps. "You scared me! Did I wake you?"

"Sorry," I say. "No... I had a bad dream, woke up and realized you weren't in bed and it's sort of an un-godly hour."

"I'm sorry," he says. "I just needed to get some bad thoughts out of my head."

Yeah, you and me both. "Bad thoughts?" I ask. "Chace, what's going on?"

"Audrey, it's really not a huge deal. I'm fine," he says. "Go back to sleep."

"Don't shut me out," I say, as gently as I can muster. "Talk to me."

"I'm just a little..." he trails off. "I'm nervous that...I don't want you to worry, but..."

"You're freaking out about us having moved in together, aren't you?" I say.

"Yeah, a little," he admits. "I think it's just cold feet though."

"Chace, this was your idea," I say, semi-exasperated. "You said you wanted to show me that you were committed, but why move in with me if you didn't want to? I didn't ask for that."

"Because I don't want to lose you," he says. "I can't imagine my life without you, and if I don't do whatever it takes to keep you, you'll find someone else."

"Look," I say. "This is New York. It's expensive to live here. I think most couples move in together far sooner here than they might in a different city...You know, to save money."

"You're probably right," he says.

"I mean, look at Jake. He almost had to move after he and Chloe broke up in the fall. If he hadn't gotten a gig in D.C., he wouldn't have been able to afford their place on his own."

"That's not helping me worry less," he says.

"What I mean to say is, can we not make such a big deal out of this? It's not like we're getting married or anything. We were spending the night together all the time anyway, and in my eyes, nothing has changed. We just share a closet now and we can pitch in on things like laundry detergent and paper towels."

He smiles. "Well, when you put it like that..."

"Let's just agree that as long as we're happy, we'll stay together. And if we get to a point where that's not the case anymore, then we'll end it and we'll figure the details out then. Okay?"

"Low stakes," he says. "I like that."

"Just less pressure," I say. "Now, will you come back to bed?"

"Okay." He smiles and takes my hand as we walk back into the bedroom together.

The next morning, I wake up with Chace holding me in our bed, in *our* apartment, and I feel resolved that we can work things out. Look at the way I talked him down from the ledge last night! We work so well as team. I'm confident now that we can get through anything.

As I gently wriggle myself free of Chace's arms, and then I grab my cell phone off the nightstand and climb quietly out of bed. I throw on my robe and head toward the kitchen to make coffee. When I open the refrigerator and pull the coffee grounds out of the fridge, I notice a voicemail on my phone from an unknown number.

"Hi, my name is Maria Elena. My daughter, Carmen, goes to school at PS 197 and it's her birthday today. I know it's so last minute, but she just loves Cinderella and I'm wondering if someone might be able to come by just for an hour to meet the kids after recess and tell a story during their reading period. If someone can give me a call, that would be great.

I'm not sure how much I can pay...my hours at work just got cut, but it would just make my baby's whole day. Just let me know. Thank you!"

I call Maria Elena's number back and she answers right away.

"Hi, Maria Elena? This is Audrey, you left a message about Cinderella for your daughter's birthday today?"

"Yes! Hi!" she says. "Oh my goodness, thank you for calling me back!"

"Of course," I say. "As luck would have it, I'm actually free before three o'clock today. What time were you hoping to have someone come?"

"Their reading period is right after their lunch break, around twelve forty-five, would that work?"

"How many kids?" I ask.

"Eighteen, I think," she says.

"Alright, no problem. I'll bring face paints and maybe a storybook?"

"Oh, that would be wonderful!" she says. "How much do you charge?"

"Where is the school?" I ask.

"95ᵗʰ and Third," she answers.

"Could you pay twenty-five to cover cab fare?" I ask.

"That's all?" she says, aghast.

"Yeah." I smile to myself. "Today, that's all. Just don't tell anyone, okay?"

"Thank you so much, Princess!" she says. "Truly, I'm so grateful."

"My pleasure," I say. "I'll be there around twelve-thirty to change into my costume, just let the office know."

When I get out of the cab at 96ᵗʰ Street, I see the school on the corner. It doesn't look like anything special, same as all the other PS number schools in Manhattan. The most beautiful schools in the city are private. Dalton, Brearley, Nightingale-Bamford, St. Bernard's, Sacred Heart, Trinity. They all look like something out of another era, which is fair to say because some of them have been around for nearly a hundred years.

As I walk toward PS 197, I think about how hard it must be

for kids in the public school system to compete with kids, who go to private schools and are Ivy-bound. The economic divide is so great in New York City, and yet, it's just part of the culture that exists here.

I start to wonder if maybe we can do more for families who are struggling in the recession. I make a mental note to look into volunteer work that the girls and I can do for the community.

As I walk into the hall of the school, I approach the counter and check in with the front desk associate named Ronda, telling her I'm a guest of Maria Elena's

Her face lights up as she tells me in a hushed whisper, "The kids are going to love this!"

"Glad I can help," I whisper back.

"You can go change in the bathroom over there. Here's the key," she says.

"Thank you very much, Ronda."

I walk into a bathroom that has junior-size stalls and sinks, intended for the smaller children. I find the larger stall at the end of the row and pull out my garment bag.

Within a few minutes I'm transformed into Cinderella and ready to go meet the kids. I walk back into the hall and over to Ronda's desk. I see a woman who I assume must be Maria Elena talking with her. She and Ronda both gasp when they see me in costume.

"Oh my goodness! Cinderella!" squeals Ronda.

"Hi! I'm Maria Elena," says the other lady. "Thank you so, so much! Come with me! Carmen is going to be so excited!"

As we approach the door, I peer into the kindergarten classroom and see a big group of kids seated on a rug in the middle of the floor. The room is decorated as any normal kindergarten class would be, with big alphabet letters and numbers pinned to the walls, small tables with small chairs, cubbies with lunchboxes and shoes in them, bookshelves with tons of picture books and big maps of the world hung up near the chalkboard.

As we walk through the door, their faces turn from

disinterest to absolute astonishment as they see me.

"Hello, everyone!" I say. "I'm here today so that we can wish Carmen a happy birthday!"

The rug erupts into screams and giggles, which is a sound I've grown to relish.

Maria Elena leads me over to Carmen and I say hello to her and give her a big birthday hug.

"Cinderella," she says. "You're here!"

"I am, Carmen," I say with a smile. "Are you having a good birthday?"

"I made a wish on a dandelion that you'd come to my birthday and you came!" she says. She reaches out and hugs me again, so tightly around my neck I can hardly breathe, but I'm so touched that I suck it up and let her have her moment.

After a few minutes, Carmen's teacher, Ms. Vasquez, helps me line all the children up for face painting. I paint Carmen's face first. A princess crown on her forehead, pink rosy cheeks and sparkles. All the girls decide to follow suit, while several little boys ask to have dinosaurs painted on their face, or a snake on their arm. Everyone is having a great time! The kids are jumping up and down, showing their face and arm paintings to each other, and all the girls gather around Carmen to giggle.

Finally the last little boy approaches me, ready for his turn. He is smaller than the others, probably one of the youngest. His skin is a deep cocoa color and his big brown eyes are shiny and bright. His cheeks have just the tiniest bit of baby fat still left in them and when he smiles up at me, my heart dissolves into dust. *That's it. I've never seen a cuter kid. Cutest kid ever.* I decide.

"Cinderella! Cinderella! It's me!" he says brightly. "Tyrone, remember? We met at Disney World!"

I feel myself melt into a puddle of adoration. Game Over, Tyrone… Game Over.

It takes a good four or five seconds before I can actually speak. "Tyrone! Of course!" I say, giving him a big hug. "It's been so long! How are you doing these days?"

"I'm good." He smiles his adorable, soul-crushing smile. "I have a baby brother now! His name's Dwayne"

"You do!" I say. "How wonderful!

"He cries a lot, and yesterday he peed on my mom while she changed his diaper."

"I've heard that can happen." I stifle my giggles.

"I'm trying to be a good big brother though… mama says I'm doing a good job."

"I bet you are." I smile.

"When will he be able to play at the park with me?" he asks.

"Probably in a few months when he can walk," I say.

"That's a long time…" he says.

"I'm sure it'll be worth the wait," I say. "So, what should we paint on your face today?"

"I'll take a rainbow, please," he says.

"Okay, hold very still," I tell him as I begin to paint his face. He looks very concentrated as he holds still, but every once in a while he looks up at me and gives me another heart-melting grin.

"How did you get here, Cinderella?" he asks. "Last time I saw you, I had to take a plane."

"Well, how do you think I got here, Tyrone?"

"Magic?" he asks.

"That's what I'd say." I smile.

"Yeah, I think you're right," he says matter-of-factly. "Your fairy godmother is powerful."

"She sure is!"

After I finish Tyrone's rainbow, I sit all of the kids down on the rug and we read a book together. When the story is over, I say goodbye to Carmen and all of her friends. As I prepare to walk out the door, Tyrone comes running over and gives my leg one more huge hug.

"See you soon, Cinderella!" he says with a big smile.

"You can count on it, Tyrone!" I say.

As I leave the school, I hope with every hope I can muster that the next time Tyrone goes to Disney World, the Cinderella there will play along and say she remembers him.

As I am thinking this, I reach into my bag to text Jake. He will love this story! But then I realize I shouldn't text him. So I text Chace instead, but he doesn't respond.

Audrey!

Thank you so much for what you did today!! Carmen cannot stop talking about how Cinderella came to her school to spend time with her and all of her friends! I cannot thank you enough for giving me a break in price and for being so flexible about coming to entertain the kids last minute. I will absolutely tell all my friends about your company, it was truly magical!! :)

Also I got a text from Tyrone's mom, Keisha. Apparently you have quite the smitten admirer on your hands. He was absolutely ga-ga over you! Too cute!

Lots of love and thank you again for making my baby girl's birthday so special!

Maria Elena

TWENTY

I've begun to learn that winter on the East Coast is a very long and tedious affair. I was comfortable with it getting chilly in October and I enjoyed some snow around the holidays, but for God's sake, it's nearly March, and I'm still wearing a parka every day, and there is still ice on the sidewalks from a recent storm we had.

I've been checking the ten-day forecast every morning to see if the temperature will rise, and today, we're barely going to get up to forty degrees. But compared to twenty-eight, I'll take it! I'm tempted to wear sandals, but I decide against it.

I grab my garment bag and supply bag before walking out the door to meet Em in Union Square. We are heading towards Coney Island today to do a birthday party.

I find her sitting at a small table inside Starbucks, drinking a hot tea.

"Hi!" I say. "Ready to go?"

"Yep," she says in a raspy whisper.

"Em, what the hell happened to your voice?" I ask. "You sound like that lady with the hole in her neck in the cigarette commercial! Are you sick?"

"No," she says huskily. "I'm not sure what happened…well that's not true…I went to karaoke last night and I might have sung 'Barracuda' with a bit too much gusto."

"Seriously? How are we going to do this party today if you can't sing or speak?" I ask. "Should I call Kay?"

"Kay has a catering gig," she whispers.

"Alright, well, we're just gonna have to tell them the poison apple assaulted your vocal chords. Do you think you can lip sync some of the songs?"

She nods.

We board the Downtown Q train heading toward Coney Island, taking our seats on the bench and stowing our garment bags between our knees. The train bumps along the track and we sit in silence.

"Should have brought you a marker board." I laugh.
She gets out her phone, presses a button and holds it up for me to see. She's opened the notepad app.

"Smart thinking," I say.

She takes her phone back and types a message before handing it to me.

Have you heard from Jake? Her message says.

"No, I think that is a lost cause. Pretty sure he hates me and thinks I'm a psycho bitch," I say.

Why would you say that? Seems extreme.

"He sort of told me."

I thought you hadn't talked to him!?

"Well, it was in a dream," I say. "But I'm pretty sure he was channeling his hatred straight to my subconscious. He hates me, Em. I'm sure of it. And I deserve it."

I know, but I initiated it," I say.

Not gonna defend what you did, but it's a two way street, girl.

"I know, but I initiated it," I say.

You didn't force yourself into his bed. He knew the risk.

"I still feel awful."

I think he's laying low because he's sad, but I don't think he hates you. Just give it some time.

"I will," I say. "Can't get much worse than not speaking. I just miss my friend," I say.

I know girl... How's it going with Chace?

"Good!" I say. "He actually just got offered a gig singing on a cruise ship, so he'll be heading down to Florida. Three weeks out and one week in New York, but we'll make it work."

That's cool! How do you feel about him being gone?

"Oh I'm fine with it," I say. "It's part of this business."

Does this mean you'll go back to auditioning now?

"What are you talking about?" I say.
She gives me a look before typing again.

C'mon, A! We've all noticed you stopped going to calls the minute Chace started struggling. Don't let your relationship dictate your career.

"I'm not!" I say, offended. "I wanted to spend some time working on my skills, so I'd be sharp."

She gives me the look again, and then she types.

You are smart, you're ready. Stop making excuses.

"Alright, let's just end this debate," I say. "I need to rest my voice since I'm gonna be speaking and singing for two."

She shrugs her shoulders as if to say, "Suit yourself."

How can she say that? How can she accuse me of giving up my career aspirations because of Chace? If anything, making sure my skills are sharp is the exact opposite of setting my dreams aside! I'm going after them even more intensely than ever.

I'm slightly peeved with Em when we get off the train in Brooklyn, but I decide I need to just relax and try and do a good job with this party.

We walk several blocks from the train station into a neighborhood that looks a little bit dodgy. When we get to the apartment building, my stomach is in knots. It's the first time we've agreed to do a party this far away, and I'm not sure what to expect. I check the address in my phone and look up at the number on the door.

"Yeah, this is it," I say grimly.

Em crosses herself and winks at me.

I text the mother and she answers the door a couple minutes later, quickly ushering us inside.

"Shhh," she says. "The kids are downstairs in the basement playroom, playing games. Can you sneak into the bathroom and stay in there until we're ready for you?"

"Umm, sure," I say.

We walk swiftly into the bathroom, shut the door and are met by a sea of bras hanging on the shower curtain.

"What the heck?" Em mouths to me.

"Who leaves bras hanging up when you have company coming?" I don't know whether to laugh or cry. We look around. The floor has three training potties on it and the sink is covered in make-up and hair product bottles. We have about four square feet to work with.

We change quickly and then sit and wait…in Brooklyn's smallest bathroom ever. Em sits on the toilet seat and I sit on the side of the tub, in full costume. We look at each other and, realizing how ridiculous the situation is, we both burst into laughter.

"I'm sorry if I was harsh," she says in her scratchy whisper.

"It's okay," I say. "You're probably right. I need to get back out there."

Another minute goes by and the mother texts me that we can come out, and just like in a fairytale, two princesses burst forth…from a tiny…bra-clad bathroom…ready to enchant and delight!

Somehow we are able to get through the party with one mute princess. The children are so enchanted with the stories and books that Em smiling, lip syncing to my voice, and miming laughter is all we need. For an apartment that looked so humble on the outside, the parents have gone above and beyond with the décor. Odd that they missed the bathroom. There's a popcorn machine, there are balloons everywhere, and beautiful streamers and gold stars hanging from the windows. The children are completely enchanted with us, but when it's time to say goodbye, the mother just tells us to go back into the bathroom to change.

"Are you going to move them down to the basement again?" I ask.

"Oh, no," she says. "It's fine."

"But… they'll see us come out and know we're not really princesses," I whisper to her.

"I think they'll be distracted with cake," she says. "Go ahead, you guys did great!"

Em and I walk back into the bathroom. Completely perplexed.

"I don't like this," she whispers to me.

"I know!" I whisper back. "We're gonna kill the illusion!"

"What should we do?" she whispers. "I can hear them right outside the door."

"What kind of princess leaves through a bathroom? We're

not gonna flush ourselves away! This isn't *Harry Potter*!"

"This whole day has been weird," she whispers with a grin.

"I have an idea," I say. "It's still cold outside. Let's leave our wigs, gloves and crowns on. Our parkas will cover our street clothes except for our shoes. We'll just say we're cold."

"Okay, take our wigs off on the subway?" she whispers.

"Yeah," I say. "I'm not blowing the magic we just worked so damn hard to create."

"Right on, boss lady!" she whispers.

We change out of our gowns, but leave our gloves, wigs, tiaras and jewelry on. In the end, we look like princesses that are wearing parkas and boots and frankly, I'll take it.

"Thanks again ladies!" I call as we burst out of the bra-laden bathroom and walk hastily toward the door, closing it quickly behind us.

As Em and I walk back to the station we are laughing about the whole situation, her laugh more muted than mine.

"What a party!" I say. "I swear, this job! You never know what's gonna happen!"

"Seriously," she whispers.

After a few minutes of our walk, the rain starts to fall and we take out our umbrellas. It's finally starting to feel like spring is around the corner. The forty-degree weather seems almost balmy.

I check my phone to see that the rain is forecasted to last through the night, which means some of this gross, dog-pee infused snow might actually melt. We round the corner toward the station and I'm feeling very positive about things.

I have new resolve to get back to pounding the pavement with auditions. My relationship with Chace is working, my company is successful, and I'm living in Manhattan again. Except for Jake, things are starting to feel solid. I'm starting to feel settled. As I put my phone back in my pocket, I feel it vibrate and bring it back out to see that it is my mom calling. Basking in the glow of my day, I feel especially warm towards her as I answer the call.

"Hey mom! How are you on this lovely spring-ish day?"

"Audrey…" Her voice sounds strained.

My heart stops. "What's wrong?"

"Honey, you need to come home, it's your father."

TWENTY-ONE

I can't believe my dad is gone...

As I sit in a chair at the cemetery, wearing black, I feel numb. It doesn't feel real. It just feels like I'm in some horribly sad dream that I can't wake up from.

"Howard Princeton was a beloved father, husband and teacher," says the minister. "Today we are all here because we share in the hollow sadness of his loss, but we also come together as a community to support each other and share our joyous memories of him."

My mother looks so stoic and heartbroken sitting beside me. She's not crying, but she looks pretty beaten down. She and my dad have had their ups and downs over the years, but they always stuck together. As I look at her, I just know a part of her heart is missing, and I worry that she may never get it back.

None of us saw it coming. My dad had been taking his meds as the doctor had prescribed. He had been exercising moderately and trying to eat better. In the hospital they said that the blood clot that caused the heart attack was just one of those rogue things. And then they couldn't pull him out of the cardiac arrest in time. Just one of those facts of life. One day a blood clot from your leg travels up to your heart, and the next day your wife and children have lost their husband and father. Simple as that.

Except it's not simple. Nothing about this feels simple or easy to understand.

Chace called the night before last and offered to fly out to California, but I told him I would be fine with just my family and not to jeopardize his new gig. Part of me hoped he wouldn't listen to me, but in reality, I'm too numb to care one way or another right now.

"And now we'd like to invite Howard's son, John, to speak about his father," says the minister.

My brother stands up from his chair and squeezes my hand before he heads to the front. He is calm and focused - my brother, the college professor. He has no problem speaking in groups just like me, but he's far less emotional, which is why we asked him to do the eulogy.

"My father, Howard, was the best men I've ever known," he says. "He taught me how to be the man I am today, and for that I will be eternally grateful. When I was a little boy, he taught me basic life skills like how to ride a bike and how to throw a ball. When I was a teenager, he taught me how to drive a stick shift and how to talk to girls."

The group gives a tender laugh, and I smile, wiping my own tears away, proud of my big brother.

"When I proposed to my wife, he told me I'd better not screw it up," he continues. "And it was just a few weeks ago when I told him how badly I wanted to become a father myself that he gave me his final words of wisdom.

He said, 'Son, none of us knows what the hell we're doing when it comes to having kids. Just love them, listen to them and protect them as best as you can.' Throughout his entire life, I believe that my dad did all of those things for us. He loved us with all his heart. He listened to us no matter what we had to say, and he protected us. Not just from physical harm, but from the hard parts of life that can leave a person bitter. He was the eternal optimist and he always made sure we saw the silver lining in everything. He was there for every one of my baseball games and every one of Audrey's recitals and plays. He'd stand in the back row and shout, 'Bravo!' after every single performance. He was just always there…And I believe he is still with us and that he will be there with my beautiful wife and me when we have our own kids…" He trails off suddenly, overcome by emotion. He takes a deep breath before he continues. "I believe he's watching over my amazingly talented sister as she fights the good fight in New York, pursuing her dreams, and I believe at all other times, he's with my incredible mother, just basking in her beauty and kind spirit. We love you dad, we miss you so much and we hope wherever you are that you are at peace."

As John finishes the eulogy, I squeeze my mother's hand tightly. I glance over at her and see a single tear toll down her cheek.

John walks over to her and kisses that same cheek before sitting down. As the minister finishes the final prayers, I find myself distracted, looking around the crowd of people that are here to support us. My grandparents on my mom's side, my cousins and their families, Logan and his mom in the back row, and countless other friends and members of the community. A few of my other Los Angeles friends have even made the trek out to say goodbye to my dad. As I scan the crowd, I notice a figure standing behind everyone else next to a tree, his face partially hidden in shadow. When I look closer, I realize that I recognize that face. How could I ever mistake those glasses?

Once the service is over, I kiss my mother on the cheek and hug Logan and my brother and sister-in-law before walking toward the tree.

I don't know what it is about Jake, but he knows exactly what I'm feeling before I utter a word. The minute his eyes meet mine, he gives me a weak smile and I feel my eyes well up with tears. The grief of losing my father is paramount, but underneath that is the ache I've been suppressing these past few months that Jake and I have been apart. As he wraps his arms around me, I realize how much I've missed him and the tears flow freely.

"I'm so sorry, kid," he says.

He holds me for a few minutes and lets me cry into his shirt. When I finally regain my composure, he lets me go.

"How did you know? How did you know where to go?" I stammer, wiping my eyes.

"Logan told me," he says. "I felt like I should be here. I only knew Howard for a short time, but he was a really great man and I wanted to pay my respects...and I wanted to be here to support you."

"Thank you." I smile weakly. "Do I look like a mess?"

"No, you look fine," he says. "Where's Chace? I didn't see him."

"He's in the Bahamas on a cruise gig," I say. "I told him not to worry about flying out; it would have jeopardized the job."

"That makes sense," he says.

"Are you coming to the house? Are you going to stay?" I ask. "Our family's favorite Thai place is catering. You'll finally get to try some of my favorite curry."

"I wouldn't miss it," he says tenderly. "And honestly, I sort of just packed a bag and went to the airport, didn't exactly make hotel reservations."

"You can sleep in the guest room." I laugh, wiping my eyes. "My mom will be so happy to see you."

At the house, we are flooded with a huge outpouring of support. Neighbors and friends come over, bringing food and sweets. My mother spends time surrounded by my aunts and grandparents and I begin to see a bit more color in her face.

I see friends from high school, old teachers in the community who knew my father. John's Little League baseball coach, my 9th grade drama teacher. The community has really rallied around us.

"Howard was such a great man," says one neighbor.

"Oh, thank you," I say.

"Such a tragic loss to the community," says another.

"It was all very sudden," I say.

"How are you holding up?" asks one.

"Oh, just fine," I say. "Getting through."

"Audrey, we need you out back," says Logan coming to my rescue with a glass of wine in hand, Jake at his side.

"Nice talking to you," I murmur, walking away. "Thank you for coming."

Jake, Logan and I walk out into the backyard and sit on the lounge chairs near the pool. The afternoon is warm and breezy – a typical late February afternoon in good ole Pasadena. The sun comes down and warms my bare feet as I lie back and just take a moment to breathe.

"Hard to beat this weather," says Jake. "Nice to have a break from the icy temps."

"I don't know if I can go back to New York," I say.

"Really?" says Jake. "It'll be spring in a few weeks."

"No, I mean, how can I leave my mom? John and Sophie are going to go back to Palo Alto in a couple days, and then she'll be all alone."

"What about your family?" asks Jake.

"They all live in Orange County and Riverside…"

"That's over an hour from here," says Logan, translating for Jake.

"Audrey, I don't mean to be indelicate in any way," says Jake. "But don't you think your dad would want you to keep pushing in New York? He was so proud of everything you had already accomplished at Christmas. I just think he wouldn't want you to give up now."

"But it's my mom, Jake," I say. "He's all she had in the world. They were it for each other."

"Holly, I agree with Jake," says Logan. "Linda will be alright. She's tough."

"I just wish she had something to focus on," I say. "She's retired; she stopped counseling years ago."

"Well, maybe she can volunteer or we can find a nice art class, or book club?" says Logan. "Hobbies are good."

"Maybe photography." Jake smiles. "She took a great photo of us at Christmas."

"Something," I say. "She needs something…"

Later that evening, after Logan and all of the relatives and guests have gone home, Jake, John, my mom and I sit in the living room drinking some of my dad's favorite wine and reminiscing about him. Jake sits beside my mom on the sofa. I'm curled up in my dad's favorite chair under a blanket and John sits on the floor leaning against the other sofa. Sophie has already gone to bed.

There's a warm fire crackling in the fireplace that casts a warm light around us. Everything feels surreal: the day, the light, the fact that we were all in New York together only two months before, and now here we are in California, one Princeton short.

"Remember when we were kids and we went to the lake?" John says. "And he wouldn't brush his hair that whole week?"

"Oh my God!" I laugh. "Yes! He'd just stick his head out the window of the car while we drove around letting the wind style his hair!"

"He called it his Mountain-Do!" John laughs.

"The man could use a pun," says Jake, laughing as well.

"When the kids were small," my mom speaks up, trying to stifle her own giggles. "Howard used to use this fake language. He invented it or something and it sounded like the Swedish Chef from The Muppets, you know the one?"

"I do!" Jake laughs. "Like, scern-da-lern-dee-flern-dee-lern, or something?"

"That's it!" John says with a guffaw.

"Except he'd sing to us in that language," my mom giggles. "Oh, Audrey's favorite was when he'd sing 'Maria' from *West Side Story* in that voice. But he called it something else. What was it, Audrey?"

"Sca-lerf-kef," I manage to get it out in between fits of laughter.

"Get out!" says Jake, chuckling.

"God, I forgot about that! It was sheer brilliance!" I say. "It was the best; our sides would hurt we'd laugh so hard."

We're all laughing and smiling and shedding a few select tears now, but mostly just enjoying being together and remembering the good times. There are so many memories to cherish.

"Mom," I say. "Maybe I should stay out here for a while until you get settled."

"Not happening, dear," she says.

"I can still run the company from L.A. and have the girls take the parties," I protest. "Plus, Chace is away on this gig. We could sublet our place."

"I don't want to hear such talk," she says. "Your father would want you to stay in New York and that's what I want too."

"But mom, you're here by yourself and I'm worried about you."

"Audrey, she's gonna be fine," says John. "Sophie and I will come down more with the school year winding down soon."

"Are you sure?" I ask her.

"Yes, love," she says. "Jake, you hear that?"

"I do," says Jake.

"You make sure you take our girl back to New York with you, even if you have to drag her onto that plane kicking and screaming."

"Yes, ma'am" he says giving her a squeeze.

"Well, I'm off to bed kids," says my mom.

"Yeah, I should go up too," says John.

"Audrey, you'll show Jake his room, right?"

"Yeah, no problem," I say.

As my mom and John head upstairs, Jake and I walk to the entry hall to grab his bags from the closet. We make our way up the stairs so I can show him to his room.

"Thank you for being here," I say, giving him a big hug.

"Of course," he says. He walks into his room and I walk across the hall into mine.

"Hey, here we are again," I say. "Right across the hall."

He smiles. "Sweet dreams, kid."

As I lie awake that night in my childhood bed, in my childhood room, my mind is flooded with thoughts. I'm thinking about my dad and worrying about my mom. I'm wondering about my future in New York, how I can make it worth it to go back there instead of staying with my mom. How I can prove to myself that it's where I need to be.

Totally restless, I look at my phone and it's after midnight. I debate it for a few minutes before I text Jake in the next room.

Can't sleep.
Still awake?

I stare at the screen on my phone, waiting to see if he'll reply, but nothing pops up. *He must be asleep.* I wait another minute before I resign myself to the fact that I should attempt to sleep. I'm molding my pillow into a comfortable shape when I hear a faint knock on my door.

"Come in," I call softly.

"Hey, kid," Jake says as he walks in the door. "Got your text. You alright?"

"Kind of..." I say. "Will you sit with me?"

"Sure," he says. He walks over to my bed and climbs in, leaning back on a pillow.

"Jake, I know this is a lot to ask, especially given what happened and stuff, but do you think you could just stay with me tonight?"

"If you want me to," he says.

"I'm not trying to seduce you or anything," I say. "I just don't want to be alone right now."

"I understand, kid."

"Maybe let's just not mention this to Chace," I say.

"Of course," he says.

"Thanks."

"Audrey… look, I know we haven't really had a chance to talk about it," he says. "But I want you to know that I'm sorry about not returning any of your calls or emails. I just needed some time."

"No, I get it," I say. "It's totally fine. I was acting crazy."

"Maybe a little," he teases.

"I just hate when things are bad and I can't fix it," I say. "I really need to be better about just letting things go and letting time work them out."

"Well, you do have a talent for writing long, poetic emails," he razzes me. "It was kind of like reading our own version of the Odyssey."

"Oh, well gee thanks," I say with a laugh. "I'll work on it, I promise."

"It's alright, kid. I behaved kind of selfishly. But I was really mad at you for what happened, and frankly I was mad at myself too. I just didn't know what to say to you. I tried to write you a response a dozen times, but the only thing I kept thinking was that I was mad at you and also that I missed you and those two conflicting emotions were sort of hard to deal with."

"I understand," I say.

"But Audrey, I want you to be happy," he says. "And if Chace is your guy, then Chace is your guy. And he's not a bad guy. I may have, you know, judged him unfairly because of my own feelings so… as long as you're happy, I'm happy."

"Thanks, Jake," I say. "But I wouldn't exactly categorize what I'm feeling right now as happy. This whole day has been so surreal… I can't believe my dad is gone."

"I know," he says, leaning over and giving me a kiss on top of the head. "I know it's hard, kid… but there's really nothing we can do right now other than make sure you're well-rested. It's much easier to deal with this kind of stuff if you're not exhausted."

"Will you hold me?" I ask timidly.

"Sure, come here." I feel his arms wrap around me and try to relax into his embrace.

"I'm so wired. I'm not sure I'll be able to sleep," I complain.

"What's your favorite color?" he asks.

"Why?"

"When I was a kid, my mom taught me this trick to help me fall asleep," he says.

"Yeah?" I snuggle against his chest, feeling it rise and fall as he talks.

"Yeah, she'd have me pick a color and then I'd think of everything I could that was that color. So if you pick red, you can think about like, cranberries, or a can of Coke, or a fire engine, Twizzlers...that Ferrari from *Ferris Bueller*, strawberries... those red velvet cupcakes from Amy's we like... or my personal favorite, Jessica Rabbit's dress. That sort of thing."

"Jake... you're silly," I mumble, feeling my eyelids grow heavy.

"So, what color do you want to pick?" he asks.

But I can't respond because I'm already drifting comfortably off to sleep, listening to the sound of Jake's heartbeat.

The next morning, I wake up in my bed alone. I grab my glasses and my phone and see that it's after ten o'clock. I wander downstairs in my pajamas, following the intoxicating smell of bacon cooking.

When I walk into the kitchen, Jake is helping John and my mom with brunch. There is a spread of bagels and all the fixings, as well as a huge bowl of berries on the kitchen island. John is mixing mimosas, Jake stands at the stove cooking bacon and eggs, and my mother stands at the waffle iron ladling on the mixture before closing the lid.

"Morning, kiddo," says Jake. "Sleep well?"

"Yeah, I did. Thanks," I say. "Wow, Jake, had no idea you'd

become such a gourmet."

"He's quite impressive at breakfast," says John.

"I can see that," I say. "Hey, why are we cooking when we have so much food from the neighbors?"

"Because Jake and I wanted to cook brunch," says my mom. "I had a craving for bagels and smoked salmon."

"Hard to argue with that," says Jake.

"John, where's Soph?" I ask.

"She's still upstairs, I think?" says John.

"Maybe she's still asleep," says my mom. "She went to bed early last night, said she wasn't feeling well."

"Soph, come down and join us!" shouts John. "There's bacon!"

"John, you doofus, mom just said Sophie isn't feeling well!" I peg him with a blueberry. "Where's your brain?"

"Audrey, I know my wife. No way she's still sleeping," he says, throwing another berry back at me. "She wakes up at six-thirty every morning on the dot."

"Sophie, love, are you alright up there?" calls my mother.

"I'll be right down," Sophie calls back.

"See, she's up," says John.

After a minute or so, Sophie appears in the doorway to the kitchen, still in her robe with an odd expression on her face.

"What's the matter, honey?" asks John. "Brunch is on! Do you want a mimosa?"

"No... I don't," she says tentatively.

"But you love brunch!" he says. "How could you not want a mimosa?"

Sophie doesn't respond; she just stands there.

"Sophie?" says my mother.

"Are you okay?" I ask.

"Oh my God," John says. "Honey...are you?"

My mom and I gasp, our hands clapped to our mouths.

"What's going on?" asks Jake.

Sophie's face breaks into a smile and she responds by reaching into her robe pocket and then holding up a pink stick with a tiny cross, imprinted in blue on the end of it.

The entire kitchen erupts into screams, followed by joyous laughter.

"We're pregnant!" says John, aghast, tears starting to flow down his cheeks. "We're pregnant! Oh Soph!"

John takes Sophie into his arms and they both hold each other as they cry. Mom and I are jumping up and down hugging and Jake comes over and puts his arms around us.

"Congratulations, you guys!" says Jake.

"A baby! Oh my goodness, a baby!" shouts my mom, looking alive for the first time this week.

"Finally!" I shout gleefully.

It's in this moment that I realize that this is exactly what I had been hoping for. A baby will be the perfect way to give my mom a purpose and something to look forward to, something to focus on. She can knit baby clothes and turn one of the upstairs bedrooms into a nursery. She'll scrapbook, she'll plan a baby shower, and she will be alright.

Well played, Dad. I smile glancing upward. John and Sophie break their embrace to come over and join in our group hug. We are all laughing and crying and holding each other close, celebrating the newest incoming member of the Princeton family.

Part IV: Spring

"She sat down on a stool, pulled her foot out of the heavy wooden shoe, and put it into the slipper, and it fitted her perfectly. When she stood up, the prince looked into her face, and he recognized the beautiful girl who had danced with him. He cried out, "She is my true love!"

- Cinderella
by the Brothers Grimm

TWENTY-TWO

It's finally spring! And it's true what they say: when you suffer through a long winter, there is no better feeling then shedding those layers and soaking up some buttery sunshine. As Logan and I enjoy a lazy Saturday strolling through the park, we find ourselves in a sea of pink. The cherry trees and Japanese magnolia trees are in full bloom. It's so unbelievably beautiful!

"I dunno," I say to Logan, as we walk along the path. "I don't want a big party. I go to birthday parties all the time!"

"But, Holly, it's your twenty-fifth! Quarter century! This is a big deal," he says.

"I know you already have something in mind," I say. "So, I might as well just ask."

"I do," he says. "Just something simple. A dinner at my apartment with the boys and the princess ladies and a few guys that I'm juggling."

"I'm listening," I say. "And you're such a whore."

"I'm thinking tapas style, small plates. So that way we can either sit down or stand around. Whatever you think would be the most fun, depending on the mood."

"Alright, fine," I say. "But nothing else, alright?"

"You've got it," he says. "No surprises, just a small gathering."

Two days later, it's my twenty-fifth birthday. My mother calls first thing in the morning to tell me the story of my birth, which she does every year. Chace rolls over and covers his head with a pillow as I lay there, listening to her story and rubbing my eyes.

"I remember the doctor telling me that it was going to take hours and I just said, 'No, that's not happening!' and I started visualizing my body making way for you…"

"Mom, seriously! You do this every year!" I say. "Why must every new year of my life begin with me having to think about your cervix?"

"Alright, fine," she says in a huff. "What else do you have going on today?"

"Logan is throwing me a little dinner party at his place with a few friends, nothing crazy."

"Sounds nice, dear," she says.

"How is the baby prep going?" I ask.

"Oh so far we're just looking at remodeling the office upstairs and turning it into a nursery so that John and Sophie can visit more often and be comfortable."

"That's great!" I say. "Do they know the sex of the baby yet?"

"They haven't decided yet if they want to know or keep it a surprise, so they've had the doctor write it down and put it in an envelope," she says.

"That's exciting!" I say. "Can't believe I'm going to be an aunt."

"I know, and me a grandma! Your dad is so proud of us all," she says tenderly.

"How are you doing with that?" I ask.

"I'm fine, sweetie. Your father and I talk every morning during my meditation."

"Oh...okay, good," I say.

"Alright, love, I won't keep you. Have a wonderful day! Check the mail when you have some time today. Your gift should have arrived."

"Thanks, mom! I love you."

I hang up the phone and roll over to cuddle with Chace, kissing his shoulder.

"Happy Birthday," he says sleepily, wrapping his arms around me. "Wanna sleep a little longer and then I'll make you breakfast?"

"Sounds good," I say.

"Hey, I've got a band practice this afternoon before we go to Logan's," he says, yawning. "Will you be okay hanging solo for a few hours?"

"Sure," I say, resting into his embrace.

After my birthday pancakes and eggs, I decide to spend the afternoon reading in the park near the Christopher Street Pier. It's sunny and warm and everyone is out enjoying the beautiful weather.

I never realized how much I took warm weather for granted growing up in Southern California. We would have a few chilly days here and there, but never five solid months of layers and hats and gloves and scarves. It all feels very glamorous when the weather starts to turn in the fall, but now that we're on the other side of winter, I cannot wait to banish all my coats and winter boots to the back of my closet!

As I lay on my blanket listening to music and feeling the sun warm my skin, I think about everything that has happened in the last few months, all the things that have been challenging and all that I am grateful for. Ever since my dad's passing I've been determined to make something of myself here. I've gone to every casting call I've found, even when I know I'm going to get typed out. I've had a few good auditions, but no callbacks. I've volunteered to act in student films at NYU and NYFA, which has been a great way for me to get some footage for my reel. I don't know why, but I have this feeling that the next year of my life is going to be a big one.

I return home in the later part of the afternoon, but the sun is still glowing bright in the sky. It's such a relief to have longer, warmer days again. I feel infinitely more relaxed than I did a couple months ago in the cold. The city feels alive again, and with it, I feel a renewed sense of vigor.

Chace arrives home shortly after me and the two of us shower and get ready for my birthday dinner at Logan's. It's strange to be heading to a birthday party that is for me. I've been to so many these past few months; I've become a bit desensitized to them. I guess the bloom is off the rose when it comes to blowing out candles on a cake.

Logan has kept his word and has restrained himself in regards to my party. When we walk in, we hear nice Spanish guitar music playing in the background, and the apartment is decorated simply with a few floral arrangements and some delicious looking tapas arranged on the table next to a small stack of wrapped gifts.

Chace and I are the last ones to arrive. We greet everyone and meet a few new faces. Em has brought a new guy she's dating, Kay has a 'friend' by her side that she recently met, and Logan has three 'friends' of his own circulating the room as well. Once we've greeted everyone, Logan brings us each a glass of champagne to kick off the evening.

"Alright everyone," says Logan, raising a champagne flute. "A toast to the birthday girl!"

"Here, here!" Jake chimes in. "Happy birthday, kid!"

"Thank you guys," I say. "This is just lovely."

"We're glad you were born," says Chace, giving me a squeeze.

"Hey." Jake is looking at his phone. "I just got an email saying there's some kind of crazy harvest moon tonight."

"Really?" says Logan. "Let's go up on the roof and check it

out."

"The roof?" I'm taken aback. "I didn't even know your building had roof access."

"Of course it does," says Logan.

"And since when are you interested in the moon?" I say.

"I'm not, but Jake seems excited about it and he's so lonely and single. I'm trying to be a good host, Holly!" he says. "Does anyone else object to taking a quick peak at the moon on the roof? For Jake?"

"I'd like to see it," says Em.

"Me too," says Chace.

"I mean sure, why not?" Kay replies.

"Yay!" says Logan. "We're going, Holly."

"Alright, alright" I concede.

"Bring your drinks, everyone," says Logan.

We walk out of the apartment and into the stairwell, climbing the four flights of stairs to get to the roof. Everyone is slightly winded, but no one complains. There's something strange about the way New Yorkers always act as if climbing tons of stairs in a walk-up is as easy as standing in line at Starbucks.

Logan opens the door to the roof and I step over the threshold and gasp.

"Oh my God," I mumble.

"Surprise!" shouts the group.

The entire space has been converted into a fairyland. There are twinkle lights everywhere. Balloon clusters are tied up along the length of the railing and there are three small tables covered with white linens, loose crystal gems and vases of pink roses on each one.

"It's your very own princess party!" says Logan gleefully.

"Logan…" I'm on the verge of tears.

"I called in a few favors," he says. "And Jake, Chace and the girls helped a lot too."

On one side of the roof is a guy dressed as a jester making balloon animals. Next to him sits a lovely girl dressed as a princess who is set up to do airbrush tattoos.

On the other side of the roof, there is a spot reserved for dancing and a bar, manned by a very handsome prince. Next to him, a small buffet table is covered in all kinds of food and a huge pink cake. Beside the balloon animal man is a backdrop and camera set up for a photo booth, and next to it sits a rack of costumes. Crowns, feather boas, gloves, swords, giant glasses, velvet petticoats, and suits of armor.

"Did you know about this?" I ask Chace.

"Of course," he says, putting his arm around my waist. "I was here all afternoon, setting up."

"You were?" I ask.

"You didn't think I'd actually schedule a band practice on your birthday, did you?" he asks.

"He and Jake carried all the heavy things up here," says Logan. "They were quite impressive."

I take another moment to soak in the sight before making the rounds and distributing hugs to my wonderful friends.

"How did you guys afford all of this?" I'm flabbergasted, knowing full and well how much parties like this costs.

"I worked out a few affiliate deals for us," says Kay. "This is their audition."

"Brilliant." I'm impressed.

"Kevin, the bartender, is a friend," says Jake. "And obviously I'll be running the photo booth."

"And Leo, the DJ, is a friend of a friend," says Chace. "We wanted you to have a special night, babe. You only turn twenty-five once."

"I haven't liked my birthday this much since I was a kid!" I exclaim.

"Except now you can drink while you get your face painted!" says Kay.

The rest of the evening is perfect. Logan has requested that Kevin create a couple signature cocktails for me. Pretty Princess reminds me of a Cosmo, but it has pomegranate juice, basil, and citrus. The Old Royal is also yummy. Jake says it reminds him of an Old Fashioned.

Everyone is having a fantastic time. We all take turns at the photo booth, snapping shots in ridiculous outfits. Logan's food is divine as always, and after we eat, we put the costumes back on and the entertainers join us on the dance floor. I'm pleased to see Jake and the princess tattoo artist chatting a bit. It might be slightly unprofessional of her, but I'm so glad to see Jake smiling that I decide to let it slide.

The night ends with Chace, Jake, Logan and I sitting on the dance floor, barefooted and picking at the giant pink cake with just forks. Everyone else has gone home, including Logan's three guests, who it turns out were more interested in sleeping with each other than him.

"I'm too tired to get up to get plates," says Logan. "But I want you all to know that this behavior is disgusting and completely beneath you."

"Thank you for this night, you guys." I take another bite of the delicious red velvet cake. "Twenty-five is off to a good start."

As the sky begins to turn pink in the East, the four of us make our way back down to Logan's apartment where we gather the rest of our belongings. Logan kisses me on the cheek and walks right into his bedroom, closing the door.

"I need to hit the bathroom," says Chace, walking out of the room.

"Hey, kid, before you go," says Jake, approaching me. "I wanted you to have this."

He hands me a rectangle wrapped in pink paper and tied up with a yellow ribbon.

"Aw, Jake, thank you," I say.

I unwrap the paper and reveal a wooden frame that looks distressed and worn down, almost like driftwood. In the middle of the frame sits a black and white photo of my whole family from Christmas Eve. All of us gathered around the tree looking happy and complete.

"Turned out pretty nicely, I think," he says. "Happy birthday, kid."

"Jake…" My voice is caught in my throat. I feel the smooth

wooden frame in my hands. "I don't know what to say…"

"Well, that's probably the best reaction I could hope for," he replies softly.

"Thank you so much." I'm still dumbfounded. "You have no idea what this means to me."

"You're welcome, kid."

"No really, this is the perfect gift. Really, Jake, it's a treasure. I love it."

"I'm so glad."

"Audrey, are you ready to go?" Chace walks out of the bathroom.

"Yes, ready for bed more like," I say.

"Jake, do you want to share a cab with us?" asks Chace.

"Nah, you two go ahead. I think I'm gonna crash here for a bit and then help Logan clean up."

"Thank you again for the party." I give Jake a big hug and kiss him on the cheek. "And echo that to Logan."

Chace and I walk downstairs into the soft, rose-colored light of the morning, where we hail a cab to take us home.

TWENTY-THREE

$\mathcal{S}$pring is by far the most romantic season. It might be the fragrances in the air, or the warmth of the sun. It could even be the increase in skin exposure as we trade in our jeans for shorts. But whatever the reason, it's the best time of year to be in love.

Nothing makes this more apparent to me than a lazy Sunday afternoon, when I receive a surprise phone call from someone I haven't heard from in over a year. My oldest childhood friend, Allie has just gotten engaged, and she wants me to be a bridesmaid in her wedding.

"I know it's a lot to ask you to fly to Texas for a wedding," she says. "But all of Greg's family is here and my relatives are in Louisiana, so as much as I'd love to do it in California, it just seems logical to keep it local."

"Allie, you were born in Texas and you're back there now," I say. "It makes total sense. And of course, I'll fly wherever you need me to. I cannot believe you're getting married!"

"I know!" she says. "And I'm so glad you'll be in the wedding. I know we've lost touch a bit over the years, but you were my first best friend and I want you to be a part of it!"

"Of course," I say, touched.

"I want to make sure that the bridesmaid dresses are inexpensive and something cute. I know you'll never wear it again, that's the biggest crock of crap, but I want y'all to be comfortable in them on the day of."

"We have some time to figure all of that out," I say.

"Can I send you some wedding blogs with ideas for flowers and colors?" she asks. "I want your opinion, Audrey, you have such nice taste."

"Oh...well... thanks," I say, surprised. "Sure! Send away!"

"Great! Well, I'm so glad you said yes to being a bridesmaid," she says. "I'll send you more info soon!"

I hang up the phone, and without thinking, peer down at my unadorned left hand. I've never really thought about marriage seriously. I've always thought it was a ways away...but now, with Chace and I living together and me being twenty-five, I wonder if maybe I might be approaching that period in life where it's time to start hoping for more.

"Who was that on the phone?" says Chace as he walks into the living room.

"My friend Allie," I reply. "We went to grade school together, but then she moved back to Texas before high school."

"Oh, how nice." He's gathering some sheet music together on his desk.

"She just got engaged..."

"Wow, good for her!" he says. "Texas weddings are a hoot!"

"Yeah, she asked me to be a bridesmaid," I say. "My first time."

"That's great, babe," he says. "You better be careful or you might steal the show with your beauty."

"Have you ever been in a wedding?" I ask.

"Sure," he says. "But I grew up in the Midwest, a lot of my

friends are already married."

"You ever think about it?" I ask tentatively.

"About the weddings I've been in?"

"No," I say. "About… you know… getting married."

"Oh," he says. "No, not yet. I'm not even sure I want to get married at all. Maybe in my mid-thirties. If the situation is right."

"I see…"

"Why?" he says. "Is this making you think about it?"

Yes. "Well, no…" I say. "Not exactly. I've never really thought about it before. I don't know anyone near my age that's married except for my brother…I just…I dunno, I love you and we live together…I mean, in a lot of ways we do the same things day to day that married people do."

"Audrey…" He pulls out his desk chair and sits down. "We agreed when we moved in together that this was more along the lines of a casual living situation."

"What's a casual living situation?" I ask.

"You said that we were spending the night together every night anyway and now we're just pitching in on dish soap and toilet paper."

"We still live under the same roof and share bills," I say. "That's all I'm saying; we are sharing expenses. I'm simply drawing a comparison."

"What are you really saying?" he asks. "Are you telling me you want to talk about marriage in a more than hypothetical way? Because I thought I made it clear at Christmas that I'm just not ready for that yet."

"You did," I say. "You made it clear. I'm not challenging your readiness. I was just asking if you'd ever thought about it. If you've ever thought about us having a future together. That's all I'm asking."

"Baby, no," he says. "I don't think about it. I'm thinking right now about the fact that I have an audition tomorrow for a national tour, and that it pays well, and that it would be huge to add to my resume. That's all I'm thinking about right now."

"Alright," I say.

"Don't be upset."

"I'm not upset," I say, getting up. "But I am late to meet Kay for lunch, so I need to go."

"Audrey, c'mon."

"I'm fine, Chace. Just need to head out…I'll see you later."

I'm not running late to meet Kay. I'm not meeting Kay at all. I just wanted to get out of the apartment and get some air. As I walk west on 23rd Street, I feel tears threatening to escape. I'm so embarrassed that I said anything to Chace. I knew what his response would be. I should have just kept the whole thing to myself.

But honestly, how has he not thought once about the possibility of us having a future? Don't you always hear couples saying, "When you know, you know."

How can he not know now, after we've been dating nearly six months and we live together? I knew I loved him within the first month we were together! And wasn't he the one who, after we moved in together, said that he couldn't imagine his life without me? And wanted to do whatever it took to keep me? Aren't we happy? Why would acknowledging the fact that we're going down the same path change that? Why is that scary?

When I get to 10th Avenue, I walk up the staircase next to Chelsea Market and ascend onto the High-Line. As I walk along the wooden path, and garden that now adorns the old elevated train tracks, I see families with children looking happy all around me. Is there anything wrong with acknowledging within your heart that you want a family some day?

I sit on the grass in the sunlight and take a few deep breaths, trying to clear my head.

Spring is the most romantic season in New York City, unless of course your live-in boyfriend tells you he doesn't want to get married for ten years and that he's never thought about you as that bride.

I take out my phone and text my brother.

How long after you started
dating Sophie did you know
she was the one?

After a minute he texts back.

Our fifth date.

I text him.

How did you know for sure?

He replies.

I just knew. Why?
You and Chace gettin' hitched?

I text back immediately.

Not any time soon.

He replies.

Well if it doesn't work out
between u 2, my vote is for Jake.
Guy knows how to make a mean
bacon and egg scramble ;)

After a couple hours of wandering around the High-Line, I head into Chelsea Market to get a sandwich from Amy's Bread and then start my walk home.

When I arrive back at the apartment, Chace is gone. Probably working on his audition material with his vocal coach.

I take Baxter for a quick walk then come back inside, kick off my shoes and walk into the kitchen to heat up my Panini in the toaster oven.

Sitting down on the couch, I flip on the TV and spend a few mindless hours watching Food Network with Baxter on my lap. Then I get up, take a shower and stand under the hot water until it runs out. Afterwards, I wrap myself in a towel and stand in front of the mirror, combing out my hair.

Chace and I have worked so hard to maintain our relationship, even thinking about ending it with him makes me feel nauseous, and all over one stupid fight? I know I'm being ridiculous to stress over this. It seems silly when we've been so solid. Our day-to-day routine has been such a comfort. I get up first, and turn on the coffee maker. Then he gets up and makes breakfast while I'm in the shower. We eat together and then go about our days. In the evening, we meet back up at home, fix dinner, open some wine and watch *The Daily Show*. I love our life together. Why would I want to mess with that, when we've been so happy?

Maybe I don't need someone who feels confident that I'm the one. Maybe no one ever really knows? Maybe I don't need to get married. I might be one of those girls who is missing the bride gene. Maybe we could just go on forever like we are now, focusing on our careers and spending time with our friends and Baxter. Maybe I don't need to be someone's wife or have any children.

At that very moment, as if to spite me, an email pings through on my phone. It's from Allie.

As I scroll through the pictures of bridal bouquets, my heart starts to ache. Of course I want to get married. My parents were married for thirty-five years and they were so happy. My brother and his wife have always had a wonderful relationship, and now they have a baby on the way. Even Chace's parents are still married and seem to be content, from what I've heard.

As I walk out of the bathroom wrapped in my robe, I feel a horrible sense of dread. *This isn't going to work long term*, I think to myself.

But when I walk into the bedroom, I spot something I hadn't seen before. There's a vase of red roses on my nightstand and a note that reads.

Let's just wait and see what happens.
I love you.
-C

By the time Chace gets home, it's after ten and I'm already in bed reading. I hear the apartment door close and Baxter runs out of the bedroom to greet him. I hear Chace walk into the kitchen, open the fridge and pour himself a glass of water.

"Hi," I say as he walks into our bedroom.

He doesn't say anything. He just takes off his shirt and climbs onto the bed. Before I can utter another sound, he takes my book out of my hands and sets it on the bedside table. Climbing under the covers, he takes me firmly into his arms and we make love.

TWENTY-FOUR

It was on a beautiful Sunday morning that we got the call. Chace and I sat at our favorite brunch spot on 9th Avenue, sipping coffee and munching on bacon when his agent's name flashed across his cell.

How do you tell your boyfriend that while you completely support his career aspirations and dreams, his good news is your own personal nightmare? A nine-month tour? Nine months apart?

I've always known that this was a possibility given our chosen career paths. I guess I just hoped that we'd have a bit more time to feel firm in our commitment to one another before one of us got shipped off on that long of a gig. I know I should've been happier for him. I am happy for him, but I'm also devastated at the same time. As irrational as I know my feelings are, I can't help but feel them.

It all happened so fast. He got the call, we paid our brunch tab, and the next day he was in costume fittings. The day after that, they sent him a contract and salary offer. And then, they sent him a plane ticket to Chicago for rehearsals. Within the span of four days, I went from having brunch at a charming sidewalk café with my live-in boyfriend, to helping him pack two suitcases so he could leave our home for almost a year.

And now a month later, I am sitting by the computer waiting for him to log on so we can see each other and talk.

I glance at my watch and see that it's one-forty and Chace hasn't even signed on yet for our one-thirty Skype date. He is always running perpetually late, so I should have expected this, but I'm frustrated because now we'll only have twenty minutes to talk before I need to leave for a party uptown.

I walk into the kitchen and pour myself a glass of water and grab an apple to munch on while I wait. As I walk back to my desk, I hear the computer ping with the Skype ringtone.

I'm slightly annoyed, but glad to be hearing from him as I click the button and his face pops up on the screen.

"Hey there," he says.

"Hi babe," I reply. "How are things in the Windy City?"

"Awesome," he says. "The weather out here is so nice right now and the show is going really great!"

"That's good," I say. "I'm so happy for you."

"Thanks baby doll."

"It's so weird having you gone." I sigh. "I still can't get used to it. I woke up this morning expecting you to be in bed with me and then I got kind of sad that you weren't."

"Aww, babe."

"This all happened so fast. It doesn't even feel like it's real."

"I know," he says. "Exciting though, isn't it?"

"I guess. It's just, if I had known last month that you were going to be leaving so quickly, I would have taken some time off to spend with you."

"Oh, babe, don't worry about it," he says. "I'm doing great here and I'll see you soon."

"When *will* I see you?" I ask.

"Well, we have a short break between rehearsals and opening," he says. "If you want to come to Chicago for a weekend next month, we can figure something out."

"Next month…"

"Yeah," he says. "I'm just totally swamped until we finish up our rehearsals."

"I haven't seen you in a month already," I pout.

"It'll go by fast, don't worry."

"How often do you think I'll see you once you're on tour?" I ask. "Will you have any time off?"

"I'm not sure, but if we're close to New York, you can fly out and visit."

"I just…"

"Audrey, please don't be upset. This show is huge for me. It's a big break."

"I know, and I'm so happy for you," I say. "But I'm just not sure you realize how long nine months is. It's going to be a lot of effort to keep things together."

"Well, we've done the distance thing before," he says.

"Yeah, when you were in Florida and the Caribbean," I say. "For three weeks at a time."

"What are you saying, baby?" He sounds a bit agitated.

"You know I'm happy for you, but the burden is going to fall on me a lot to come to you," I say. "And it's going to be taxing flying around all the time, and finding a dog sitter for Baxter, and trying to get time off from my day job and running my company remotely. I think I just need to know that it's going to be worth it."

"Why would you even say that? Of course it will be," he says. "You know when you come to visit I will do everything I can to make it worth your while. Nice dinners, romantic evening walks, city tours, you name it!"

"You're not getting what I'm saying…"

"Is this about your friend who got engaged again?" he asks.

"No, it's not," I say. "Well, maybe a little."

"Baby, I thought we were past this! I thought we were going to wait and see what would happen."

"Chace, I don't want to get married any time soon, I'm only twenty-five and I'm not looking for that right away, but if I'm going to be putting the money and effort forth to stay with you, I need to know that we're on the same path… that we want the same things…"

"You know we want the same things," he says. "We work in the same field, we both love New York."

"That we want the same things in life, I mean…long term," I say.

"Audrey—"

"Look, I'm not asking you to be sure, but I am asking for you to tell me that when you think about what you want down the line, you see me, that you see us…. that we could maybe plan a vacation for next summer and both be confident that that trip is going to happen."

"I don't know what I want," he says, resignation in his voice. "I'm not ready to promise you anything."

I feel my heart drop at his words. It's a minute or two before I can speak. "I know," I say, understanding, for the first time, exactly what those words really mean. Especially now, with so many miles in between us. As much as we've been fighting the inevitable, sometimes loving someone just isn't enough and logistics become important.

"Audrey, I'm so sorry," he says looking somber. "I hate that we're talking about this on Skype."

"It's alright," I say. "It is what it is."

"I love you so much," he says, his voice catching slightly. "But I'm still figuring myself out. I'm still blazing this trail and I think you need something more than what I can offer. You deserve something solid. I feel like a dick that I can't give that to you, but I just can't…"

"So, this is it," I say, taking a deep breath.

"I'm so sorry, Audrey, I am," he says. "If you want we could just take some time apart and see if that helps."

"I don't think so, Chace." I sigh. "I think I'm finally realizing that while we might love each other, we just want different things and there's no way to force this. We'd just be delaying the inevitable."

He takes a deep breath. "I know you're right," he says. "But

I just can't imagine you not being a part of my life."

"I think at some point, we'll be able to be friends," I say.

"I hope so," he says. "Look, I don't want to put you out, so I'll pay rent while I'm on tour if I can keep my stuff there."

"Thank you," I say. "I really appreciate that."

"I'm sorry about all of this," he says. "I feel awful. I do love you. I do... it's just a timing thing."

"We'll be alright." I look at my watch and see that I need to leave in a couple minutes. "All will be well in time."

"It just sucks," he says with a dry laugh. "I feel like I let you down."

"Chace, if anything you've gone above and beyond trying to make this work for my sake. Letting me down is the last thing you've done. I appreciate how hard you tried."

"Hey, can you hold on a second..." He stands up and walks away from the screen.

"Okay," I say.

He walks back over to his computer, after a minute, holding a stack of papers. "Listen, would you mind if I do a monologue right now?"

"I'm sorry?"

"I just really want to channel this raw emotion," he says, his eyes lighting up. "I think it will work perfectly with this one scene in the show..."

"Okay, that's my cue to go, Campbell," I say.

"No? That's not cool?" he says. "Okay, we can keep talking."

"It's OK," I say. "I think we've said all we need to say."

"I know it will take some time, but don't be a stranger," he says. "And can we not un-friend each other on Facebook? I hate when people do that."

"Of course." I say. "We can stay Facebook friends."

"Take care of yourself, doll."

"You too. Good luck with the show."

I take a deep breath, close out the Skype screen. I close my eyes, waiting for the tears to come, but they don't. So, I grab my party bag and head out the door.

As I walk along 23rd Street toward the subway, I'm surprised to find that I feel somewhat relieved. Sad, but relieved at the same time. If I'm being completely honest with myself, it has been a struggle with Chace since Vermont. After that whole experience, the magic was just sort of gone and I've been on edge waiting for the other shoe to drop. Did we have passion? Yes. Was it exciting? Yes. But did I feel safe? No.

Maybe I should have just followed Logan and Jake's advice and stayed single for a while longer, really gotten in touch with myself and what I want alone. Isn't that why I moved to New York in the first place? But then again, they say no man is an island. And haven't I always known how to be happy alone? I was single throughout all of high school, and a couple of years in college before I met Brent. Maybe I'm just getting to that age where people are starting to think about partnering up. And don't I want to build a life with someone at some point?

As I get off the train at 72nd Street, I remind myself that I don't need to figure any of this out right now. Maybe I can just give myself the afternoon to do this party and enjoy bringing happiness to others.

I walk into Wonderland Teahouse, ready for anything, and am greeted by Pam.

"Audrey," she says. "Get ready because I'm about to tell you the most precious thing ever."

"Okay," I say.

"Your booking this afternoon is only two people," she says.

"That's it?" I'm obviously surprised.

"It's a father and his daughter," she says. "And my heart is about to explode because listen to this. They live in D.C. but he's taken two days off of work to bring her up to New York for her birthday. They're having some kind of epic day. They've done a trip to FAO, carriage rides, boat excursions on the lake, and they're finishing here. But wait until you see him."

"Why?" I ask. "Is he hot?"

"I don't want to tell you anything," she says. "I just want

you to see it for yourself, because it's unbelievable."

"Alright." I shrug.

I spend the next few minutes changing into my princess costume and readying my supplies. According to Pam, I'm just going to have tea with the two of them and paint her face.

I walk out of the changing room and over to the hostess stand where Pam is.

"Ready?" she says.

"As always," I reply.

"Look over there." She points.

I turn around and in the back corner booth I see what is easily the cutest thing I have ever witnessed.

"Shit, you were right," I say under my breath. "That's adorable."

The little girl is at the booth in a beautiful pink princess dress; she has ribbons in her hair and a tiara on her head. Next to her sits her father, decked out in a royal velvet robe draped over his shirt and a crown. He is dressed as the king.

"I'm pretty sure I'm in love with him," Pam whispers from behind me.

I approach the table and greet the adorable duo. I learn that her name is Madeleine and she's turning five. Her dad's name is Vincent and he's brought his darling girl up to the city to give her a fairytale birthday she will never forget in the wake of her mother's unexpected passing.

"B-R-E-A-S-T C-A-N-C-E-R," he says to me as Madeleine colors the princess coloring sheet I've brought for her. "We didn't see it coming."

"Gosh, I'm so sorry," I say. "How long ago?"

"Almost a year," he says. "I work in government, so Maddie spends a lot of time with her grandparents. But I know that this girly stuff is important. She loves princesses. I just decided that if I needed to wear a king's robe and bring her to New York City for her birthday, then that's what I'm going to do."

"It's incredibly sweet," I say.

"I want her to know that even though I'm not around as

much as I'd like, that she's my princess and that she's the most important thing in my life," he says. "I don't really have time to date, and I don't want her to be confused, so I've sort of just remained married to my work and every free moment I have, I spend with her. You have no idea how many princess songs I know."

"Well, you win 'father of the year' in my book, hands down," I say. "And if you decide you might want to take a crack at dating, my friend Pam over there thinks you're very H-A-N-D-S-O-M-E."

"That's nice to hear." He smiles. "She seemed really nice over the phone when I called to set this up."

"So, Maddie," I say. "Are we ready for some dessert?"

"Yeah!" she says.

I signal Pam and she comes in with a giant cupcake covered in pink sprinkles with five candles in it.

Madeleine blows out her candles and I pose for pictures with them both. When it's time to leave, I give her a big hug and her father a warm handshake.

"It was really nice talking with you," he says.

"You as well," I say.

"Would you mind giving my card to your friend on your way out," he says, handing it to me. "You never know…"

"I will," I say, with a smile. "You never know indeed."

Hi Audrey,

Sorry that we didn't have more time to chat at the cast party, but I wanted to write you and tell you that you did a great job in our little workshop and I'd like to have you come in to read for me for an upcoming production of *Into The Woods* we'll be sending to D.C. in October.

I understand you already have a bit of princess experience, so I think you'll be a great fit for the show.

Rehearsals begin in September and it's an Equity Show. Jeff Chamberlain told me you don't have your card yet, but we think we can pull some strings and get that taken care of if you're able to do this.

Also wanted to tell you that I was really impressed with your website. Can you tell me who shot your headshots? Really fine work.

Lastly, would you consider coming out to Long Island to do a princess party for my niece? She's in a huge Sleeping Beauty phase right now!

Speak soon,
Annie

TWENTY-FIVE

I'm out of breath by the time I run up the subway stairs and out onto the street at 23rd and Broadway. I've just come from a great meeting with Annie. She's very excited to have me come in and audition for *Into The Woods*, reading for the part of Cinderella, naturally.

I'm so glad that Jake has called me to have lunch with him today; I cannot wait to tell him this news! He will be so proud.

As I walk into Madison Sq. Park, toward the tables set up for Shake Shack, I see him sitting at a table waiting with two drinks and matching plates of burgers and fries.

"Hey! I'm sorry I'm late. Subway," I say.

"It's okay, kid. I had some emails to send out." He pushes one of the cups and paper plates my way.

"Thanks." I smile as I lift the cold drink to my lips. "Guess what!"

"What?" he says.

"I just had a meeting with Annie Crawford, the director

from the reading I did."

"Yeah?"

"She wants me to come in next week to audition for *Into The Woods* in D.C.! They want me to read for Cinderella! How perfect is that?"

"Wow!" he says.

"She says it's between me and one other girl, but that calling in the other girl is really a formality. They want me!"

"That's amazing, kid," he says. "When is it?"

"In the fall, it's just a few months. Rehearsals start in a month and then we'd open in D.C. in August for a six-week run. And the show is Equity, so I'll finally get my card!"

"Audrey, that's great news… I'm so happy for you." He takes my hand across the table and gives it a squeeze, but something is off.

"Are you okay?" I ask. "You seem a little weird."

"I'm good," he says shifting slightly in his seat. "Did you want ketchup?"

"Jake, what's going on?" I ask.

"Nothing is going on." He looks nervous. "I might want some ketchup."

"Spit it out!" I'm growing irritated. "You're wigging me out right now."

He takes a deep breath. "Something happened with work…"

"Oh my God," I say. "They didn't fire you, did they?"

"No, no, kid. It's nothing like that," he says. "It's… well, I got offered a job. And it's a pretty big deal."

"Really? What is it?" I ask

"It's a gig with National Geographic. They liked my café culture idea," he says, still sounding oddly hesitant.

"Jake! That's amazing!" I reach out my fist to bump his. He keeps his hands on the table, leaving me hanging.

"Yeah. I mean, it's pretty huge… we'll start in Paris, but they want to extend it to a few other cities as well," he says tentatively. "For six months…"

"Oh. Oh gosh," I say. "Well, even so, that's incredible! I

mean, I'll be sad to have you so far away though. I was hoping you'd come see my show in D.C., but that's alright."

"Well, that's the thing," he says. "I'm not sure I want to go."

"Why not?" I ask. "It's such an amazing opportunity for you. And you've been talking about wanting to do this since I met you."

"Of course it is. But the thing is, I would be gone for six months," he says. "That's a long time to be away."

"Well, it is a long time, but New York isn't going anywhere," I say. "We'll still be here when you get back."

"Right. But...people can change a lot in six months," he says. "Things can happen. Hell, you'll be an aunt by then."

I laugh. "That's true. But what does that have to do with you being offered your dream job?"

Jake pauses for a moment, taking a sip of his soda, and then he sets it down and takes my hand. "Audrey, I'm in love with you. You have to know that, don't you? I've been in love with you for a long time, but I had to make sure you knew before I actually considered leaving. I was trying to give you some time and space, after your breakup with Chace, but...you might be with someone new by the time I get back. I just...I couldn't risk missing my chance with you again."

"Jake..." I pull my hand away and scratch my forehead.

"I wanted to ask you to come to Paris to visit me," he says. "I wanted to take you there. I don't know, maybe you'd still be able to come before you start rehearsals for your show?"

"Jake..." I'm looking down now, attempting to avoid his eyes. "I'm not really sure what to say."

"We'd travel so well together..."

I sigh. "Jake, I thought we were OK? I thought we got past what happened...I don't want things to get weird between us again."

"Can you at least look at me?" He sounds hurt.

"It was a moment," I say looking up. "We had a moment... I don't regret it, but that's all it was, and we've come so far since then! We've been good!"

"Audrey, I was willing to swallow my feelings as long as you wanted to be with Chace. I knew you had some things to figure out there. But we both know that our 'moment' meant something," he says. "And if you really think it didn't, you're kidding yourself."

"I'm still getting over Chace." I say. "It's only been a few weeks and I think I need to be single for a little while, like you and Logan have both said before. I need to figure out who I am before I jump into another relationship."

Jake runs his fingers through his hair and heaves a big sigh before looking up. He lets out a short laugh and shakes his head.

"You know what your problem is, kid?" he says patiently. "It's not that you don't know yourself, because you do. You know who you are, but what you haven't grasped yet is that you owe it to yourself to be with someone who treats you the way you deserve to be treated and who will love you the way you deserve to be loved. Your problem is that you're scared to actually let someone in who might be right for you, because then if they leave, it will break your heart. You've been attracted to the wrong guys because when they inevitably bail, it's not a surprise. And it doesn't hurt as much."

"What?" I stammer, cutting my eyes to the side, suddenly self-conscious about the other people around us.

He lowers his voice. "You knew Brent was wrong from the day I met you, and you knew Chace was wrong the night we slept together…"

"You're out of line, Jake."

"I've been right here, Audrey," he says, defeated. "This whole time… but now… I need to *not* be for awhile."

I stare at him, tongue-tied.

"I gotta go," he says. He stands up from the table, tosses his full plate of food in the trash and walks away.

I sit at the table for a good twenty minutes in a huff. How could he say something so mean to me? I'm not attracted to the wrong guys! Am I? I'm convinced he's dead wrong, but his words linger in the air and they sting with a little bit of truth.

Logan and I spend the evening packing up Chace's stuff and storing it in the hall closet so that I can fill the drawers and shelves with my own belongings. The first week after we broke up, I avoided moving Chace's things into the closet. But over the last few days, I've felt ready to start moving on and claiming the space as my own, at least until I have to move again when he gets back. The apartment is finally starting to feel like mine, and I'm happy to once again have a fresh new start, as the weather turns hot and sticky again. I would be feeling very positive if I hadn't had that unsettling conversation with Jake over lunch today. I wish things could just normalize between us. I hate all this fighting.

"He Varjack'd you," says Logan, sealing the final box with packing tape.

"Who? And what?" I uncork a bottle of wine.

"Jake," he says. "At lunch...he one hundred percent Varjack'd you."

"I don't know what that means..."

"Where is your copy of *Breakfast At Tiffany's*?" he asks.

"On my bookshelf." I point to his left.

Logan jumps up and grabs the DVD, popping it into the player. "I'll show you."

"Okay..." I pour two glasses of chardonnay and walk back over to the sofa.

Logan selects the DVD menu and chooses the final chapter of the film. Then he fast-forwards into the middle of the taxi scene and stops just as Paul gets out of the cab.

"You know what's wrong with you, Miss Whoever-you-are? You're chicken. You've got no guts. You're afraid to stick out your chin and say, 'Okay, life's a fact. People do fall in love, people do belong to each other, because that's the only chance anybody's got for real happiness.'

You call yourself a free spirit, a wild thing, and you're terrified somebody's gonna stick you in a cage. Well, baby, you're already in that cage. You built it yourself. And it's not bounded in the west by Tulip, Texas, or on the east by Somali-land. It's wherever you go. Because no matter where you run, you'd just end up running into yourself."

"Oh my God…" I mumble. "He totally Varjack'd me."

"Yup!" he says.

"Holy shit."

"Do you remember what you said to me last time we watched this, after you got fired from the Hamptons gig?"

"I said that I loved how Paul calls her out and walks away," I say.

"Bingo, and you said, 'that's what I want. That's a real man.'"

"I did, didn't I?" I say.

"I know you don't want to hear this, Holly," says Logan "But I'm with Jake here. He's one hundred percent right about you. You've been choosing relationships that have no chance, subconsciously, because they're less threatening. If something goes wrong and it ends, it's a lot less painful to lose someone you didn't love all that much to begin with."

"Are you saying I didn't love Chace?" I say, frustrated.

"No, I'm not saying that," he says. "I think you did love Chace, but I think it was a love that was turbo-boosted by lust and heavy infatuation."

"It was more than that!" I protest.

"I think that so much of what you loved about Chace was the fantasy you built in your own head, love, and not who he actually was to you or how he actually treated you. You loved the idea of him, and unfortunately, he just didn't have the headspace to work through a real relationship. I don't think Chace was a bad guy. I think he genuinely means well; he's just not ready for someone like you."

"I hate when you're right," I say with a smirk.

"Look, even I got a bit swept up in Chace!" Logan admits. "He was a beautiful man-specimen!"

"God, he was so pretty," I say.

"He was…But Jake is a real man," he says. "He's solid as a rock and his love for you runs deep as the fucking Atlantic Ocean. He flew to California to support you at your dad's funeral. And you know how much those last-minute tickets cost!"

"I know… and Chace wasn't even there." I lament. "I mean, I told him not to come…he'd just started that job…"

"Audrey, don't make excuses for Chace. His girlfriend's father passed away. Job or no job, he should have been on the first flight out."

"I don't know, Paulie…what's the point? Jake's leaving tomorrow. He's going to be gone for six months, and I'm so messed up in my head right now. I'm so confused. I don't know what I want," I say.

"Maybe sleep on it, love," he says. "Wanna watch this from the beginning?"

"Always," I sigh.

TWENTY-SIX

Today I'm doing a Cinderella party in Brooklyn and I'm multi-tasking. And by multi-tasking, I mean that I'm performing this party and doing everything I possibly can to not think about Jake. He's leaving today for Paris. By the time I'm done with this party, he will already be headed to the airport.

It's just as well. Things have been so difficult between us, that maybe it makes sense for us to have another break from each other. I still don't feel like my mind is totally clear, and I think it would be unfair to put him through my indecision one more time.

"Cinderella!" says the little brother of the birthday girl.

"Oh, sorry Sammy, what did you say?"

"I said Grimaldo's," he announces. "You asked what kinda pizza we having today. I asked my mom for a special kind because I don't like regular pizza, so she gets me the Magita from Grimaldo's

"Do you mean the Margherita, from Grimaldi's?" I ask. *Jake's favorite.*

"Yeah, thas what I said," he replies.

"Oh, I have a friend who likes that kind too," I say.

"Cool," Sammy replies.

As the kids sit down at the table, I excuse myself to the restroom for a moment and pull out my phone to text Jake.

When do you leave?

He replies.

2:30 train, 5pm flight

I glance at my watch; it's just after one o'clock. He'll be heading out soon.

**Have a safe flight
and a great trip**

A moment passes before his reply pings through.

Thx, kid.

I walk back into the dining room and over to my chair.

"Cinderella, will you tell us a story while we eat?" asks Sydney, the birthday girl.

"Sure!" I reply. "What kind of story would you like to hear? The story of me going to the ball maybe?"

"No. Make one up," says Sydney. "A new princess story!"

"Wow, a challenge!" I reply. *Oh lord, here we go.* "Okay, once upon a time, there lived a princess in a magical land. She loved to sing and dance and play with her animal friends in the woods." *So far, so good.*

"What kind of animals?" asks a little girl who's got pizza grease running down her chin.

"Well, she liked all kinds of animals," I say. "Doggies and

kitties, squirrels and bunnies. Birds, chipmunks; pretty much most animals."

"What happened to her?" asks Sammy.

"Hmm. Let's see. Well, she um…" I trail off. "Well, she met a handsome prince."

"Did they kiss?" asks Sydney's older sister Maggie.

"Ewwwww!!!" all the kids squeal at the thought.

"We won't get into that, but she thought he was the perfect prince."

"Was he?" asks Sammy.

"Well, no…" I say. "He wasn't."

"What did he do to her?" asks Sammy.

Oh, ya know, Sammy, he couldn't commit… "He… he was very busy focusing on doing prince-things and he wouldn't…share his…crayons and stuff with her, and that made the princess sad."

"My teacher says that sharing is caring," says the pizza-faced girl again.

"Yes, that's right. Sharing is very important and so is having good manners and saying 'please' and 'thank you.' Can anyone think of some other important manners?" I ask, hoping to move on to another topic.

"Cinderella, why would the princess like a prince who wasn't nice to her?" Maggie is keeping me on task.

"Well, it's not that he wasn't nice to her…I mean, listen, he wanted to be nice to her. He tried to be nice to her, but he just didn't know what he wanted. And, I dunno, maybe it was the princess's fault for not seeing him very clearly. Maybe she was a little blind to what was really going on and maybe she should have been a bit smarter with her choice in princes."

"Oh no," says Sydney.

"Okay, maybe she thought he could change," I continue. "That he might change for her. I mean is that so awful? That I thought he could be better?"

"Cinderella, my mommy says you can't change a man," pizza-face girl chimes in.

"Your mom is a smart lady then," I say. "Maybe I can learn

something from her."

"Think you gotta find a prince that is the right prince from the start," says Maggie. "Then you can live happily ever after."

"Well, maybe there was a second prince," I say without thinking, Jake's face popping into my head. "A prince who really cared about the princess...but she didn't know at first that he cared for her."

"She should be with him," says pizza-face girl. "Maybe he'll share his crayons with her."

"And maybe his coloring books and his toys and his pizza too!" says Sammy.

"Or maybe the princess should just be alone for a while," I say. "You know? Spend some time with her friends and focus on princes later."

"Is that what you want to do?" asks Maggie skeptically.

I feel a tightness in my throat. "No..."

Damn, she's good.

"I think if you love him, you should be with him *and* your friends," says Maggie. "My yoga teacher at school says it's all about balance."

"I think that's a good happy ending, Cinderella," says Sammy. "They can all go have pizza together at Grimaldo's!"

"I'm so stupid," I mumble.

"Cinderella, you said a bad word," says pizza-face girl.

"Oh my gosh!" I shout. "You guys! I'm such a moron!"

"What's a mor-on?" asks Sydney.

"I have to stop him," I say. "Sydney, I have to stop my prince before he leaves for Europe for six months and ends up with some French hussy."

"I think you need to go, Cinderella," says Maggie.

"I'm sorry, Sydney," I say, giving her a big hug

"Is otay. Thanks for coming to my party."

"Mrs. Burns, I need to go!" I call over my shoulder as I walk toward the coffee table where I've left my bag.

"What?" she says. "We still have twenty minutes."

"Mommy! Cinderella needs to go stop her prince before he ends up with a French husky."

"Excuse me?" says Mrs. Burns.

"I don't need you to pay me!" I grab my bag and throw the books and stickers back into it. "This one is on me!"

"Cinderella, this is extremely unprofessional." She is standing over me now.

"I know, I'm sorry!" I say. "I'm so sorry, but I have to tell this guy that I love him before he goes to the airport, or I'll miss my chance."

"Is this part of the act, Audrey? Because we never discussed this," she whispers.

"I know it sounds fake," I say to her. "But I'm serious. My best friend told me he's in love with me and I'm such a J-A-C-K-A-S-S. I need to make this right!"

I look up at her, begging her with my eyes. For a moment she scowls down at me, looking perturbed, but then her face softens and she smiles. "Go on."

"Thank you!" I say as I grab the bag and head for the door.

"Byeeee Cinderella!" scream the kids. "Good Luck!"

Jake. Please don't leave before I have a chance to tell you how I feel!

I fly out the door of their apartment, still dressed as Cinderella. I don't care that there are stickers and glue and dried macaroni stuck to my skirt and that running full speed in a blonde wig and tightly-corseted, tulle-infused ball-gown should be considered a new Olympic sport.

I make a break for the 7th Avenue subway station, praying that I haven't missed one of about five weekend trains going into Manhattan.

As I run, I try calling Jake's cell, but it goes straight to voicemail. He's probably already underground heading to Penn Station to catch his train to JFK. I wait to leave a message, hoping maybe he'll get it in time.

"Jake, it's me! I need to talk to you! Please wai-"

"We're sorry, but your message did not record either because you were not speaking clearly or because of a bad connection. Please try your call again later."

"Dammit, phone!" I yell. At this point, my best shot is to try and catch him before he leaves Penn Station. There's no way I'll beat him to JFK in a taxi, during Memorial weekend traffic; plus once he's through security, I'm screwed.

I round the corner and pound down the station steps in a full sweat. *Please, MTA! Please be on my team today!*

TWENTY-SEVEN

Excuse me!" I shout as I push past a large crowd of people filing through the turnstiles slowly. They all have Brooklyn Botanical Gardens stickers on their sweaters and they all look about ninety years old.

"I'm sorry! I need to get through!" I shout.

No one moves.

"We're in line, here," says one of the women.

"Please! It's an emergency!" I say, hoping it will get me through faster. "I need to make this train!"

"Get in line, Princess!" snaps a disgruntled man. Clearly he's a local and is as annoyed with the crowd as I am. A bead of sweat drips down my face as I hear the rumble of the train coming into the station.

"You don't understand. I need to get through! The train is coming!" I'm frantic now. If I miss Jake's train to the airport, then he's off to Europe for six months. And who wants to confess their love for someone over Skype?

And then there's always the possibility that he'll meet some sexy Parisian chick named Jacqueline, who will say things like

Oui, oui Jake! C'est bonne! In a sexy accent, and who will wear Chanel No. 5 perfume and cigarette pants without underwear. *No!* I have to get to him now!

The train is pulling into the station and I'm still about seven people back. An old lady tourist is having problems swiping her metro card and my head is about to explode.

"You have to swipe it with purpose! *With purpose!*" I shout from the back of the line. I can't help but voice my frustration.

The train doors are opening and commuters are beginning to file out into the station. I'm going to miss it. I'm going to miss Jake. I'm going to miss my chance. I'm the biggest idiot I know.

"Hey, Princess! Over here!" I hear a voice to my left. "Quick, I got you."

A saint of a man in a Knicks jersey, holding a boom box, opens the emergency door for me and pushes me through so quickly that I tear my skirt. But I don't care because I'll make the train.

The conductor hears the sirens go off and begins to object when the Knicks fan guy jumps in.

"She said she had an emergency," he says. "So I opened the emergency door! Let her on the damn train, man."

"Hurry up!" the conductor yells at me through his tiny window. *Thank you all that is holy and good!* I've made it on the train.

"I'll swipe my metro card twice later, I promise!" I shout into the conductor's box.

"Yeah, yeah, yeah," he replies.

I turn around just in time to shout "thank you" to the Knicks fan.

As the doors close and the train begins to move, I see that the group of tourists are still stuck behind the lady who can't swipe with purpose. *There's a chance I might make it.*

As I collapse against the subway bench, I have a brief moment of wondering if I should try to take off this wig and fix my hair, but as I pat my head and do a mental count of how many hair pins I'd have to pull out, I decide against it.

I close my eyes and spend the ride into the city thinking about how stupid I've been. All the times that Jake was there for me and I overlooked him. How many times he let me crash at his apartment, how he took care of Baxter when I couldn't, how supportive he was of my business, how he treated my family so warmly at Christmas, how he came to my dad's funeral. The night we cuddled in my bed at my parent's house, everything he did to make my birthday party happen, the photo he gave me... He's been such a selfless friend. And I've been so unfair to him.

I hear Logan's words in my mind: *"Jake is a real man. He's solid as a rock and his love for you runs deep as the fucking Atlantic Ocean."*

How had I just overlooked him for so long? Of course I love him! He's one of my best friends. He would do anything for me. Why did it take a conversation with a bunch of kids for me to finally get it?

I just hope that I'm not too late. That I catch him before he leaves, but also that he will hear me out. Even if he tells me there's no chance, I still need to tell him how I feel. I tap my foot impatiently against the front of my seat as we rumble under the river. *I'm almost there.*

As the train pulls in to the West 4th Street station, I grab my bag and what's left of my skirt, hike it up and get ready to make a full-blown sprint up two flights of stairs hoping to catch an Uptown A.

I look at my watch. It's two-fourteen. Sixteen minutes before Jake's train leaves. The doors open and I fly out of the subway car so fast that I nearly trip on the platform. I jump the stairs two at a time, willing myself to keep moving faster. *C'mon, c'mon! Go! Go! Dammit, Go!*

"Congrats on your wedding day!" a man yells at me as I run up the stairs. "Hey! You dropped your shoe!" He's right, one of my shoes has fallen off, but I keep going, leaping the last three steps at once.

I hit the top of the platform and to my horror, the A train is already in the station and the doors are closing.

"NO!" I scream as I hurl myself toward the closed door, slamming into the glass with my hands. "Please! Please!"

The people inside look at me terrified. I nearly burst into tears as the doors fly open and I tumble forward into the train. *Thank God!*

"Sorry," I say as I crawl to my feet. "Dinner theatre gig."

The intercom of the train crackles as the doors close, "*This is an uptown local A train. We will be making all local stops. Next stop is 14th Street. Stand clear of the closing doors, please.*" Click.

Ping-ping! I stand leaning against the doors of the train as it juts forward violently and then begins to bounce noisily uptown, my heart still pounding.

As we pull into the 14th Street station, I glare at my watch hoping to intimidate it enough that it might tick the seconds by more slowly. Two-twenty-one. I have nine minutes. The doors close and I silently will the train to move. *Please move. Please!*

The garbled sound of the intercom rings out in the train car again. "*Due to weekend construction, this train will be bypassing 23rd Street. If you need to get to 23rd Street, please take this train to 34th Street and transfer to a downtown E train, repeat a downtown E train! Stand clear of the closing doors, please.*" Click.

Ping-pong! With eight minutes to go, Penn Station is the next stop! As the doors close and the train moves forward, I feel a tiny twinge of hope.

The train begins to move forward but doesn't pick up pace. I look out the windows to see men working construction, waving flashlights so the train conductor knows she can pass safely. With six minutes to spare, we are barely passing through the 23rd Street station. *No, no, no, no. Please! I'm so close!* I'm ready to throw my hands up in resignation when the train lurches forward, knocking every passenger violently backward. *Go train, go train, go train.* Five minutes. I have five minutes.

The train blasts through the tunnel and into the platform area of Penn Station. I jump up and wait, poised by the door and ready to sprint. The doors open and I hurl myself onto the platform.

I've made this dash many times before, so I know the route

with confidence. I race gingerly down the stairs, along the long corridor to my left. Running at full speed, I throw myself at the emergency door, which swings open. I turn left and run up the ramp towards the Long Island Railroad announcement board.

I see the sign flashing, **Jamaica Train Now Boarding Track 19.**

I can't hold back anymore. Like a complete idiot I'm running through Penn Station, shouting his name, "Jake! Jake! WAIT!"

I run past a Hudson News stand, Dunkin Donuts, Hot & Crusty and Sbarro's pizza. I'm basically carrying what remains of my skirt so I won't trip over it.

My one bare foot must be bleeding because it's killing me, but I don't care. I hurl myself towards Track 19, pushing past people to try and get to the track faster. I round the bend at Track 19 and make a sharp turn to race down the stairs.

"Jake! Jake! Please, wait!"

"Watch out!" yells a lady that I nearly bowl over.

"I'm sorry! I'm sorry! JAKE! I'm sorry!"

"Look where you're going, lady!" yells a man.

I'm alternating between screaming his name and apologizing for knocking people off their path.

I take the last two stairs in one leap, landing on the platform clumsily.

I run down the station platform, frantically searching windows of the train for him. I see families sitting together and couples and teenagers sitting side-by-side sharing ear buds, but no Jake.

"Jake! I'm here! Jake!"

I'm starting to cry now. I run frantically all the way to the front of the train, and then turn around and run back towards the other end. But he's nowhere to be found.

Maybe he took an earlier train. I'm too late.

I slump down on the ground leaning against a poll, exhausted. Surrounded by a sea of crinoline, tulle and satin, and the tears start flowing freely. He's gone…

"Audrey?"

I freeze at the sound of his voice. I turn around and see Jake staring at me with a look of amusement mixed with bewilderment. He's standing on the platform with his suitcase next to him. The doors to the LIRR train close and it begins to leave the station, but Jake doesn't move.

I can't even find the words. I nearly trip as I attempt to stand up. I wipe the tears from my face, even though it's useless when I've got mascara tearstains down the front of my dress.

He approaches me slowly and straightens my crooked tiara. He brushes a strand of wig hair out of my face and smiles.

"What in the world?" he looks at me in astonishment.

"Jake…" I choke out. "I'm so sorry. I'm so sorry. You were right. You were right about everything. I just didn't see it. I don't know what I was think—"

Before I can even finish my sentence, his lips meet mine and his arms encircle me as he pulls me tightly towards him.

I've made it. I've made it in time and I'm safe in his arms and he's kissing me. We're kissing!

He pulls back slightly and nuzzles his nose against mine. Then he takes my face in his hands and looks me in the eye. "You're a mess."

He kisses me again and pulls me tightly to him, lifting me off the ground. His arms hold me and I never want this moment to end. My heart swells in my chest and I know this is right. He is right. We are right.

He sets me down and we both start laughing.

"Wait," I say. "What about Paris? What about the project?"

He takes my hand in his, grabs his suitcase in the other and leads me towards the stairs. "I'll re-book my flight. We don't start for a week anyway." He laughs.

"Does this mean I'll get to come along until my rehearsals start?" I ask.

"Only if you let me take you to a real Parisian brasserie for something other than Nutella crêpes."

"I think we can work something out." I smile.

"Let's go get you cleaned up first. I can't take you anywhere looking like this," he says, teasing me. "Hey, where's your shoe?"

I look down at my one shoe-less foot and we both giggle as the hilarity of the situation washes over us. "Who needs the glass slipper when you've got the prince," I say with mock sincerity.

He chuckles, rolling his eyes. "You're ridiculous."

"You know you love it!" I retort.

"I do." He takes my hand. "Let's go."

As we walk, I peer down at my Cinderella dress, surveying the damage. It's covered in stickers, glue, macaroni, and some trash I picked up along the way. It's ruined.

But I don't care.

I don't care one bit, because Jake is holding my hand.

We walk up the platform stairs, through the hustle and bustle of Penn Station and out into the brilliant sunlight of the busy Manhattan street.

ACKNOWLEDGEMENTS

To my wonderful family, the Gutmans, the Shaws and the Gonzales families, for always loving and supporting me in every creative endeavor I put before you. You guys are the best family a girl could ask for! I cherish you all.

Particular huge amounts of love to my mother, Paula and my brother Casey James, who always have my back, whether I'm starting a new creative project or packing up to move across the country again to another new city. I realize I'm a lot to put up with. You guys are my heart and soul and I love you! Also big shout-out up to my father, Gary Shaw, the man behind the genius that was "ska-lerf-kef" and the "Mountain-Do." He is always with us in spirit and we love and miss him. And to Wikket, my perfect man.

To my friends in LA, NYC, NOLA and everywhere in between. Thank you to those of you who read pages and gave your time and energy to help me formulate this project. Thank you to those of you who housed me this past summer while I traveled across country working on this story!

SAVES + AJ, est. 1999 eternal love and gratitude, you guys are my heart and soul and I'm grateful for you every day. Tigers 4 Life, son!

My 'other, other half,' thank you for your wisdom and for letting me journal vent to you when life goes Nicholas Sparks > Stephen King.

Work Wife, thank you for all your help with this story! You are such a fierce friend and champion of a business partner.

To JJJ, the straight man, who read this entire manuscript and gave the most wonderful honest feedback, thank you for always being there!

Nerd besties, Ms. Stark, Ms. Jackman and Ms. Lynch thank you for teaching me the power of a perfectly timed pop-culture reference and for amazing years of nerdy friendships that never fails.

Lots of love to all of my Play Club friends, spread all over the country. Thank you for always making me laugh and keeping my love of theatre alive!

To the city of New Orleans, thank you for taking me in with such open arms and making me feel so welcomed. Mr. Dudley, you have been instrumental in that and I love you dearly.

To the city of New York, thank you for kicking my ass for four great years and giving me so many stories to tell. Special thanks to the Evans family for taking such good care of me while there.

To the city of Los Angeles, particularly Pasadena/South Pas, you are and will always be home. Huge shout-out to Saladang Restaurant on Fair Oaks Ave. Your yellow chicken curry continues to inspire this foodie.

To my editors! Leah Campbell, thank you for being my biggest champion with this story! Your support and wisdom mean the world! Laura Silverman, thank you for having incredible patience with me and my nasty habit of over-using ellipses!

Finally biggest of hugs to my New York Princess girls, who lived a lot of these hilarious/horrific tales! Without your stories, this book would have been very boring. Keep partying!

SPECIAL THANKS TO:

Maria Aparo, Joni Aparo, Aaron Aragonez, Meghan Allison, Samm Bahman, Rachel Barker, Shannon & Kristopher Lee Bicknell, Maureen Brady, Claire Broderick, Leah Campbell, Olivia & Erik Campbell, RJ Castaneda, Emily Clark, Lori Spurlin Clark, Linda Clemens, Suzi Cohen, Ashley & Daniel Curran, Sophia deLaat, Andrew Devine, Sam Dudley, Kara Durrett, Pamela Quinn Eberhardt, Ashley Eskew, Jeanine Espejo, Ariel Evans, Christina Evans & Family, Gale Fenton, Chris Fore & Family, Courtney Foster-Donahue, Cruz Fuentes, Adam 'George' Founier, Kathy Giangregorio & Family, Andrea & Bob Gonzales, Quinn and Cynthia Gonzales & Family, Roman Gonzales, John F. Goff, Jo Goldfarb, Jack & Jo Gutman, Marilyn & Craig Gutman, Jenna Gutman, Chris Gutman, Patrick Gutman, Katie Grimmer, Malynda Hale, Jeanne Hall, Leslie Hall, Courtney Harper, Drexel D. Heard II, Ness Hernandez, Dave Howe, Sarah Horng, Ashley Hufford, Jeni Incontro, Laura Jackman, Steven Jacks, Jackson James, Casey Jones, Kathleen Kiralla, Shane Lynch, Vikki & Brian Marsee, Nicole McCreary, Alex Mohajer, Ana Maria Muñoz, Stina Nelson, Shauna & Jeremy O'Brien, Kavin Panmeechao, Nicole Pasquale, Fanny C. Pearce, Nicole Pearce-Coarsey, Matthew & Brittany Petrone, Kai & Joe Roderick & Family, Tripp Pettigrew-Rolapp, Debbie Radvar & Family, Travis J. Riner, Lance, Suzanna & Dylan Roll, Brandon Ruiz, Lesley Schiedow, Mary Ellen Schneider, Kiri Shaw-Allenbaugh, Caitlyn Silhan, Laura Silverman, Allyson Stark, Susan & Oliver Stark, Taylor Sternberg, Michael Stimpfel, Laura Swan, Kathryn Turner, Constance Turpel, Jonathan Vandercook, John Volk, Brittany Walter, Haley Webb, Lisa White, Vincent Yun Zou, and, the incomparable Mr. Logan Yost.

ABOUT THE AUTHOR

Erin Shaw is a freelance writer and performer, who naïvely moved to New York City in the midst of the 2008 recession with dreams of gracing the Broadway stage.

Once there, she learned this was a task, far more difficult than she anticipated, and so she started a princess party company to help her stay on her feet, while she worked as a nanny.

While she never made it to Broadway, except the actual street, which she walked down constantly, her company became very successful. She lived happily in the Big Apple for nearly four years before returning home to Los Angeles, where she started writing *Party Girl* in 2012.

Erin now resides in the great city of New Orleans, where she continues to write, teach and perform. She has since retired from doing princess parties. For the record, she *loves* Brooklyn.

erinashleyshaw.com

MUSICAL INSPIRATION

Music is such an important part of my personality and life experience. To me it's one of the most powerful tools for nostalgia and tapping into memories. Because I wrote a lot of this book about experiences I had five years ago, I chose to write while listening to the music that had the most plays on my iPod my first two years in NYC.

I count 2008 and 2009 as the years that I fell in love with Indie music. I had spent so many years in college listening to Broadway cast recordings and classical symphonies, that moving to New York City felt like a re-awakening for me musically. I credit a few specific friends with introducing me to these musicians and I'm ever grateful.

New Yorkers always have their ear-buds in. It's the best way to block out the constant drone of the city so you can stay sane. Each time I listen to these songs, I have very specific memories of the city – riding the subway, walking through the park, waiting in the snow for a bus, waiting in line at Whole Foods in Columbus Circle, walking home etc.... Just by putting myself back in that timeframe, the story came through. So I credit a lot of these songs in helping this story come to life. Here is my "Party Girl" playlist, which you can listen to via Spotify. The link is on our website. PartyGirlBook.com/music

THE PLAYLIST

1. "75 and Sunny" – Ryan Montbleau Band
2. "A Fuller Moon" – The Sea and Cake
3. "All My Stars Aligned" – St. Vincent
4. "Be Good Or Be Gone" – Fionn Regan
5. "Blizzard of '77" – Nada Surf
6. "Boat Behind" – Kings of Convenience
7. "California English" – Vampire Weekend
8. "Don't Wake Me Up" – The Hush Sound
9. "Dig" – Incubus
10. "Either Way" – Wilco
11. "Eriatarka" – The Mars Volta
12. "Flume" – Bon Iver
13. "Hazy Jane II" – Nick Drake
14. "Horchata" – Vampire Weekend
15. "Impossible Germany" – Wilco
16. "Killian's Red" – Nada Surf
17. "Love Hurts" – Incubus
18. "Lighthouse" – The Hush Sound
19. "Mientras La Veo Soñar" – RX Bandits
20. "Mrs. Cold" – Kings of Convenience
21. "Northern Sky" – Nick Drake
22. "Noticed" – MuteMath
23. "On a Letter" – The Sea and Cake
24. "The Party" – St. Vincent
25. "Place To Be" – Nick Drake
26. "Punk As Fuck" – American Analog Set
27. "Put a Penny In the Slot" – Fionn Regan
28. "Re: Stacks" – Bon Iver
29. "Skinny Love" – Bon Iver
30. "Stretch" – Ryan Montbleau Band
31. "Typical" – MuteMath
32. "We Intertwined" – The Hush Sound
33. "White Lies" – RX Bandits
34. "White Sky" – Vampire Weekend

Proof

Made in the USA
Charleston, SC
26 February 2014

27108055R10176